The Cardinals of Schengen

For the one and only Yvonne.

Michael
xx

Michael Barton

authorHOUSE®

AuthorHouse™ UK Ltd.
500 Avebury Boulevard
Central Milton Keynes, MK9 2BE
www.authorhouse.co.uk
Phone: 08001974150

This book is a work of fiction. People, places, events, and situations are the product of the author's imagination. Any resemblance to actual persons, living or dead, or historical events, is purely coincidental.

First published by AuthorHouse 10/8/2008

ISBN: 978-1-4389-0646-1 (e)
ISBN: 978-1-4389-0645-4 (sc)

Printed in the United States of America
Bloomington, Indiana

This book is printed on acid-free paper.

About the Author

Michael Barton is married with a son and a daughter, both in their early twenties. The majority of his working career has been spent trading the financial markets of the world, or advising clients on investments. He enjoys reading, with his favourite modern day authors including Michael Connelly, Dan Brown, and Lee Child.

Now that both his children have flown the nest, Michael is able to concentrate on his writing. He currently lives in Spain with his wife for much of the year, where the more relaxed lifestyle affords him the time to concentrate on putting the life of Peter Hudson on to paper.

Acknowledgements

A friend once informed me that writing is a lonely business. He told me that undertaking to be the author of a book would necessarily mean hiding oneself away from the real world that exists beyond a closed door and removed from a computer keyboard. I have discovered the words to be entirely true, but not just for the author.

I want to thank my wife, Evie, for all the long hours of solitude this book has given her, for her belief in me, and for her unending words of encouragement. Also my children, Tara and Gareth, for being at least part of the reason I write.

To all my friends and family, especially those that have done such a good job at being the original audience for my work and pointing out any errors there may have been. I thank you all for your time and patience.

To my brother-in-law John who, after years of waiting, has finally got his "Hud" – thank you: I needed a surname for the hero.

But most of all I want to thank one person - my very best friend - without whom this novel, and all others that follow, never would have been possible. Courage and mental attitude to adversity is what makes a hero. It is to you more than any other that I dedicate this book.

Peter a hero in your lifetime, an inspiration after, missed everyday.

PROLOGUE

May 13th 1944. The docks at Stralsund, Baltic Sea coastline, Germany.

Gerhard Schneider sat watching the bubbling sea, transfixed on the scene unfolding through the morning mist. Beneath him a melee of panicked Dockers and Port Guards ran first one way and then the other in reaction to instructions bellowed from an unseen voice. As he watched, Schneider tore another handful of dry black bread from the half loaf he had saved from the previous day.

He liked the salty smell of the cooling breeze that rolled in from the Baltic with the rising sun, and would often come to the docks in the early hours before he set off to work in his baker's shop.

But he had never witnessed scenes like the one he now observed.

Gerhard had often dreamed of becoming a sailor

when a young boy, of working his way to captain of his own vessel and serving his country across the oceans in pursuit of adventure and fame. But severe and uncontrollable sea-sickness had crushed his hopes, and so ever since his teenage years he'd had to content himself with watching the sea traffic arrive and depart the busy port. Cargo ships bought goods from across the globe, and trawlers took their loads of brave fishermen away to return them with their haul sometimes weeks later.

Having built friendships over the years, he was on first name terms with many of the Dockers. Even though the war had changed the port from a bustling commercial wharf to a heaving naval base, he rarely had problems with entering the docks. Each morning he would complete his ritual of an hour contemplating a life that might have been, before returning to the real world and the life that was.

But this morning had been different. There seemed a larger contingent of guards than normal, and even Manfred - the friend he had known since they had schooled together - was unable to spirit him to dockside. And so Gerhard had used an unknown hole in the wire mesh fencing to enter the port and now sat silently, watching the scene below him unfold.

Less than an hour earlier he had watched through the mist as the U-boat had docked, unloading a huge cargo of tea chest sized crates on to two military lorries. He counted them off the boat as they were hurriedly manhandled into the waiting vehicles. Twenty-seven square cases, all labelled as ammunition. But to Gerhard, they did not look like ammunition packaging. He had seen enough of that through this port to realise that these boxes contained something other than military shells or rifles.

The whole operation had been overseen by a young Officer, who had been addressed with the well respected naval surname of "Doenitz". He was a hard taskmaster, castigating any tardiness as the crates passed from sea to shore. When the last of the boxes had been securely tied down, the young man had stayed with them. The Captain of the U-boat had said his goodbyes and wished the young officer a happy birthday before the lorries had departed, taking Doenitz away with them.

The morning had been different from all others because the submarine had been the only vessel in port.

Gerhard had never known Stralsund with only one ship in the dock, in peace time or in the years since the war had broken, and so had sat intrigued for longer than he should. He had lost track of time and was already late for work.

But work could wait.

Now he watched as out to sea the water eddied around the stricken submarine. Near to port and so still surfaced, the vessel had been ripped apart by an immense explosion in its midriff that had rocked the wooden piers it had left behind moments earlier. Then a second and a third blast had torn the sub in smaller pieces. Huge blasts that reverberated through the sea to the land, and echoed upwards through Gerhard's feet. The yellows and oranges of burning fuel now encircled the steel shell as it fell from sight, underneath an ever increasing cloud of thick, tar like black smoke.

Men along the docks were preparing rescue vessels, to pick up the survivors. But Gerhard could see that there would be none. Flailing arms disappeared as the flames from the burning gasoline shot ever higher and engulfed the few heads that bobbed on the surface. He could hear the screams of men as their flesh melted in the heat.

The smell of burning, and death, stretched from the sailors' watery grave to where Gerhard sat. He had never before witnessed such destructive power.

He turned away, the grief for his unknown countrymen twisting his features. Suddenly he felt thankful that he was blessed with his "mal de mer". Never again would he waste his hours on this earth dreaming of a life at sea.

As he unlocked the door to his shop, Gerhard would not have known that more of his countrymen had lost their lives in the English Channel as the U-boat had exploded before his eyes.

An ill-conceived raid on Selsey on the south coast of England had gone horribly wrong, and the German Fast Boat had gone down with all hands.

Two simultaneous but separate incidents isolated by hundreds of miles across land and sea.

Two identical outcomes. No survivors.

ONE

The present day, somewhere in the Kent countryside, England

The assassin looked at his watch. It was fifteen minutes before midnight. That meant he had a clear fifteen minutes to reach his destination, a little short of a mile away through open countryside. He would move swiftly, unseen by human eyes on this leg of his journey.

He had to reach the farmhouse by midnight, for that's when the guard dogs would be let out for their ten minutes free exercise. After silencing the dogs, he would then have all the time he required to find and eliminate his target, complete his mission and make his exit unseen before the dogs' owners missed them.

Dressed in black fatigues, black leather gloves and a black balaclava he blended in with the pitch of the unlit land. The Director had chosen the time well:

together with the lack of moon, the thick cloud cover had presented a night as black as tar. All movements in the Kent countryside would be masked from prying eyes.

The assassin flipped down his night vision goggles, and surveyed the landscape that came into view, a multitude of luminous greens and yellows. He performed a speedy 360 degree sweep. Aside from a nearby herd of deer he was alone, just as he expected to be.

Time to move.

He travelled light on such missions. On his back a specially customised pack holding in place all that he would need in a polyfoam surround to protect against damage. He had placed the skeleton key and torch in the upper chamber of his pack, with the most deadly items in the lower casing. Tonight he would be using specially prepared darts of snake venom: two for the dogs and one for the target. No room for error. But just in case he carried a hunting knife with a six-inch blade, and had holstered his favoured Glock 38.

His handgun, however, would only be used in absolute emergency. Compact and lightweight, it was easy to conceal on those missions which demanded public execution. A favourite amongst many law enforcement and military personnel, the 38 had a cartridge capacity of 8 rounds. No matter what mission he was on, The Assassin always carried two spare magazines. He knew, however, that he would not need this firepower tonight. But it made him feel more relaxed, and that was important in his line of work.

He moved off, keeping low against the horizon. His direction of entry to the target was through what had once been a National Park, with sporadic woodland and wide open grazing areas. For many years now it had been closed to the public, but still the old footpaths remained. The wildlife had thrived even more since the park's closure, with a burgeoning population of pheasant and rabbit - and the foxes that fed on them - complimenting the deer.

He ran with increasing speed, taking care not to trip in the potholes caused by the hooves of wild deer on wet autumn days, the holes then being sun-baked and hardened like concrete.

He knew the path he should take, having been this way in preparation for the task ahead every night for the previous fortnight.

He also knew what he was to do, and understood that planning of such missions was the key to success. Particularly when the target was so high profile in public life.

About to vault a stile, sudden movement to his left stopped the Assassin in his tracks. Instinctively he slowed his breathing to a steady, shallow sigh. The sound of silence cracked through the night air. He crouched by the stile waiting for a sign, any sign. Flipping his goggles back down from atop his brow he turned his head to the left. A patch of warm yellow stood in front of him, no more than ten yards away. Piercing eyes stared, waiting for movement. A fox, lurking for its prey.

He calmed himself, jumped the stile and carried on. On towards his prey and his next big pay day.

Soon he came to the road. Now he needed to take extra care, be more vigilant than during his run here. There would be security on the other side. He had to hope that they would now follow their normal routine, and not break from the natural order of their nightly tasks.

He glanced at his watch. Two minutes before midnight. Bang on time. He pulled his sleeve down over his watch and the gloves up to make sure that the luminous dial would not give his position away.

Peering through his goggles, he saw the door to the main house open, no more than 50 yards away. The glow from the hall lights lit the pathway. Two large Dobermans sped out, and down towards the Assassin's vantage point at the front west flank of the grounds.

Darting across the road, crouching low, the assassin threw two lumps of lean steak in the grounds. The dogs had been conditioned over the last couple of weeks to accept the offerings. Indeed, they expected it, like the dogs in Pavlov's experiments. What they didn't realise was that all that prime steak had been in preparation for their benefactor's next offering.

He crouched low as the hulking hounds fed without restraint on the raw meat. Unloading his pack from behind him, he shimmied the zipper down. One of the dogs looked up from his food, as if in suspicion of this odd movement. No sooner had his eyes met the man's than he returned to his midnight snack.

The assassin pulled out two of the darts, and held them gently in his left hand. He put his right back into the bag and pulled out a twelve-inch blowpipe. He loaded the first dart, and placed the end of the pipe between his lips.

The dog froze the very second the dart hit, and keeled over to the ground, a blank expression adorning his face. Unperturbed, the second kept gorging on the fresh meat under his nose. Seconds later, this sentinel too was prostrate.

The assassin knew that he had eight minutes to achieve his aim, and be free of the grounds before the absence of the dogs was noticed.

Skirting the flint wall he moved furtively round the property, halting only when one of the security guards opened the door to extinguish his cigarette. He held still and silent as he watched the guard take one last drag on the butt before dropping it casually on the floor and stamping the burning embers, and only moved off again when he knew it was safe to do so.

The assassin knew that he could have taken both guards out. They had got complacent through the passage of time on such a cushy job. They were no longer highly trained professionals. They were a disgrace to the uniforms that they had once been proud to wear. Typical army turned security: lazy. Over time becoming inept with the knowledge that they were employed for show, not for any real practical purpose.

Eliminating these guards would be as easy as ridding the threat of the dogs had been. But he had his orders. Only the target was to be eliminated. Not the guards, except in absolute emergency. The Director knew that such a scenario would not occur.

Not tonight.

And not with the Assassin on the job. The best of the best, and tonight's result would push his price up even higher.

The door closed behind the guard, and the Assassin moved again toward the back of the house, watchful that his steps did not grate against the gravel underfoot.

It was at the rear west wing that he stopped and once more delved into his bag of tricks, this time extracting a pair of lightweight long nose pincers.

He ran his left hand across the wall, three feet above ground level, and found the junction box that housed the cable to the external rear camera. All other cameras pointed away from the house, this was the only one that covered his path to his goal.

He placed the nose of the pincers around the base of the cable, and gave a little tug. The cable moved, and fell out of the socket in to which it had run. He replaced the pincers in his pack. Taking out the skeleton key and a ring that he slipped on his index finger of his left hand, he immediately set off seeking the rear door that he knew was just yards away.

He knew it would be locked, but slipped the skeleton into the keyhole. With a deft little jiggle and a turn of the doorknob, he was in. He waited. No alarm, exactly as the Director had said it would be.

He moved quietly to the front of the house through the darkened corridors, passing the enclosed hallway where he could hear the guards laughing at some programme on the television set.

Inept, out of the zone.

No wonder they had not yet noticed the lack of feed from the closed circuit television at the rear of the house. Too long on easy civilian jobs, where their once honed skills were being allowed to rot like carcasses in the searing heat of the dessert.

He finally came to the study entrance. The Director had told him that this is where his prey would be, preparing for more rounds of publicity after the sun had risen on a new day. Only he would not see that sunrise.

The adrenaline flowed through the assassin's body. He could feel it. Every time it was the same, a feeling better than any snort of cocaine, or puff of weed could ever give. He craved these moments, and was addicted to them the way a serial killer would look forward to his next victim. He didn't know whether it was the knowledge of the pay out, or just the thrill of the impending kill that made him feel this way. He suspected it was the latter.

He slowly pushed the door open. There sitting at his desk was the victim, looking at the figure in the doorway, dumbfounded. A desk lamp half lit his face and the Assassin could see the look of horror in his prey's eyes. It was always like this: a split second or two of utter bemusement, before returning to the land of the living with the realisation of impending doom.

Before he had time to awaken from his cerebral hiatus, the masked intruder was upon him, covering his mouth with his right hand and placing his left around his neck. He was sure that he saw a smile spread across the intruder's face as a small pinprick dug into the right side of his neck.

He tried to struggle, but the heat that coursed through his veins was unbearable. He couldn't move, not even his little finger responded to his thoughts.

The intruder let him go, placing him gently back to his seat, unmasking himself at the same time.

'I really wish it wasn't you, Jack. But these things have to be done. You've got too close to the truth, and you wouldn't play ball with the Director. Now all I'll take is the file that you have, and then I'll be on my way.'

Jack Hudson, Foreign Secretary, could no longer see his assailant, though he could hear him. He had no way of fighting back. Paralysed in body, though able in mind. He tried to place the voice that he had heard. He knew the man was still in the room. He could hear him, he could feel his presence. How had he got in? How had he evaded security, and the dogs? A dreadful thought entered Jack's head. "What if this madman had killed all in the household on his way to the study?"

Hudson could hear his attacker rifling his files. One after the other was being opened and plundered, the search becoming more feverish as the seconds ticked by. Seconds that seemed like hours.

Hudson knew that what was being searched for would not be found. Not here. That was the only solace he had. At least he had set the ball in motion. He smiled inwardly at the thought.

The Assassin went from one drawer to another. Only half his job had been done. He knew what he was looking for, but it was nowhere to be found.

Time was running out.

Very shortly the guards would be recalling their hounds from the grounds. They would not come. The Guards would go looking, and it wouldn't take them long to discover the bodies. At that point, the useless pair would then enter the Secretary of State's study.

'Where is it old man? Where have you hidden the treasure? I should have made you squeal before killing you.'

He glanced at his watch. Time had run out. His mission was only half accomplished, but the file had not been where the Director had said it would be. Had the Director been outmanoeuvred?

He looked at the Secretary of State before making his way out of the French doors that would lead him around the east wing of the house and to the safety of the road and the park beyond.

He could have sworn that he saw Jack Hudson smile. But he knew that was impossible.

'About time those dogs returned. Go get them, Charlie.'

Charlie got up out of his seat, and went to move to the main external door, glancing at the monitors as he stretched his weary body.

'That damn rear camera's out again,' he said as he exited the security room to the main garden.

He called the dogs to order.

Nothing.

He called again.

Once more nothing.

This was not usual. Even if the dogs had found a stray rabbit, they always returned when ordered.

Charlie entered the room, and stared at the blank screen once more. He picked up his gun, and held it by his side.

'We've got problems, Jones. Full alert. Let's get and check the old man.'

The two guards left the confines of their security room by the internal door, exiting directly to the corridor leading to Jack Hudson's secure office. The corridor was in darkness, save for a sombre primrose glow emanating from the open door of the study, bathing the corridor in an eerie gloom.

A breeze blew gently in their faces. Charlie glanced at Jones; beads of sweat on their brows belied their calmness. Jones put his finger to his lip, and pointed for Charlie to travel one side of the corridor as he took the more open side toward the study.

The breeze grew stronger as they approached the open doorway. Peering in, Charlie crouched, gun pointed in toward the Secretary of State, with Jones similarly pointing his firearm into the room but from a standing position.

The midnight breeze played with the nets that hang from ceiling to floor in front of the French doors. To the guards this merely confirmed the gravity of their situation. Jack Hudson never had these doors open.

Charlie moved toward the desk, and stared in disbelief at the sight of his charge sitting bolt upright in his leather Captain's chair. He tried his pulse. Although Jack Hudson was still breathing, there was no pulse. Nothing.

The man's hand was still warm, though no life coursed through its fingers. It was limp, with no intent left in its sinew. The eyes, too, told the tale of death, staring fixedly at a point in the distance, unblinking. Just there, two lifeless black orbs in a sea of snow. His cheeks were an ashen grey, the colour seeping out of them with every passing breath.

Within seconds he was gone.

Jones and Charlie just stared at each other. After a time, Charlie looked out toward the blackness through the French-doors.

'Shit!' he exclaimed.

'I think its worse than that,' stated Jones, a tinge of despair in his voice.

A Police helicopter buzzed overhead, but the escape had already been made.

The Assassin drove at a steady pace in his car. Twelve Forty-five. Half the mission completed.

His identity intact.

It bothered him that the file had not been retrieved. But then, it had not been there. In the few minutes he had, a thorough search of the office had been conducted. The file had simply not been there. Could Jack Hudson have known what was about to happen? It didn't look like it, the way the horror had spread across his face when he had seen the masked intruder standing in his doorway.

He also had not expected the 'pin prick of death', as the Assassin liked to call it. The Mojave rattlesnake has highly neurotoxic venom, causing rapid paralysis, eventually leading to suffocation.

When released by his specially commissioned ring, it was one of his favourite methods of killing. It gave him pleasure to think that his victim was in a semi-conscious state whilst he watched him die.

And the missing file? The Director would know what to do. And he would soon know that at least part of his problems had been dealt with. But he would not hear the news from the Assassin. There would to be no contact for two days, and then the Director would find him. That was always the way.

He looked in his rear view mirror, to see the helicopter circling with search-lights on in the distance behind him. Two police cars sped past him travelling towards the scene of the crime, blue lights flashing.

The Assassin laughed to himself. It was always the same.

A world full of incompetent security.

No wonder men like him existed.

TWO

The young soldier stood there, listening intently to the orders being given to him by his Commanding Officer. Peter Hudson was a fine military brain, a man who not only commanded his troops with profligate efficiency, but also one who commanded their respect with unbound compassion. He had risen through the ranks and knew what it meant to be in a position of unswerving obedience, to put your life in the hands of those that would lead you to glory or death.

And now he was the leader of a crack force of troops, the elite of the British Military, The Special Air Services, SAS.

Motto 'Who dares wins.' Hudson preferred 'Proper planning prevents piss poor performance.'

The air felt heavy under the weight of the mid-afternoon sun. There was never any breeze at this time of year to refresh and discharge the stench of weaponry mixed with the sweat of both Arab and Christian militia. Sweat caused by both the incessant beating of the sun, and the unending tension of each day.

Iraq. Bloody Iraq.

And now his elite force of himself and seven men had got caught up with manoeuvres of American troops

Hudson's patrol was the now unheard of 'Bravo Four Zero', one of four patrols sent behind enemy lines in late January 1991 to gather intelligence on the movement of Soviet Scud missile launchers.

Further objectives included disrupting the enemy by blowing up various strategic targets, such as the fibre optic communications systems that lay in pipelines all over Iraq.

Hudson's patrol had somehow been dropped directly over an advance force of the United States' 2nd Brigade, 1st Cavalry Division, on reconnaissance for impending operations.

They were now all holed up just a couple of miles away from a whole Battalion of Saddam's Republican Guard.

Hudson was debriefing the young officer standing ahead of him. They had to get away from here and continue their mission.

The flies swarmed round the officers, like vultures waiting for their prey to drop. The march from the drop point to their current location went unhindered, but was slow and painful progress as soon as Hudson had realised that they were not where they should have been.

They had been due to be dropped behind enemy lines near the Rumala oilfields. Instead they had found themselves to the North East of Umm Qasr, Iraq's only port, on the border of Kuwait.

The fighting was heavy along the border, and the American force had been deployed ahead to try to cut off supplies to the front line.

It was a damn mess. The 1st Cavalry had been besieged for two days now, pinned down by the ferocious fighting of the Republican Guard, and Hudson had been dropped slap-bang in the middle of the stalemate. Despite several air attacks on the enemy, they still held the upper hand in this particular dogfight.

Umm Qasr stands on the banks of the Khawr Az-Zubayr, on the Khawr Abd Akllah estuary, which leads to the Persian Gulf. It had been bombed heavily in the first days of the War, but still had not fallen into coalition hands, although the Iraqi troops had pulled back into their own land from the Kuwaiti side of the small inlet that separated the two countries at this naval port.

Hudson's plan was both simple and daring. During nightfall his patrol would head toward the port on foot, and dig in before sun rose the next day. From their vantagepoint they would be able to assess the best way back across the border, whilst at the same time spying opportunities to wreak as much havoc as possible on the surrounding Iraqi troops. Perhaps their mission would not have been entirely in vain, after all.

Hudson stood explaining his motives and the escape plan to the younger man. A spark of light from a distant point on the horizon pierced Hudson's eyes. Before he could push his charge to the ground and out of harms way, the young officer's face disintegrated in front of him.

The bullet had entered from behind, just under the neck of his helmet, and blown away his face as it exited. Blood and tissue splattered Hudson's face. The boy fell backwards, with Hudson falling on top of him. The boy's body pulsated to the rhythm of its final heartbeats.

Blood and brains fused into one horrible mess, the boy unrecognisable...

Peter Hudson opened his eyes, awaking from the dream; the horror of reality that visited him in the early hours of every morning as it had done for the past 16 years.

He would never be able to eradicate the memory of that moment. He should have been more vigilant. He knew the dangers. They had been in a war zone. He had made a personal promise to the boy's brother that he would bring him home safely. Home to his bride to be. Speaking to her had been almost as terrifying as seeing his protégé's face blown off.

Sweat seeped from every pore of his body as it always did at this point. He could not stop the memory reappearing each morning, but he could deal with it. His Army Councillor had advised him to find a coping mechanism.

He swung his legs out of the bed, and unscrewed the cap on the waiting bottle of Southern Comfort. Picking up the tumbler waiting on his bedside table, he poured himself a large mouthful and gulped the brown liquid in one. It no longer warmed his throat as it disappeared. He was too used to it for any effect like that. It was more like a child's comforter, a security blanket that had the psychological effect of dulling any pain he felt.

The sleeplessness, the bad dreams, and his own brand of medication had been the downfall of his marriage. All that coupled with the fear of being widowed that his wife felt constantly. He didn't know which was the biggest contributor to the split.

At least the divorce had been amiable: he couldn't have stood the fight. And he guessed that Judy knew this. She had made it easy on him, and he on her. They still kept in touch. She still phoned him daily to make sure he was alright. He looked forward to her calls.

Like him, Judy had not got together with anyone else since the divorce. Sure, she'd had a couple of boyfriends, but nothing serious. In fact, he was sure that she still had feelings for him. He knew he had never fallen out of love with her.

The early morning sun drifted through the curtains, slowly breaking into the darkness. Peter stood up and walked naked to the adjoining bathroom. As he entered he pulled the light cord and strode to the sink. He turned the cold tap on and cupped his hands underneath the flow.

Three times he repeated the process of collecting a reservoir of cool clean water and dispersing briskly over his face. He looked in the mirror.

Although no longer twenty eight as he had been in the dessert on that fateful day in 1991, he still kept himself fit. His cropped blonde hair stood a little spiky early morning. He had little facial hair, but would shave none the less. Many military habits were hard to break.

He was still toned like an officer. Broad shoulders being the mantle for a cut torso, six pack still firm. He breathed in, proud of his physique. Well built, but without the extra trappings that a man his age ought to have. He kept himself well, regularly working out at his local gym. He knew that Judy would not entertain having him back any other way.

After shaving he completed his daily bathroom routine by showering, again in cold water, and patting himself down with the clean white towel that he laid out every night in readiness for the following day.

Routine. Routine and normality. The two things that the Army shrink had told him were key to his recovery.

Returning to the bedroom, he pulled the drapes wide allowing the day to flood in. He lit a cigarette, a habit that had only taken hold after the Iraq incident.

He sat, staring at the local inhabitants beginning their daily business below.

When he and Judy had split, he had told her to keep the house. He now rented an apartment on the upper floor of a block in Clerkenwell Green, London. He liked the traditional look of the building, whilst at the same time enjoying all the mod cons that a refurbished building should accommodate.

His loft space was well appointed, with a large bedroom and en suite, and a combined open plan lounge/ dining room/ kitchen.

The bedroom was simply furnished, with a white metallic double bed and a small pine bedside table on each side. He had a table and chair at the window, again in pine, and where he now sat. Built in wardrobes, with mirrored sliding doors to open up the space even further completed the look.

He watched as the fishmonger who lived across the street from him used one of the public phones in the street below, calling a cab as he did every morning. The traffic was becoming heavy in the street below as was its want on weekdays, circling the small plaza where the two old style red telephone boxes stood. Peter particularly like these. Traditional: and offering the occupant more privacy than the more modern three-sided perspex variety.

He looked down the street to where his local bakers stood. He'd soon be at the counter ordering his croissant to have with his morning coffee.

Routine.

He stubbed his cigarette, and walked over to his wardrobe. Today he would wear a freshly pressed white shirt with cut away collar, his navy blue suit with thin grey pinstripes, and a blue and grey woven silk tie. But then again, working the security desk at one of the major city investment houses meant that he wore the same every day.

Normality.

Having dressed he moved to the lounge, surveying his property as he went.

The walls were open to brickwork, and the floor a veneered pine. He had a small bar in the far corner of the lounge area, next to the floor to ceiling windows. The windows had remote controlled full length cream blinds to protect one's privacy, which Peter tended to leave only half open at all times. On the bar stood three optics, dispensing Vodka, Whiskey and Southern Comfort. The southern comfort was three quarters empty. Tumblers and wineglasses sat on the glass shelf to the rear of the bar.

Mounted on the rear wall of the lounge was a thirty six-inch flat screen plasma television, with surround sound speakers. A mini sound system was set on a white pine counter below.

Peter picked a remote from the arm of the brown leather sofa and flicked the compact disc player on to play.

He adjusted the sound level to something appropriate for James Morrison's 'You give me something.'

Peter never watched the news at this time of the morning, preferring to percolate his coffee to soft music. The news of the day could wait until he was on the tube.

He walked past the dining table, with chairs for four. He didn't know why he had indulged in this. He usually ate dinner on his own, and only occasionally would he have company: even then it would most likely be Judy for Saturday lunch if she were in town doing some shopping.

Flicking the switch on the percolator, Peter opened the fridge and retrieved a pint of full cream milk. It was then that he noticed the flashing red light from his telephone answering machine on the far wall of the dining area.

He always had his phone on silent at night, figuring that any emergency could wait until the morning. He walked over. The display read '10', the most messages that his phone would allow. He was perplexed, and pressed play, fast-forwarding to the most recent.

'Hud, as soon as you pick this message up, turn on the television. Watch the news, BBC1. Call me, please.'

It was his sister in law, Amy. She, like everyone he knew, called him by his schoolboy nickname of "Hud". In truth he liked it better than his given Christian name. He had never heard his brother's wife so panicked. And it was certainly not usual for her to call him. Amy was Judy's best friend. That's how Hud and Judy had first met, at Jack and Amy's wedding. Since his marriage had ended, Amy had always held the divorce against Hud. As far as she was concerned, Hud had never made any effort to be the man that Judy deserved.

Confused, Hud used the remote that he still held in his hand to turn the volume down on the sound system whilst simultaneously switching the television-set on and changing channels to BBC1.

There, on the screen in front of him was a picture of his brother. Nothing unusual there. Being a member of the British Cabinet he was often on screen. What was different was the flash below:

'Jack Hudson, Home Secretary, found dead at his desk in the early hours of this morning. Suspected heart attack'

Peter Hudson collapsed to his knees. This couldn't be right. His brother was almost as fit as he was.

He picked up the handset of the cordless phone, and dialled Amy's number. The number was answered within two rings.

'My god, Hud, where have you been. I've been waiting for your call,' the tearful voice at the other end cried out.

'Amy, you know I never have my phone on at night. I've only just got your message. I've seen the news. How the hell did it happen?'

'Hud, not on this line. Get in your car. Come down. When can you be here?'

'Amy, calm down. What do you mean 'not on this line'? Of course I'll come down.'

'Now Hud, hurry.'

With that the line went dead.

Hud looked back at the television screen.

Routine and normality.

It would seem that his recuperation would have to wait a while longer. He had never had much faith in his shrink, anyway. The last sixteen years had proved him to be right on that score.

THREE

When he arrived at his late brother's house, Hud was amazed to find a multitude of security surrounding the large abode and grounds of a man who had died form a heart attack in the middle of the night. Even though his brother had been so high profile, in full public view – particularly with the heightened terror alerts of the previous weeks – this seemed a little extravagant. The place was positively swarming with police and the more secretive plain-clothes security forces that such a man seemed to have with him everywhere he went.

Hud had made the journey from his flat in London to the mid-Kent countryside in double quick time. He was aided, of course, by the fact that the majority of the traffic was flowing into London during the morning rush hour and he was travelling out.

Once he had negotiated The City, and made his way over Tower Bridge, he had found the remainder plain sailing and had been able to push the speed limit of seventy miles per hour.

What his sister-in-law had said to him bothered him. And her *wanting* Hud to be there as soon as possible didn't make sense. Ok, so Jack had been Hud's older brother, but Amy had family nearby living at Aldington, a small village a few miles South of Ashford. Surely she would have called upon their support first?

As he rounded the corner toward Jack and Amy's house, Hud noticed a silver BMW 5 series. He was almost certain that the car with blacked out windows had sped past him along the M20 between Maidstone and Ashford. But then again, BMW's were now almost as commonplace as Ford Mondeos.

Hud was stopped at the head of the driveway by a policeman wearing the obligatory yellow safety jacket, his head protected against the rain by the regulation peak cap.

All told, there were four marked police cars, and two black Jaguars that Hud guessed belonged to high level security. Above he could hear the drone of at least one helicopter, possibly a pair. The police numbered ten, and with the security guards as well, Hud reckoned there to be at least fourteen personnel guarding a dead man.

As he pulled to a halt in front of the large country house, the Coroner and his assistant were wheeling the covered body to the waiting ambulance, followed by Amy.

She seemed not to notice Hud at first, with tears streaming down her face and pale as a ghost.

The realisation of Jack's death caught up with Hud, like a tidal wave washing away the trappings of civilisation from the golden sands of one of those popular Costa Blanca tourist destinations. Up to this point he had been almost in a trance of disbelief, as if the whole affair had been just a bad dream. At the moment of realisation, he wished that Judy had been sitting at his side.

'Hud, you've got to see him before they take him away. You've got to Hud, it's important!' cried Amy through the glass of the driver's side window, banging on the pane with her clenched fist.

The younger Hudson composed himself, and stepped out onto the gravel drive. His leather soles crunched against the small stones. Amy flung her arms around him, holding him tight for just a second, and whispered in his ear.

'They're putting out that it was a heart attack. But you've got to look at him. Look at him Hud, then you'll know.'

Hud took Amy's hand and moved toward the ambulance, where his brother's body was being unceremoniously shunted through its wide-open double doors.

Amy knew the task that she had asked Hud to perform would be sickening for him. She knew the fear that would permeate through to Hud's most inner self, to the core of his being.

'Let me see him. Let me say goodbye to my brother.'

The coroner stopped and turned to survey the man who would have him disrupt his job, a look of disdain upon his face. Without speaking he gave a sideways glance to one of the plain clothes boys, who nodded approval.

'Sir,' the coroner said, unzipping the black body bag that lay half in and half out of the ambulance.

Hud walked over, every step harder than the one before. Everything seemed to have stopped, waiting on him. The wind no longer blew. The rain no longer wet his face to mask any tears that might appear. Eyes burned into the back of Hud's head. The world moved in slow motion, perhaps because he was willing it to. Perhaps he wasn't up to this task.

All focus was on him, just as it had been that fateful day in Iraq. He had seen plenty of death throughout his life, but none since Iraq. None since that young soldier in his charge had bought it. He felt nauseous, gastric bile building up in the back of his throat. The shape of his brother within the body bag pulling him nearer, and yet at the same time pushing him away.

With one last effort he was there, standing next to his brother. Hud lent forward, in close now. Unblinking, lifeless eyes stared back at him. Lips were blue, cheeks a pallid grey drawn in at the bones. Hud leaned closer still, resting his forehead against Jack's. Cold.

He placed a hand behind his brother's head, and one on the opposite side of the cot. He couldn't make out whether it was the need to hug his brother one last time, or the inability to stand unaided that made him adopt such a position: head bowed, arms akimbo.

He raised his brother's head off the bed of the cot, and that's when he saw the red mark upon the right side of Jack's neck. Small but with a little bruising around. No bigger that half the diameter of a five-penny piece.

He looked again at the eyes. There was a fear in them that he had never seen before. It was as if Jack were able to see his fate before it had happened.

He looked at Amy. She viewed him intensely. Looking in his eyes, she could see that Hud knew this was no heart attack. She was satisfied that she wasn't going mad.

Hud looked once more at his brother. He felt the surging desire to vomit, and cry at the same time. He did neither.

Releasing his grip from the back of Jack's neck, he kissed him on the forehead. He slowly pulled the zipper back to its sealed position, and negotiated the few paces back to Amy.

The world came to life again.

The wind blew, the rain fell.

Helicopters buzzed above, and the police carried on about their duties.

Hud looked at Amy, her tear stained face a little less pale than before. Where a moment ago there had been despair, there was now determination. Amy had always been strong. Sometimes a little too single minded for Hud's liking, but always the woman that his brother had needed. Hud gripped Amy at the elbow and led her in to the house, away from the confusion in the courtyard.

'Let's get a cuppa,' he said, making their way to the back of the house and to the relative sanctuary of the kitchen. As they crossed the main corridor of the property, Hud spied a small army of forensics working feverishly away in Jack's study. He hoped that they would find clues that would lead to the killer. But somehow he doubted it.

Once in the kitchen, the younger Hudson picked the kettle from the side and filled it from the cold water tap, letting a little water drain the pipe before placing the kettle underneath.

He placed it back on its base and flicked the switch down, to the on position. He took two cups off the tree, and placed them on their saucers. He turned to Amy, who had taken a seat nearest the door that led to the rear garden. She looked up at Hud, her arm resting on the informal dining table next to her.

'Tea bags are fine,' she said, second-guessing his question before it came.

He carried on in silence, and when the tea was finally made – which seemed to take an eternity – he picked the saucers holding the cups and walked them over to the table.

Usually he would sit as far away from Amy as possible, but not today. Today he sat on the corner nearest Amy. He placed his hand on hers, and she looked up at him. Her eyes were bloodshot, but the tears no longer flowed. Perhaps she was all cried out, at least for now.

'Thanks, Hud. Thanks for coming.'

'Why me? Why not your sister? She's only lives a few miles away.'

'Hud, your brother would have wanted it this way. Jack was a good man, and loved you. I knew that you would see what I saw. His eyes, Hud! Did you see his eyes?'

Hud looked at Amy. There was that steely determination again. She knew more than she was letting on. There was something that she was holding back.

'What is it, Amy?'

'Tell me you saw it. I know you did, I can see it in your eyes. Judy always said that for a second she would know whether you were lying or not, just by looking at your eyes. They are so like Jack's. You two are so alike in so many ways.' She spoke as if Jack were still alive.

'Yes, I saw it, Amy.'

'I knew it. I knew you would. My sister wouldn't have. That's why I needed you here, Hud. When they were putting Jack in that goddam ambulance, I thought you would not get the chance to see for yourself.'

Amy blaspheming took Hud by surprise. Amy never swore.

'Calm down, Amy. Let's drink our tea, and then we can talk.'

'My sister would have been useless. She phoned, you know. Wanted to come over. I told her no, not yet. Later. I'll give her a call when you've gone.'

'No Amy', replied Hud, 'I'll call her before I've gone. You shouldn't be alone. And having the police here isn't the same as having a friend or family with you. Trust me on this one. I know.'

They finished their tea in silence, the only disturbance the sound of the forensics team working away toward the front of the house. They seemed to be getting closer, moving toward the back of the house through the corridor.

Hud pondered the strength of the police and security. And all this forensic science stuff going on. It seemed that it was not only Hud and Amy who believed that this was no heart attack victim.

'Excuse me, Sir! Madam!' a booming voice from the kitchen doorway awoke Hud from his pondering.

The man stood nearly six feet tall, and filled the width of the entry. One of the plain-clothes boys, his tie neatly hiding an unbuttoned collar. A mop of mouse brown hair, which had the look of having dried naturally after a good soaking, told the tale that he had been conducting himself both in and out of the house. As did the rain splashed mackintosh that the detective wore.

'DCI Borden, Sir. We'll be out of your way shortly. We're just finishing up. We'll leave a couple of uniformed officers on scene for a day or two to deter the hacks and photographers from the tabloids.'

He turned to leave, his job done for the day.

'Officer,' called Hud.

The officer turned abruptly, and eyed Hud.

'Yes, Sir?'

'Tell me, why so much fuss? Why all the forensics, and the number of police? It seems rather heavy handed for a heart attack victim.'

'Yes, Sir. It would seem that way. However, you're brother was a very prominent figure around these parts, as was he in Westminster. We are merely following the prescribed route of investigation for such a person.

'All the forensics, well that's to ensure that we have covered all bases.

'And the security? And the police? As I've just stated, we must ensure that there is as little intrusion from those that want to profit from your family's misfortune as possible. By showing our strength and determination to keep such profiteers away from the scene early on, its easier to then use a lesser presence and achieve a similar result later.

'I'm sure you can appreciate what a sensitive situation this is. If we showed too little regard, the press and public would hang us.

'We hope to have the household back to some normality as quickly as possible, Sir.'

With that DCI Borden left the room and disappeared down the hallway, passing the last of the forensics team as he went. To Peter Hudson, the explanation – whilst plausible – seemed a tad too scripted. He didn't need to ask what Amy thought.

When the last of the police had departed, and Borden had said his farewell, the house was finally peaceful. He had been true to his word, and left just two uniformed officers at the front door. The security that had been there when Jack was alive had now departed.

Amy's sister had telephoned three times during the early part of the afternoon, and each time it had been Hud that answered. He would soon be calling her over, to spend the night with her sister.

'Before you go, Hud, I need to speak to you. Now that all the commotion has died down a bit.' Amy said, still sitting in the same chair that she had first occupied when they had entered the kitchen some hours previously.

'Amy, if I could I would stay the night. You do know that don't you?' Hud answered an unasked question.

'I know, Hud. I Know. But you need your routine. I know that as well. Jack was so worried about you. So mindful of the things that you went through all those years ago. But you are the only one he trusts. Trusted.' She corrected herself to use the past tense, and Hud could see how much it hurt to do so.

'It's time we left the kitchen. Let's go to the sitting room. We can have a quick drink before you leave. Just the one, mind, you're driving. We've still got that Southern Comfort from Christmas when you were here last.

'I wish I'd allowed Jack to have you here more often. Maybe none of this would have happened. I'm sorry, Hud'

'Hey, no matter. You had your reasons. And let's face it, not without foundation.'

Amy stared at Hud. This was the first time that he had ever admitted to her, or anyone for all she knew, that he'd had a problem, that any of his troubles could be of his own making.

Amy poured herself a large gin and tonic, without the ice or slice of lemon, and fixed a Southern Comfort for Hud. Placing her drink on a coaster next to her armchair near the fire, Amy announced that she needed to fetch something from upstairs and left the room.

Hud stood near the open coal effect gas fire, which he had ignited when he and Amy had entered the room. It wasn't cold, but there was a chill to the house that needed ridding. He looked at the photograph of him and Jack together at Jack's graduation ceremony. His brother had always been the most intellectual of the pair, and had graduated in Law from Cambridge University. From there he'd had a brief spell in a City Law firm before swiftly moving into politics.

His politics was often a bone of contention with his younger brother: Jack hosting such socialist beliefs and yet with all the personal trappings of one of the gentrified classes. Four by four car, big house (far more bedrooms than he required), a lover of fine wines and champagnes, high salary, and massive perks, and so the list would go on.

To Hud none of this went with the politics of socialism, and he could not understand why Jack had chosen to be a Labour candidate all those years ago. In defence Jack would contend that all these 'extras' were self-made, and so were actually as a result of his socialist ideologies rather than in spite of them. It was an argument they had never been able to resolve, but had learnt to ignore.

Jack had been a fine orator, one who could captivate his audience in a sentence. That was certainly a detail that

Hud had admired without exception. It was the gift of public speaking that had allowed Jack Hudson to climb the ladder to political success so rapidly.

If only Jack could speak now.

As Amy returned Hud was still reminiscing, staring at the photograph on the mantle.

'That was Jack's favourite picture of you two together', Amy stated, fingering the frame. 'He would look at it almost every evening, and describe how full of life you looked at that time. You can see that you are so proud of each other.'

They stood silently for a moment, both remembering happier times.

Finally Amy asked Hud to hold his hand out, and placed a key on a fob in his palm.

'Apart from the look in his eyes, which I shall never be able to erase from my memory no matter how long I live, this is the other reason that I know Jack was murdered.'

Hud looked down. It was a simple key, very much like the type that you would get at a swimming bath, to open the lockers where one would store belongings for a pound while enjoying the pool. It was attached to a small brown leather fob with the name 'Viv' in capital letters embossed in gold.

'What's it belong to? And who's Viv?' Hud enquired of Amy.

'Jack gave that to me a couple of weeks ago. He said that should he ever run into trouble, that I ought to give the key to you, and that you would know what to do. I asked him who 'Viv' was, too. He just said that you would figure it out. I was hoping that you would be able to tell me what on earth was going on?'

'I haven't the foggiest. But If Jack felt that I would work this little conundrum out, then I had better not disappoint him!'

Their conversation was cut short by the ringing of the doorbell.

'That will be Chrissie. I phoned her when I was upstairs. Put the key in your pocket, Hud. I'll see you out.'

With that Hud followed Amy to the door, where she greeted her sister with a hug. Her sister burst into tears.

"Time for me to go", thought Hud to himself. He said his hellos and goodbyes to Chrissie in one sentence, and Amy told her to go into the house.

'Hud, be careful. Whatever you have to do, do it for Jack. But don't go getting in too deep,' Amy said giving her brother in law a hug, as if it were the last she would give him.

'I'll see you soon, Amy. Take care.'

With that, Hud got into his black Lotus Exige S and keyed the starter. This car was the one real luxury that Hud had allowed himself. Built in mid 2006, the car benefited from a supercharged 1.8 litre engine that produced a 0 to 60 time of 4.1 seconds, and a top speed of around 150 miles per hour. He loved the feel of the raw power that the car produced: to him it was like being in the cockpit of a superjet, except without the fear of being off terra firma.

He felt inside his trouser pocket, and touched the locker key on its fob.

'Viv. Who the fuck is Viv?' he asked himself under his breath.

He looked back at the front door, where the two policemen stood. Amy had already followed her sister into the house.

Hud slipped the motor into first gear and eased away from the drive, collecting gravel stones in the tread of his tyres as he went. He cursed the day that his brother had persuaded him to help stone the drive. A distant memory. His brother now gone.

Hud turned left out of the driveway, flooring the accelerator. He just wanted to get away from here. Two hundred yards along the road he did a right onto the main 'A' road, heading north toward Ashford. Since the main trunk road had been completed between Ashford and Folkestone, this road was often deserted but tonight there seemed more traffic than he would have hoped for a Sunday evening.

He travelled along, passing a derelict roadside café that had once been a thriving stop off for the lorry drivers that travelled from the industrial heartland of the Midlands down to Dover, where they would take their truck loads of manufactured goods to the Continent.

As Hud was contemplating the day's events he was only semi-concentrating on the road ahead. He certainly wasn't paying attention to the road at his rear.

From behind the disused blue and white café, the silver BMW 5 series with blacked windows silently advanced onto the road travelled by Hud's Lotus.

Sitting three cars back from his mark, The Assassin permitted himself a wry smile. It had been most unusual for the Director to make contact so soon after a kill. He now had new instructions to follow.

FOUR

Peter Hudson pondered the day's events as he drove. Nonchalantly he slipped down a gear to aid the Exige's ascent up a small incline, tickling the accelerator as the car shifted through neutral.

Riding on the almost deserted B road, he peered to his left and saw the headlamps moving at speed on the motorway below. A constant stream of traffic flowing both toward and away from the port at Dover, people leaving the country on holiday as well as the humdrum heavy goods vehicles transporting goods for import and export.

He slowed as he neared the roundabout that would divert him onto the M20, and lead him past Ashford without the necessity of negotiating the roads through the conurbation. He timed the lights on the entrance perfectly, which allowed him to avoid bringing the car to a halt, and carried on effortlessly, taking the third exit onto the fast route home.

Hud eyed the rear view mirror and saw that there were three cars going the same way as him. His mind wandered back to the riddle that his brother had set him.

Clearly Jack had felt in danger. What possible other reason could there have been for him to be so cryptic, and leave the key for his brother, not explaining even an iota to his wife? Jack and Amy had been so close, and shared everything. Amy knew all the innermost cabinet secrets and Hud would often discuss the affairs of state with his wife into the early hours of the morning. As far as he was concerned, Amy was the perfect sounding board.

Hud often thought that it was Amy that was helping to mould New Labour's Britain at least as much as the members of the Prime Minister's cabinet.

He felt the key in his pocket again.

Pulling into the right hand lane, he rounded a Land Rover Discovery. Four by fours, the automobile of choice for the well to do, were commonplace in this part of the world. This was indeed the heartland of Conservative Britain, and had not been out of Tory hands since 1931 when Michael Knatchbull was elected to Parliament. The Knatchbulls had been a prominent family in these parts, and a Grammar school in the town had been named after Norton Knatchbull, Michael Knatchbull's son.

Hud had often thought that his brother choosing to set up home in this area, so Conservative blue in its outlook, had been Jack's way of sticking two fingers up to the voting public. Hud had many times argued that his elder sibling, in order to be true to his party and his political convictions, should relocate to the Labour controlled boroughs to the North of England.

'Viv? Who is Viv?' Hud asked of his invisible companion.

He pulled the fob from his pocket, and held it to the windscreen. The key shot blades of light across Hud's face as it spun to the tune of the passing headlights. He rolled the fob between his forefinger and thumb, so that the embossed name was uppermost.

'Viv. I've got to find Viv.'

A car with full beams lit crested the uneven road on the opposite side of the central reservation, and the flash of bright yellow light temporarily blinded Hud. As his eyesight returned, the letters on the fob hit him, and its meaning became clear.

'VIV!' he exclaimed, tugging the steering wheel sharply left, narrowly missing the offside wing of a Hertz rental van. Horns beeped and headlamps furiously flashed behind him. He didn't care. He knew where he was going.

'It's not Viv! It's not a name! It's a number! Five – One – Five!' He informed his companion, who sat there: unseen, unheard, imagined.

When they had been younger, their parent's had insisted that Jack help Hud with homework at every opportunity. Hud had always resented his brother's help, and had found ways of irritating his would be tutor. One such way was labelling all of his books, sections of work and pages in Roman numerals. Jack had hated this, espousing the virtue of modern language, modern numerals, and modern thinking in a modern age. He felt that the use of such antiquated systems had no place in the world in which they grew up.

Hud looked skywards.

'You sly old fox! You knew that no one else would get it. And I know just where you need me to go.'

He braked hard as he approached the next exit, to the north of the town. He veered off the motorway and onto the slip road, taking the left bend at speed and against the natural camber of the tarmac surface. Turning sharp left at the next roundabout, he entered Ashford from the north side and found the ring road that circled the town centre. Travelling clockwise, he would be where his brother wanted him to be in less than five minutes.

The last manoeuvre had been both dangerous and erratic. Perhaps he had been dazzled by the oncoming headlights, or perhaps fallen asleep at the wheel. Whatever had happened, the sharp left steer in front of vehicles had been out of character, and the driver behind the wheel of the silver BMW had been forced to follow suit, dipping in behind the rental van that Hudson had swerved in front of.

The Assassin sat behind the Exige, just one car in between now providing his mask. He dropped back a little way, trying to figure out if he had been spotted and if this was the reason for the sudden volte-face toward the town.

He followed Hudson onto the circular, and made sure that there were cars between. It was easy to keep tabs on where his target was headed on the highly lit road, and then again it would be easy for him to be spied himself. He hated following in such conditions. It would be normal on surveillance jobs to have several tails, each taking turns to follow so as to not be noticed.

But this was no ordinary job. The ramifications of errors would be huge for the Director and his plans. That is why he chose his best man for the task.

Hudson carried on the route, ignoring a left turn and continuing clockwise. The Assassin darted to his right at the latest possible moment, remaining Hudson's hidden shadow.

He stopped on a double yellow, a hundred yards short of the left turn that Hudson had pulled into. He waited a few seconds and then resumed, a steady pace taking him into the car park of the community leisure facility.

He would park and observe Hudson's next move. Perhaps he would be able to deliver the file the Director sought tonight.

Peter Hudson pulled into a space in the car park in front of the newly finished leisure centre. He was sure this would be where he would find whatever it was that his brother had wanted him to find.

The Stour Centre was not actually a new facility, but rather a completely refurbished existing community sports centre. As he drove in, Hud couldn't help but admire the glass fronted edifice. During the remodelling, which had begun in June 2005 shortly after Labour's third election win on the spin, Jack Hudson had been a big supporter of the new space for the community. All that was left to complete the building works was for the scaffolding to be dismantled at the rear of the building in preparation for the official opening by Jack Hudson in a month's time. Only now that ceremony would be conducted by someone else.

Although he wasn't the local MP, Jack took it upon himself to be involved in the community in which he lived. Hud thought that his brother had ideas of removing the incumbent Tory MP from office at the next election, and becoming Labour's first representative in the House from this Kentish constituency.

Jack had become a leading champion of the leisure centre and the benefits to the town during the period of his residence in the district, and had also been a frequent visitor to the centre's Contours Health Club, taking up a full membership package. The centre itself boasted three pools with flumes, a sports hall that catered for court sports and indoor football, as well as the fitness studios. It was the changing facilities of the fitness studios to which Hud needed access.

He locked the car with the remote, and strode over to the large entrance foyer. As he was about to enter he stopped a second to examine the reflection of the silver BMW 5 series in the glass of the spring-loaded door.

The car proceeded past his parking space and to the rear of the car park. Hud walked in, approached the reception desk and positioned himself so that he could watch the car park whilst quizzing the young girl on duty.

He had come to the Leisure Centre to find a locker, and remove its contents. Now he had another objective. He needed to either find out who was tailing him, or lose him. As he smooth talked the receptionist, he continued to spy the BMW that had parked the other side of the car park.

No one exited the car, which convinced Hud that he had been followed. The same car that had sped past him earlier that day and that he had seen moments prior to seeing his brother's body for the last time.

Hud thought about the possibility of some type of governmental security, perhaps a guard to ensure the same fate that had fallen on his brother did not meet Hud also. He dismissed this notion as implausible: all press releases were categorically stating that Jack Hudson had died from a massive and unexpected heart attack.

No, Hud knew that his pursuer would be someone far more sinister. He knew his brother had been murdered, even if the rest of the world didn't.

He watched, and waited. He looked at the clock on the wall in the foyer. He had been talking his way into a free pass for five minutes. He'd explained that he didn't want to use the facilities, but was considering becoming a member. All he wanted to do was have a look around to see if it would serve him well. He had promised that if he decided to take a membership, then he would sign there and then, that very evening, allowing the receptionist to claim the commission. Finally she had agreed on ten minutes. His cause had been helped by a group of teenage boys complaining that the refreshment machine had eaten their money.

'Sir, you have ten minutes. By the time you return I'll have sorted these boys out, and we can complete your membership application. We take all major credit cards or cash. No cheques, I'm afraid.' With those words she buzzed him through, the turnstile rotating as he walked.

He looked back. Still the BMW remained, its occupant hidden by the black glass of its windscreen. Hud needed a plan, and quick.

FIVE

Walking through the turnstile, the smell of chlorine hanging in the air grew stronger with every step. Hudson was a very good swimmer, but hated the sterile overtones of manufactured pools. He had always suffered from adverse reactions to swimming in chlorinated water, and his eyes would redden and tear-ducts stream within minutes of diving in when he was a child. Consequently his father had taught him to swim in the sea, and in his early army years he had twice swum the English Channel from Dover to Calais.

Hudson looked up at the direction signs swinging in mid air above his head, ensuring the information given to him by the receptionist was correct.

Taking a left at the first set of stairs he climbed two flights to the top floor. The air was cooler here than below, and less acrid to his nostrils. He passed two glass-fronted gymnasiums before entering the third door on his left, an aluminium door with 'Men's Changing' embossed in blue capitals.

As he turned the knob he eyed the corridor in both directions. At the far end was a fire exit, which had a yellow and black striped 'no entry' tape stuck across it. The corridor from the direction he had travelled was empty.

The changing facilities were white and pristine: white walls, white benches, even white lockers. The benches were positioned in three tiers in the middle of the room, with pegs above. The lockers lined the walls, from floor to ceiling two lockers to each column. In the far corner was the exit from the changing room to the exercise rooms. Hud walked over to this door, opened it and stood in the doorway.

There were half a dozen machines being used by patrons of the centre, and two staff monitoring progress. Hud looked at his watch: eight forty five in the evening. The fitness centre closed at nine. His guess was that all the exercise junkies would stay occupied on their machines until closing. He had time to locate the locker, remove the contents and make his get away. He shut the door, and turned to survey the lockers. Starting at the closest he located the number by the key and read out loud to himself.

'One hundred and five.'

He moved to the other side of the room, to find locker four hundred. The final wall took him close to the fitness room exit once more, where he located locker five hundred and fifteen.

He placed the key in the lock and turned. The door popped open to reveal a small grey and black sports holdall. He pulled it out from its hiding place and sat down on the bench opposite with the bag on his lap.

Hud stared at the soft leather sack in front of him, his eyes trance like as if he could see through the outer skin to the contents inside. About to pull the zipper open, a noise from the corridor outside startled him. The door started to open.

Hud sprang to his feet, and faced the path to his freedom, eyes wide, heart pumping.

Through the doorway a man of stocky stature, dark hair and a full beard appeared. Behind him he pulled a silver bucket on wheels, using the handle of his mop to guide his water receptacle.

Hud calmed himself, breathed deeply and picked the bag from the bench.

'Sorry, Sir. I didn't realise anyone was here' the janitor said.'I hope you had a good workout.'

'Sorry? Uh, oh, yes. Yes, thank you' Hud replied, brushing past the cleaner and heading for the door. He could not afford the time to make small talk. He had to effect his escape. Examination of the bag could wait.

Exiting the changing room, Hud looked through the glass to the swimming pool below. People dressed in just their bathing costumes were starting to clamber out of the water, driven by the two lifeguards. The last session was ending. Soon the corridors would be full of people fresh from their once a week exercise, trying to make their way out of the building and homeward bound.

Hud knew that he could not afford to go with them. He had to find another way out. He looked to his left at the taped fire exit door. Ensuring that there was no one watching his movements, he made his way to the door. It was not chained. He lent on the push bar, and the door popped open.

Outside a black expanse greeted him. For a moment he saw nothing, just air ahead of him. No stairs or emergency ladder. As his eyes acclimatised to the darkness, he saw his escape route.

To his right, about a yard away from the doorway, stood scaffolding. Hud swung the bag out and dropped it onto the first board. Smartly, his left leg followed suit, as Hud held the doorframe with his right hand. His foot hit the solid scaffold. He now hung there, pinned by his right hand and his left foot. He moved his left hand to grasp the scaffold pole, but gripped only thin air. Hud's grasp of the doorframe slipped. For a split second he stayed forty feet above ground, as if he were halfway through a mid-air star jump. He felt himself falling backwards.

Instinct took over, and he pushed away with his right foot, spinning himself in a pirouette. He pressed hard against the scaffold board with his left foot, the momentum caused by his movement enough to bounce him above the scaffolding. As he fell earthbound, Hud reached with both hands. They caught the feel of cold steel.

He wrapped his fingers around the scaffold tightly, his legs falling from above and behind to crash into the wood and steel erection. He clambered up, hauling himself with his arms until he could rest his feet against the boards.

His heart thumped fast, his breathing making steam patterns in the cool night air. He sat silently, watching, listening: nothing. Light shone from the open door. From his vantage-point he could see only darkness below. Looking across the expanse of blackness, he saw the lights of Ashford International Railway Station. Just a couple of hundred of yards away was his ticket to freedom. At least for the time being.

Hud pushed his arms through the straps of the holdall, so that he wore it on his back like a rucksack. It was not overly heavy, but certainly enough for him to know it was there.

He hauled himself onto his feet and, gripping the horizontal bar above him, swung his legs away and down to feel for the next steel rod. Silently he moved down the scaffolding until he felt terra firma beneath him.

Above he heard voices, and could see the shadows of the janitor and one other in the open fire exit. It would not be long before security would be sent to inspect the ground below: the ground where Hud now stood.

With his back to the building he ran across smooth tarmac before coming against a wire mesh fence. He stole the bag from his shoulders and heaved it over, following with himself dropping the six feet the other side onto wasteland.

In the pitch black he had to tread carefully, the ground littered with all manner of waste material. Several times he slipped and fell, his legs scraping against some old masonry, or brick work that had been left for others to dispose of.

Finally he reached the other side. He heard footsteps on the tarmac behind him. In front of him the lights of the railway station. He was on high ground standing against another six feet wire mesh fence. He fell to the ground, on haunches so his silhouette would not give him away. He looked back toward the rear of the sports centre where two guards and a van were inspecting the area below the swinging fire exit door.

Torches were shining up the scaffold, and around the perimeter road.

Hud threw the bag over the fence, and once more heaved himself behind. He slid down the grass bank and made his way to the entrance of the station.

This was his most dangerous time. He did not know what his pursuer looked like, so any one of the people around might have been his foe.

He hurried to the ticket counter, and requested a one way ticket to London Victoria Station asking what platform the train would leave from.

Hud dug into his trouser pocket to retrieve payment for his ticket. This was the first time that he noticed the rawness of his palm. As he passed the money over, the ticket master too noticed.

'That's a nasty graze you've got there. Fell over when you were running, Sir?' the balding man asked Hud.

'Yes, just outside, actually. Should have left more time for the train. How long have I got?' he answered, deflecting further questioning.

'Two minutes from Platform Five. To your left and second stairway from the end', came the reply with Hud's change and ticket.

Hud hurried down the stairs and to the platform edge as the train pulled into the station.

He looked behind him. The stairs were empty.

Hud climbed aboard and found a seat near the toilet. He positioned himself so that he was looking forward, next to the window nearest the platform.

The train sat there as he willed it to move.

The driver started to announce the stops and destination.

'This is the 21:05 service from Ashford International to London Victoria. Calling at Charing, Lenham...'

The driver's words were lost to Hud as he noticed a lean but well built man dressed in a leather coat with leather gloves reach the base of the stairs. He looked up and down the train before opening the nearest door to him and jumping aboard.

'... Due to arrive at London Victoria at 22:32.' finished the driver. The train lurched away from the station.

Hud watched the door that connected his carriage to the one the late arrival had entered. He saw the man take a seat just the other side of the glass-fronted door, and facing Hud.

Hud stood up intending to take the holdall into the toilet behind.

As he rose, so too did the leather clad man in the next carriage.

Hud sat again. The connecting door opened.

The man strode through looking at Hud all the while, walking toward him. Hud placed the holdall on the floor behind his feet, and clenched his right fist in his jacket pocket.

The stranger passed Hud and entered the toilet behind. Hud moved so he was the opposite side of the aisle, so that any surprise attack from behind would be mitigated.

The man came out, and walked down the alley back to his seat in the next carriage. Not seeming to notice that Hud had moved.

Relieved, Hud looked at the holdall. He had to know what was in this bag. What was it that had caused his brother to be murdered?

He looked down the carriage to where the late arrival was sitting. Now was not the time to examine the contents of the holdall. That would have to wait.

Hud picked the bag from the floor and wrapped the straps around his right arm, keeping the bag secure and away from the aisle.

He sat watching. He started to consider the events of the day:

The murder of his brother;

The cover up of the murder that was being perpetrated by the police, and governmental security;

The key with the cryptic clue that his brother had left him;

The holdall that he now held firmly in his possession;

The way that he had been followed;

And now the late arrival to the train.

As he sank deeply into his thoughts, the adrenaline that had been pumping through his body for the last few hours started to ebb away. His eyes felt heavy. He started to breathe deeply as he drifted to sleep.

The late arrival looked back and saw Hud's eyes closed fast. He moved so that he had a better view of his target. He never liked travelling by train and facing the way it was moving. He picked up a nearby paper and began to read, every now and then looking up from the printed pages and eyeing Hud. He tried to get a signal on his cell phone, but still there was nothing.

The Assassin sat in his car, waiting for Peter Hudson to emerge from the sports centre. There had to be a reason that he'd suddenly diverted from the motorway and headed back into town.

For a short while he thought that Hudson had spotted him, hence the sudden and dangerous manoeuvre on the busy road. But he was now convinced that he hadn't, but rather something had sent Hudson to this sports centre.

It had been 20 minutes since Peter Hudson had walked in through the glass-fronted doors, and still no sign of him. It would not be long now, though. The centre was emptying of its customers for the day. It was now gone nine o'clock, and the early evening security van had already disappeared behind the building.

The Assassin knew that Hudson could not get away. He was convinced of that one fact. There was nowhere for him to run. But just in case he had put other plans into motion.

The Assassin looked at his cell phone. He was expecting a call from a colleague. A colleague who had been deployed to watch the only other nearby escape route, the International Railway Station in the town.

The Assassin had given clear instructions.

He continued to wait. Wait for either Peter Hudson to appear, or for his cell phone to ring.

He knew there would be no escape for Peter Hudson.

SIX

Hudson woke with a start, beads of sweat running from his hairline down his forehead. His recurring dream had shaken him to consciousness.

Only this time it was not the young soldier's face that had startled him awake. This time the faceless soldier had been transformed into the staring eyes of his brother.

Hud shook his head in an effort to come fully to his senses. He looked down at his arm. The holdall was still there. His hand stung from the grazing he had received on the wasteland between the sports centre and the station.

He looked through the carriage. The late arrival was still there, sitting with a newspaper in his lap and talking on a cell phone.

He seemed to be still watching Hudson.

Hudson looked out of the window, at the houses speeding past. City houses, old terraced tenements, bricks thickened with the smog of the city and years of steam trains passing this way before diesel and then electrification cleaned up rail travel.

He narrowed his line of focus and saw his reflection against the darkness outside. He did not look good. His hair was matted, his face dirty where sweat had carried down his cheeks. A five o'clock shadow had started to appear around his chin.

The train started to slow.

'Bromley South' came the announcement from the driver. 'Next stop London Victoria' he finished.

Hudson stood up from his seat, and without looking at the late arrival, turned to the left and through to the exit door. He turned away from the platform and half turned the handle to release the door on the opposite side.

As the train stopped, he flung the door wide. It cracked against the outer skin of the train. Ducking down, he peered round the corner toward the carriage where the late arrival had been.

The seat was empty.

Hud darted back and opened one of the toilet doors, slipping in and closing behind him.

Now he just had to listen.

It was only a few seconds later that he heard the platform door open and agitated steps taken into the carriage.

'Shit, he's gone out the other way. There's no sign of him,' he heard a voice screaming.

Hud sprung out of the cubicle and in front of his follower, who had turned back to head toward the platform again.

The late arrival looked dumbstruck, his mouth agape at the sudden appearance of his game ahead of him. He held his cell phone to one ear, which is where it remained as Hud struck an almighty blow with a right handed upper cut.

The leather-clad assailant fell back through the door, landing headfirst between the rails of the second track. Out for the count, his phone broke into pieces beside him.

Hud closed the door, and retrieved his holdall from the toilet. He moved through the train to the front carriage as it pulled away, and chose a seat that had no occupants close.

He would be at Victoria in about twenty minutes. From there he would take a taxi to Islington. Public transport was getting a little too dangerous to risk the tube.

He also knew now that there were at least two people following him. The late arrival's words had given that away.

Hud wondered how much time he had bought himself by fleeing from the sports centre earlier in the evening.

He also needed desperately to know what he had got himself into. Or what mess his brother had left for him.

He looked at the holdall sitting in his lap. Inside would be some answers. At least that's what he hoped as he pulled the zipper.

SEVEN

As he opened the bag, a sense of trepidation came over Hud. He couldn't help but pause with the zipper half open, half closed.

So much had happened that day, culminating in him dumping an unknown man off the train. Hud didn't know whether he had killed his pursuer, or just knocked him out.

He looked at the bag again.

Whatever the bag contained must hold the key to everything that had gone on in the last 24 hours.

He looked up, and around. The carriage was empty.

He pulled the bag open.

Inside there was another bag, smaller and made of polyester. On top lay a large brown manila envelope, sealed, and with the words 'Peter Hudson' written in capitals across the front in thick black marker pen.

Hud carefully prised the envelope seal, and took out the file inside. Printed in red on the front was 'Eyes Only.'

He opened it.

The file itself was split into three sections, separated by card dividers, the sort that schoolchildren use on their homework assignments: one red, one black, and one white.

The file was about an inch thick and held both typed and hand-written papers, and clear plastic sleeves with old black and white photographs. Hud flicked through, before deciding to start by examining the first section.

Firstly he looked at the photograph. It showed a stern looking man in, perhaps, his mid fifties. The man wore the insignia of the German Military of the Second World War, and round his neck sat the Iron Cross. Atop his head was a highly decorated peak cap. The man stared to his left, not looking toward the camera.

Hud started to read the accompanying articles. The first of which read as follows:

'There have been several books written about Grossadmiral Karl Doenitz. What you are about to read is a précis of his life.

Note the high esteem in which he was held by the Fuhrer, Adolf Hitler. A man who is willing to reciprocate can only gain such esteem.

Doenitz was born on the 16th of September in 1891, in Grunau, near Berlin, Germany.

He joined the German Imperial Navy (the Kaiserliche Marine) in 1910, and rose to the rank of Second Lieutenant by the time war broke in 1914.

He began the First World War on the light cruiser SMS Breslau, and in 1916 was promoted to First Lieutenant and transferred to U-boat UB68. This was the real start of a highly decorated career in the German Navy.

Doenitz was a loyal subject of the Kaiser and an imperialist at heart. When the war ended, Doenitz had been captured and remained in a POW camp in Redmires in England until his release in 1919.

By this time, the Kaiser had been deposed, and the rule of Germany was by the so-called Weimar Republic (more correctly known as Deutsches Reich). This was the first attempt at a true German liberal democracy, and many - such as Doenitz - despised its constitution seeing it as an attempt by foreign powers to take away German autonomy.

Doenitz married his wife, Ingeborg, in 1916, and their first son, Klaus, was born on 14th May 1920. His second son, Peter, was born on 20 March 1922. Although he remained married until his wife died in 1962, the marriage was not a happy one, and he cared more for his children than anything else.

Doenitz had been bought up in middle class Germany, with a father that was truly master of his household. Whilst not tyrannical, his father had taught him to be a good follower of orders, and Doenitz continually looked for a leader figure in his life.

He continued in the Navy and was promoted to Full Commander by Hitler in 1933, rewarding him for his service to the Nazi Party cause. Hitler's dictatorial methods suited Doenitz's need to be led, and he was further rewarded with promotions through to Rear Admiral by the time that the Second World War broke.

Doenitz was charged with commanding the German U-boat flotilla, and was continually in Hitler's favour for the results that he achieved during the war.

His second son, Peter, was killed in action in 1943 when aboard U-954, and this prompted Doenitz, who had by this time replaced Erich Roeder as the

Oberbefehlshaber der Kriegsmarine (Commander in Chief of the German Navy) to command that Klaus be removed from active duty.

However Klaus remained in contact with his former Naval colleagues. It is believed that he was aboard a German 'Fast Boat', the S141, for his 24th birthday treat which went down with all hands after being sunk by the French Destroyer La Combattante defending Selsey on the South Coast of England from German attack.

Before his suicide, Hitler decreed that Doenitz should become Germany's Head of State, effectively his replacement, and so it occurred that on 30th April 1945, Karl Doenitz did, indeed, succeed Hitler.

Doenitz ordered his two great friends, Alfred Jodl and Wilhelm Keitel to sign the unconditional surrenders that ended the war in Europe on 7th and 8th May 1945, believing that he would escape trial for war crimes.

However, with the war won, the allies of the West needed also to have convictions for the huge losses suffered. It was, if you will, a show of strength and the final nails in the coffin of the Third Reich. The end of Germany.

Doenitz was charged on several counts, and finally imprisoned for 'conspiracy to wage aggressive war' in 1946 at the Nuremburg Trials.

Released form prison in 1956, he published two books about his life during his retirement in Aumuhle, Germany. The first, "Ten years and Twenty days", published in 1958 followed by "My ever changing life" in 1968.

Doenitz died of a heart attack on December 24th 1980, and was buried on January 6th 1981 in the cemetery in Aumuhle. Many thousands attended funeral including former servicemen and naval officers.'

Hudson finished the second page of the first section and looked again at the photo of the dead Naval Officer.

He then continued to read the notes, only what followed had been written in ink, and not typed as before.

Hud clearly recognised his brother's handwriting:

'Promoted to Oberbefehlshaber 1943.

Saw end of war approaching.

Wanted to save only surviving son, so commanded that he was not to see active duty.

Why then was Klaus allowed back on ship that was to attack Selsey?'

The final part of this section again was a plastic sleeve with a black and white photograph. This time it was a picture of a funeral procession, pallbearers carrying a coffin.

Surrounding the coffin as it emerged from a church were the grief stricken faces of old men. None wore uniform, but Hud could see that they all had the stature of ex-servicemen, and all looked as if they were in their eighties and nineties.

All except the one in the left hand corner of the picture. The one with his face circled by red ink looked nearer sixty than eighty. And, to Peter Hudson, he looked strangely familiar.

Hud stared at the photograph, trying to make sense of the passage that he had read. Thoughts racked his brains. Why would his brother be collecting files on a dead Second World War German Naval Officer? What did this have to do with his brother's murder? What was so important that meant Hud had maybe killed a man that evening?

The train began to slow.

Hud placed the file back in the envelope and returned the contents to the holdall. Answers would have to wait. Right now he needed to get home.

Then a thought struck him.

He had been followed from London in the morning. Perhaps there would be someone waiting there for him now. The thought sent shivers through him. He could only hazard a guess as to the enormity of his situation.

He moved quickly off the train and to the exit of the station, hailing a taxi-cab as he went.

EIGHT

Although he was sure that he hadn't been followed on the last leg of the journey from Bromley South to Victoria, Hud couldn't be certain. He now knew there was a second follower but didn't know if he had hopped the train, or indeed maybe waiting for him to arrive at Victoria.

He hadn't looked back whilst walking through the station, but had been vigilant all the same. As he had emerged from the entrance, Hud had swept past an elderly couple to make certain of getting the first possible taxi.

On sitting in the back seat of the black cab, he didn't really care for the look of bemusement on the driver's face when asked to drive around for five minutes before returning to the front of the Station.

All the while that they were touring, Hud kept a wary look behind, trying not to appear too obvious.

At one point Hud thought that a dark blue Volvo was following, when upon asking the Cabbie to take a sharp right down Chester Street and then doubling back via Wilton Street, the Volvo kept on the cab's tail. However, he was relieved when the Volvo driver eventually stopped next to a parking meter in order to ask directions from a passing Traffic Warden.

Satisfied that they weren't being followed, Hud allowed the driver to make his way toward Clerkenwell Green, asking him to pull short at the Three Compasses Public House on Cowcross Street.

During the journey he allowed himself several drags of a cigarette, his first since the start of the day. He was trying to give up, and Amy never permitted smoking in her house. The Cabbie gave a disdainful look, so Hud dropped the slide window in the rear to expel the ringlets of smoke that had formed in the rear.

He took one long last draw and held the smoke in his lungs for a few seconds. The head rush caused by the nicotine made him feel light and hollow, the trials of the day being expelled from his mind for a brief while. They returned to him as he pushed the remaining dregs of smoke from his chest.

He considered his next move as he examined the red glow dying away from the cigarette which by now he had smoked down to the filter. Holding the butt between his thumb and middle finger, he flicked the dead end out the window.

Hud didn't want a drink, nor to sample the gastropub's Thai cuisine, but was wary that whoever it was that had been following him for the last 24 hours probably knew where he lived. He wanted to make sure that he would be entering a 'clean' house.

He paid the Cabbie from inside the taxi, through the window that separated passengers from driver. Hud would usually leave a tip, but decided not to on this occasion. The cab pulled away, leaving Hud standing outside the pub clutching the leather holdall.

Hud eyed the newly decorated exterior of the pub. With gleaming cream masonry and dark green woodwork and boasting two entrance doors, the downstairs had recently been returned to a pure bar whilst the floor above had become a dedicated restaurant. The bar staff now all wore green shirts and black trousers.

He could see through the glass front that there were few patrons inside. During daylight hours this was a favourite haunt of the suited employees from the nearby office blocks that had spread from the inner sanctum of the square mile, being invited in by the eclectic mix of traditional pub and modern wine bar. At this time of night, just before closing, the patronage tended to be the market workers soon to start their day in the nearby Smithfield Meat Market.

Hud decided against a swift drink, choosing instead to walk toward Farringdon Station and then turn right into Turnmill Street. He continued to observe closely both occupants of vehicles and pedestrians as he walked briskly toward the Green and his loft apartment.

Many of the three storey Georgian houses - large grandiose buildings in white masonry or red brick with copious four quartered sash windows - that line the streets in this area of London were in darkness, the roofline obscured from the prying eye by the brightness of the street lamps below. He passed several pubs on the way, each time resisting the temptation to partake of a little Dutch courage.

He crossed at the junction of Clerkenwell Road, and made his way to the corner of the Green, where he stopped to survey the area.

It was quiet now, people preparing for the working day that would be carried by the next dawn. Save for the usual street cleaners, there seemed to be nothing unusual to disturb him.

Hud paid particular attention to the cars parked around the Green, but saw no sight of the silver BMW.

Still holding tightly to his brother's holdall, he crossed and made his way to his block, keyed the security code into the box on the wall by the main door, and climbed the stairs to his apartment.

Again he stopped, holding his breath and placing his ear against his front door. He strained to hear, pressing harder against the cold wood, closing his mind to the faint sound of the street below and concentrating his efforts to behind the locked entry.

He heard nothing.

He carefully turned the key in the lock, letting the door swing gently open and stepping to one side as it did so.

The flat was in darkness.

He moved in, holding himself fast against the wall. The door gently snapped shut behind, as his eyes searched the darkness ahead. He could see into the lounge, where the half light from the night outside partially invaded giving an eerie feel to the emptiness within. And it was this half-light that told him what he wanted to know.

The flat was empty.

He moved toward the window and fully closed the blinds. Once more the blackness blinded him. He felt his way to the wall and fingered the light switch. Suddenly the place came alive, now temporarily blinding him through the brightness.

Once his eyes had grown fully accustomed to the brilliance of his spot-lit room, he picked up the bag and carried it to the bedroom, where firstly he slid the door of his wardrobe open and threw the bag inside before returning to his bed.

He poured himself a large slug of Southern Comfort and kicked his shoes off. He finished the drink and returned to his front door where he made certain that the security bolts were securely fastened.

Felling certain that he was safe from intruders - at least for the time being - he padded in be-socked feet back to his bedroom.

Replenishing his glass he caught sight of himself in the full-length mirror of the wardrobe door. He looked dishevelled, dirty, and unkempt.

He finished the drink, his throat coming back to life as the warm wetness of the liquid reinvigorated. He disrobed, leaving his clothes in a pile on the laminated flooring, and moved to the bathroom.

He stood, hands pressed against the wall, as the hot water from the power shower washed away the day. The steam dug deep into his skin, blood from his hand making a pale pink water colour running down the tiles, curdling with the dirt from his body to create a stream of rust coloured water beneath his feet.

When it finally ran clear, and when not a patch of wall or ceiling was not covered in droplets of steam, Hud stopped the shower and stood in front of the mirrored cabinet above his sink. He looked at himself once more and filled the sink with hot water, lathering his chin as he did so.

After shaving and cleaning his teeth, and now feeling refreshed, even if still tired, he moved to the lounge. He flicked the music system and poured himself another drink, this time using the optic on his bar. He wanted to conserve the remains of his 'bedroom bottle' for the morning.

He sat, and finally relaxed. He was safe. At least for the time being. At least until the morning.

Hud thought about retrieving the holdall, and investigating further, but decided that he could wait until after he had slept. He needed to clear his mind before taking in more information, to dissect the day before moving to a new one.

This was all part of his routine. A routine that had been shot to shreds with the events of the last twenty-four hours.

He looked over toward the phone. He hadn't yet thought about listening to any messages, but the available message light wasn't flashing.

As his mind worked, his eyes grew heavy. With half a tumbler of his favourite beverage in one hand, Peter Hudson suddenly felt very much alone in the world.

NINE

Hud woke with a start to the rapping of his door. He could hear a voice calling his name, a voice that he half recognised.

He felt groggy but at the same time assuaged that he had not had to fight the demons of his nightmares in order to come to life.

In his hand remained the half tumbler of Southern Comfort. His neck was stiff from the awkwardness of his sleeping position, his legs too.

The door once more rang out to the urgent knock of his unknown visitor.

Hud rose from the sofa, and noted the time. Eight O'clock. The light was still burning and the blinds closed tight. He didn't know whether it was morning or evening.

He shook himself awake, stretching skywards and rotating his head to dispel the rigidity bought from his involuntary hibernation.

He looked at his hand, which had begun to scab after the cleansing of the shower and the dowsing of antiseptic he'd administered. In stretching he had spun the tumbler so as not to spill any of the stale drink. He swigged the last drops, immediately wishing that he hadn't and yet thankful he had.

The door-knocker again thudded four or five times.

As Hud's senses returned he could make the noise of the street below. People talking, cars moving. Footsteps as if an army were on the march in the distance. The sounds of the morning.

He moved to the doorway, placing his spent glass on the lustrous granite top of the adjoining kitchen as he passed.

Even though the concave of the little door window distorted his visitor's face, it was instantly recognisable to Hud. A face from the past, from a time which Hud now longed for. A face that he had never thought to see again.

He released the deadbolts and turned the handle. With the door open he spoke, holding his hand out as he did so.

'Chatters! You're the last person I expected, though it's good to see you.'

Mark Chatfield stood over six feet tall. Muscularly built, well-groomed, short dark hair and piercing blue eyes. His jaw was square and thick set, with perfectly white teeth showing through his smile. He had a deep scar to his left cheek, caught by a wayward piece of shrapnel during the Falklands conflict in nineteen eighty-two.

Hud had served with Mark Chatfield on that campaign, and it was mainly because of Chatfield's recommendation that he had moved to the SAS some years later.

The last time they had seen each other had been at the graveside of Mark's younger brother: the young soldier that Hud had promised to keep safe in Iraq. 'Chatters', as all his friends knew him – not just because of his name, but also his propensity to over-egg a debrief – had never held his brother's death against Hud, but they had drifted apart after the funeral. Hud had not known what to say to him, and felt deeply personally responsible for the fate of his charge.

There had been a time, a year or so prior to the door knocking today, that Chatters had phoned Hud to offer him a position in his security firm. But Hud had turned him down. The Saville Row suit that Chatters now wore clearly indicated that he was doing well from his firm.

Chatters held out his right hand, and Hud moved to shake it. He saw that the hand was not empty, but instead held a bottle.

'I heard about your brother. Let's get wasted. I guess you could do with it?' he said, more as a statement than a question and taking a step over the threshold.

Hud invited Chatters to sit, whilst he freshened up in the bathroom.

During the few minutes that he was alone, Mark Chatfield walked the open plan floor of the apartment. It was as he had imagined it: clean, simple, everything in its place, except a lone short glass on one of the kitchen surfaces.

He remembered that Hud had started drinking heavily after Iraq, and remembered too that this had been a big contributory factor in the divorce from his wife.

The light streamed through the windows when Hud returned to the lounge. Chatters had opened the blinds fully. He pointed to a freshly poured drink on the table by the sofa, and beckoned Hud to take a seat.

Hud picked up the glass and moved to a chair away from the windows. He didn't want to be in full view of any prying eyes from street level. He would have liked to pull the blinds again, but did not want to arouse suspicion from his companion.

The two sat in silence a few minutes, before Hud spoke first.

'Your brother. I…I'm so sorry. I tried to protect him, I really did. The bullet just came from nowhere.'

'Listen, Hud, I've said before. Shit happens. That's the game we soldiers play. We all knew the risks we had to take to do our jobs, our duty. Even Jim. He wouldn't hold his death against you anymore than I do. It's over. I just wished you'd taken the job I offered last year.'

'The time wasn't right, Chatters. I explained that to you.'

'I know, Hud. Listen, the offer's still there.'

'I can't. Not now: not with Jack gone. I know how you must have felt now. God only knows how Amy's going to cope. I went to see her yesterday, she's a mess. They were so close, and now her world's turned upside down.'

A couple more minutes of silence followed. Hud wanted to tell Chatters about the file that Jack had left for him. About the red mark on his brother's neck, and about being followed. But something held him back from being too open. He didn't know what that something was, but felt that perhaps it was the need to understand things more clearly himself before discussing it with his friend.

Finally, it was Hud who again broke the silence.

'I don't know if Jack died naturally. I mean, I know what the television is saying, and the newspapers. But they didn't see him. I did.' His admission surprised even himself.

'What do you mean, Hud?' enquired Chatfield.

'His eyes, Chatters. He was, like, staring at somebody. Scared, like in some horror movie. And there was a tiny red mark on his neck.'

'Well surely that could be anything? A spot or something? There'll be an autopsy, I guess?' Chatfield retorted.

'Yeah, your right.'

'Hud, when was the last time you saw a heart attack victim?'

'Well, I haven't'

'Exactly! You and I, we've seen death a plenty, but none of it's natural. It's always been because of a bullet, or shell blast, or a grenade going off. How can we judge a heart attack? The autopsy will tell you for sure. Until then don't beat yourself up with guesswork.'

'It's not just that. There's something else.'

'What?' asked Chatters, seemingly determined to help his friend.

'My brother, Jack, he left......'

His words were interrupted by the shrill call of the telephone.

Hud spun round in his chair, alarmed by the sudden disruption to his conversation.

He lifted himself from his seated position and moved to the telephone table. He picked the receiver from its cradle just as the answer machine kicked in. He had to listen to his own voice before speaking.

'Hey whoever it is, don't hang up. It's Hud here.'

'Hud, thank God you're there! I've been going mad trying to get hold of you. Amy said that you'd been there, but left yesterday. Where have you been? Why haven't you returned my messages? And what's wrong with your mobile phone?'

'Hey, Judy, calm down. You worry too much,' Hud interjected, 'I'm fine, in one piece, and sitting having a drink.'

'Hud, it's not even nine in the morning. It's a bloody good job I'm on my way. I'll be there in ten minutes. Don't go anywhere!'

With that the line went dead.

He knew he shouldn't let his ex-wife bully him so, but had always been hopeful that they would get back together. He knew it was a long shot, but figured there had to be a reason that she hadn't dated seriously since they split. He looked forward to her arrival now.

'That was Judy. She's on her way.' Hud explained to Chatters as he crossed to the kitchen.

'We better get rid of the evidence,' he said, sweeping the glasses under a running tap and simultaneously filling the kettle with water, 'and have a coffee. Sugar?'

As the water ran, part of Judy's conversation came back to him.

'*Why haven't you returned my messages?*' she had asked.

'What messages?' Hud questioned out loud.

'Pardon?' Chatters requested.

'Judy asked why I hadn't returned my messages. What messages? I didn't have any. The phone was clear when I got home last night.'

'She's made a mistake, probably phoned the wrong number. There'll be some old guy wondering who the hell Judy is as we speak.'

Chatters looked at his watch. It was time that he made his excuses and left. Judy had never trusted him, and he certainly didn't want to be in the flat when she arrived.

'Look, Hud, I won't stay. You know how Judy is with me. I'll leave you to it. I'll give you a call in a day or two.'

'Hey, Chatters, she'll have to put up with it,' Hud replied, secretly thankful that his friend would be leaving before Judy arrived.

'No, Hud, I'll be gone. Speak soon. You make the coffee, I'll see myself out. I'll leave the bottle for you. Looks like you could use it,' he said, pointing at the empty optic behind the bar.

'Thanks, Chatters. See you soon.'

As Chatfield made his way to the door, so Hud walked the bottle to the optic, replacing the empty with a barman's expertise and throwing it in the waste bin underneath the bar.

He heard the door shut behind Chatters and continued with the coffee. Although Judy preferred percolated, he had run out of beans. Instant would have to suffice.

TEN

Mark Chatfield started his engine and pulled away, driving the three hundred yards to sit at the end of Clerkenwell Green where he could spy Judy's approach. As he sat in his car waiting for her to arrive, he thought about times past.

Judy had long since ceased to trust Hud's friend, and Mark did not want to be in the flat with a bad atmosphere hanging between the three of them. He had made a snap decision to leave immediately that Hud had confirmed Judy was on her way.

It had been a long time since he had last seen her, and he was curious to know if she had lost any of her looks. Mark had always been a little envious of Hudson's wife and had once made an ill advised pass at her. It was this that had given her such a mistrust of him. She had been a real catch for his friend, and everyone agreed that they had made the perfect couple. But that was before Iraq. Before Peter Hudson's life had turned sour.

Now Mark waited to see if she had changed any since they had all last been together in happier times.

After a short while, a taxi pulled to the kerb outside Hudson's apartment block and Judy emerged on the passenger side. Even from this distance it was easy to see that she was still an attractive woman, tall and slender with high cheekbones and perfectly formed shoulder length blonde hair.

As he watched, Mark placed a small earpiece to his left lobe. This would enable him to listen to the conversation between Hud and Judy, from the transmitter that he had placed in Hud's phone the previous night. In doing so he had wiped its messages, and now had to hope that Hud wouldn't tamper with the equipment.

Mark Chatfield had left Ashford for London as soon as his colleague first called in shortly ahead of midnight the previous day. Hud was on the train, sleeping and clutching tightly to a black leather holdall. Mark hadn't seen Hud go into the sports centre with a bag, and so it followed that whatever was in the bag was important to retrieve for the Director.

The previous evening he had arrived at his waiting place when he received the second call from the watcher on the train, a call that mysteriously had cut short.

Mark had then gone into Hud's flat, the lock easy to pick with his skeleton key, and planted the bug.

He had left the flat as he had found it, and returned to his car. It was just a question of the rabbit returning to the hole, which he had done twenty minutes after Mark had vacated the building.

As he now watched Judy enter the building, Mark's mind drifted to the unfinished business with Peter Hudson. It was a matter of family pride.

His younger brother's death in Iraq had led to his Mother dying. Once Jim had died in the name of duty, his mother had just given up. She wouldn't eat, or drink, and just retreated into a shell. Eventually she had contracted pneumonia and died whilst in a coma.

Yes, Peter Hudson had a lot to answer for. He had to pay for the suffering that he had caused. When the end came, the look on Hudson's face would be more than adequate payment. This was a kill that he had been fantasising about for the last sixteen years, and he would make sure that he got the utmost pleasure from it.

Mark Chatfield wondered how Judy would feel when Hud was dead.

ELEVEN

Judy sat on the sofa where Chatters had been seated minutes before, whilst Hud finished stirring in the milk to their coffees. Once finished, he replaced the milk bottle in the fridge and bought both mugs over. He kept one himself and positioned the other on a nearby coffee table for his ex-wife.

Hud looked at Judy, and immediately felt the need to be in her arms. She still made him feel passion that he had never felt for anyone else, even though they had been separated for several years now. The way that he felt about her had made the divorce easy. They had both wanted to remain friends, and had only resorted to lawyers to put the divorce agreement in print: they had thrashed out the details themselves in the time it had taken to consume a three course meal at their favourite Italian restaurant.

Her blue eyes sparkled as they always did, hypnotising Hud through the steam of his coffee. The heave of her bosom underneath her pale blue blouse told Hud that she had raced the stairs rather than accept the elevator. Judy had a fear of confined spaces, and once confided in Hud that the fear was down to being locked in an understairs cupboard by her brother when they were playing a game of hide and seek when young children.

' Sorry about the coffee, I've run out of the real stuff', Hud apologised.

'And cream, I see.' replied Judy, with a smile. 'Hud, how are you?'

'I'm fine, honestly. But it's been a funny few hours.'

Hud took a sip of his coffee and proceeded to tell Judy about the goings on of the previous day, finishing with Mark Chatfield's arrival, and subsequent sudden departure, that morning.

'Well I don't trust him Hud. He's a snake. I know he offered you that job last year, but why all of a sudden do you hear from him now? It's not like you're as close as you used to be, is it?'

'Judy, leave it, please. He was in the area, and knows what it's like to lose a brother. Whatever you say, he's a good mate.'

Judy stood and moved to the kitchen. Holding her mug in the air, she asked if Hud wanted another coffee also.

He nodded and walked his mug over, holding it out for her to take. As she did so her fingers seemed to linger on his a little too long.

'Tell me more about this bag that you picked up from the sports centre', she asked, oblivious to the spark that Hud had felt.

'Well, not much else to tell really. As I said I haven't really looked inside, save for the file I've told you about: and even then it's just the first few pages that I've read.'

Judy looked at him, and smiled.

'Hud, why don't you go and get it while I finish the coffee. I trust that it will only take the time that it takes to put a spoonful of instant in a cup,' she finished, sarcastically bemoaning Hud's lack of fresh 'proper' coffee.

When Hud returned with the holdall, Judy had already pulled the coffee table in front of the sofa and cleared the top leaving just the two coffees that now stood at either end.

She beckoned Hud to take a seat next to her.

Together they opened the bag, pulled the file out and laid it on the table. Hud went to open it, but Judy held his hand.

'We know what's in that, or at least partly. It doesn't make any sense to you, and nor does it to me. Let's get everything out so that we have a better idea what we're dealing with. Then we can start studying it all, and come to a decision how we should proceed.'

'I'm not sure this is something you want to be mixed up in, Judy' Hud said, almost sincerely. Deep down he was pleased that he had Judy by his side, and that she wanted to help him.

Judy just looked at him, the sort of look that said 'get on with it, I'm with you.' She didn't have to speak, Hud did what her eyes wanted him to.

Next out of the bag came the smaller bag that had been stuffed inside. He pulled the velcro tabs apart, making a rasping sound as he did so.

They sat wide-eyed, staring with inconceivability in both their faces.

Hud turned the bag upside down, and poured the contents on top of the manila file. They sat in silence, just looking at the heap of money in front of them.

'Wow!' Hud exclaimed, picking up some of the Euro notes, and placing them in neat piles.

By the time they had finished sorting the money, they had counted twenty five thousand in Euro notes ranging in denomination from five to one hundred, and now neatly placed in ten piles. Beside this they had placed a grey money belt that had also been in the smaller of the two bags. On top of the folder, there now sat a passport and a sealed brown A4 envelope.

Hud picked up the envelope and looked at the writing on the outside. In his brother's handwriting were etched the words 'For Hud, in case of emergency.'

Judy noted the hesitation.

'Hud, if this isn't an emergency, then I don't know what is. Open it. Let's see what you've got into.'

Pealing back the seal, Hud reached inside with his right hand and pulled out a single sheet of paper. It was a letter written to Hud, in black ink. His brother always used the fountain pen that Hud had bought him to congratulate him on his first Cabinet job:

Dear Hud,

If you are reading this, then you will have solved the clue that I left you. I have no doubt that you have, and knew that 'VIV' would hold a real meaning for you.

Hud, I trust you more than anyone. Having opened the bag that I left you, you will have found a file, cash and a passport that you may need to use.

Do not let the file fall into anyone's hands.

You need to get to Paris Charles de Gaulle Airport within 48 hours of my death, where you will be met by a friend. You can trust this man with your life, and he will make himself known to you. I can't tell you anymore than this, but have to trust that you will do the right thing.

You are the only one I can trust, Hud.

Good luck and Godspeed,

Jack x

Hud re-read the letter, then handed it to Judy to read. A tear welled in his eye, and he had to sweep it to one side in the hope that Judy would not see this weakness in him.

'Hud, when did he die?'

'The early hours of yesterday. It was announced at around five in the morning.'

Hud could see Judy's mind beginning to work.

'You've got to get to Paris pretty damn sharp. It says here within 48 hours. It's nearly 10 in the morning. You've got to be there by five tomorrow morning at the very latest.'

'That's if I go, Judy. So far since my brother died I've been followed – twice – nearly fallen off high rise scaffolding, pushed someone out of a train, read half a file about some old Nazi, and been landed with 25,000 Euros. I don't know if I need this shit right now.'

'You're forgetting something' Judy replied with a steely stare. Hud hated it when she looked like this.

'You're forgetting that your brother was murdered yesterday, and he has trusted you to unravel why. That's what all this is about, don't you think?'

Hud looked blankly for a moment, then picked himself off the sofa and stepped over to the bar. He poured himself a glass of Chatters' southern comfort, and downed it in one.

'Hud, this is no time to be drinking!' Judy cried.

'If I'm going to do this, then I need a drink first. I'm going to pack.'

With those words Hud strode past Judy and toward his bedroom.

He returned with his brother's black holdall. He'd packed all that he felt he would need: socks, underwear, trousers, tops, a couple of pairs of trainers and a pair of his old army boots.

Judy had neatly put ten thousand Euros in the money belt, and packaged the remainder in the A4 envelope that had housed the letter from his brother. She passed him the fake passport, but held back the file.

'I don't need that passport, I have my own,' Hud said.

'Take it.' Judy ordered. 'If your brother went to the trouble of having it made for you, then the least you can do is take it with you. He'd have done it for a reason.' Of course, she was right and Hud knew that she was.

Since Hud had returned from Iraq after the incident his life had turned upside down, and that included the way he was with company. He used to be a leader of men, natural to make quick but logical decisions. Now he tended to be a follower, and this was most obvious in his relationship with his ex wife. Sometimes Hud had the feeling that this infuriated Judy, and at others she seemed to thrive on the responsibility.

'I've booked you a flight, it takes off at five o'clock this afternoon from Heathrow. There's a taxi outside waiting for you.'

It seemed to Hud that Judy had taken command, but it felt good to him that she wanted to help. Before the split they had made a good team, and Hud desperately wanted her back in his life on a more permanent basis.

'Judy..' Hud started, but could not finish his sentence.

'I know, Hud.' Judy said looking into his eyes and seeing a look of hopelessness that had been evident for far too long. 'Listen, I'll keep the folder here, and try to make some sense of it. Keep your mobile phone on, and I'll call. Whatever you do, call me when you are safely landed in Paris.

'Oh, and Hud. Take care' Judy lent forward and kissed him on the cheek, at the same time pressing herself against him as she put her arms round him and hugged.

Hud held her for a second, looking into her eyes, and then reluctantly released his grip on her.

In silence he picked the waiting bag from the floor, and made his way out of his apartment. He knew Judy would be safe, and also knew that her analytical mind was better equipped to decipher Jack's notes.

Stepping into the black cab that had been waiting for him with the meter running, Hud failed to notice the silver BMW that was parked at the side of the road not a half mile away.

TWELVE

Mark Chatfield had heard all he needed to, and alerted colleagues in Paris to Hudson's impending arrival. He would be there a little later, having booked a seat on a flight to Orly from Heathrow. It meant that he would arrive in Paris an hour later, by which time Hudson would be in the clutches of those loyal to the cause, and then the Director's instructions could be completed.

But not before he had his hands on the file that Hud had left alone with Judy.

He looked up towards the flat, and saw Judy at the window watching the departure of her ex. As the engine of the BMW silently started, he dialled with the thumb of his right hand on his cell phone.

As he pulled away from his watching position at the end of Clerkenwell Green, he was confident that all his dominoes were in place bar one, the one that would take care of Judy. He knew just the man to do the job required, and now placed the call giving firm instructions of timing, method of entry and the information to retrieve.

Frank Rogers was a sadistic beast of a man. A man that enjoyed inflicting pain and suffering on his targets. A man not to be messed with. And he enjoyed his women, especially if they fought back, which Mark knew Judy would do.

Three of the best men his organisation had to offer, and three of the most loyal. Rogers would take care of the London end, while Jean-Pierre and Michel would capture and hold Hudson in Paris awaiting Chatfield's arrival. Finally both Judy and Hud would meet their ends, and he would have the file to return to the Director.

He smiled as he thought about the ways in which he might kill Hudson, and the look of hopelessness that Hudson would have when he heard about Judy's fate in London. He pictured Hudson's face in his mind's eye, the look of horror as his heart was ripped from him.

Chatfield turned the air conditioning to full, ice cold. He switched on his in car music system, and flicked through the tracks on the cd until he arrived at his favourite swing number 'Mack the Knife' by Hudby Darin.

He was on his way to gaining revenge for what he considered to be the murder of both his brother and his mother, and the destiny of Europe would soon be in the Director's hands.

THIRTEEN

The change in air pressure as the plane started its descent into Charles de Gaulle Airport woke Hud up. His head felt heavy as his ears blocked. He could see people talking and the stewardesses walking the aisle ensuring that belts were fastened. Magazines were being replaced in their netted hiding places on the back of seats, and the 'fasten belt' lights had joined the no smoking lights above heads.

He pinched his nose, closed his mouth and blew hard into his nostrils several times. On the third or fourth blow his ears popped, the rush of peoples' voices and the low humming of the air conditioning straining against the pressure change exploding in his head.

The stewardess approached his seat, looking left and right as she moved down the aisle warmly smiling at her clients. She held the same expression for Hud as she looked in his lap, ascertaining his belt to be tightly fastened in readiness for the runway approach.

Hud had spent the entire journey in an unforced siesta, as was his custom on flights. He generally fell asleep before even taking off, to awake as the jet fell earthwards on the last leg of its journey.

This trip had proved no different, despite the feeling of uneasiness that his predicament gave him. That feeling was now compounded by the closeness of reaching terra firma once more.

Deep in thought, he processed what the next few minutes might hold for him. He needed to ensure that his luggage had not been tampered with.

At Heathrow he had taken the precaution of putting all but a thousand Euros of his cash in the holdall, along with the fake passport and his money belt. He reasoned that he was less likely to have his bag searched than undergo a full body frisk as he went through the tight security land-side of the departure lounge. Never the less he had stood in front of the check out and watched his belongings disappear a little too intently. He now worried that an over eager security guard may have gained suspicion from this and checked the black holdall in any case. He was anxious about passing through customs with such copious amounts of cash, and feared being called to have his bags searched.

Throughout his time spent waiting for his flight to be called, he had sensed that he was being followed. He had circled the departure lounge several times, visiting the same coffee bar twice and taking the same stall to consume a luke warm, frothy cappuccino. Despite his anxiousness, he had not been able to pick a pursuer from the throng surrounding him. Eventually he had put his tension down to paranoia.

Whilst he had been contemplating his predicament, the plane had hauled itself gently to a standstill in front of the terminal. His fellow passengers had begun to unbelt, standing with arched backs as they emptied the overhead trays of their belongings.

Hud stayed put, feeling no need to rush from the plane. He watched his travel companions as they first queued and then filed out both fore and aft. When most had left, Hud unclipped his own belt and squeezed from his window seat to the aisle. He looked up and down the plane and decided to exit at the front. His decision to do so not swayed by the numbers waiting to disembark, but more by the flowing blonde locks of the stewardess bidding farewell as her charges moved from the cool of the plane to the balmy air of Paris in the spring evening.

He made his way from the gate in terminal 2F to the baggage collection. The terminal itself was one of the most modern in Europe, and also one of the busiest. Glass and steel accentuated the feel of space and openness, and the escalators were springy underfoot, and well lit by luminescent side panels of opaque perspex.

It wasn't long before his bag emerged on the turntable. He took it to the nearest toilet and chose the cubicle farthest from the entrance. He made sure the door was locked behind him by tugging on the aluminium handle, then placed his bag on the white plastic lid of the toilet pan.

He took the money belt from the holdall, and refilled it with as many notes as he could. Once satisfied that the belt was packed solidly, he let his trousers fall to his ankles and lifted his shirt. Carefully he wrapped the belt around his waste and pulled the buckle tight.

Once he had pulled his shirt into place and refastened his trousers he felt a little more at ease. He kept the thousand euros in his right hand trouser pocket, and his passport in his inside jacket pocket. He pushed the fake passport in his rear trouser pocket and re-zipped the holdall.

He flushed the toilet for good measure and made his way out of the cubicle, walking over to the wash basins.

Standing in front of the mirror he placed his hands under the automatic tap and adjusted to cold. He rinsed his face and hands several times, preferring to dry with the paper towels available to him rather than the hot air dispenser.

He surveyed himself in the mirror one final time before exiting. The money belt, whilst well concealed, gave the impression that the flight had added a few pounds to his midriff. It felt a little uncomfortable, but also gave him a sense of wellbeing: even in France cash could speak louder than words.

He walked out of the toilet and through to the European Union customs exit. One thing that the European Union had achieved was the freer movement of its peoples around its countries, without the need for rigorous passport and customs checks. Hud was pleased about this as he moved to walk through, holding his passport open at the photo page ahead of him as he went.

Hud noted a security guard observing him as he neared the head of his line. The guard wore the uniform of the French Army and carried a semi-automatic rifle. Hud had forgotten that all airport security across much of Europe had been strengthened again since the recent Islamic Fundamentalist Terrorist alerts.

As Hudson made his way to the passport checker, he saw the guard move forward, to stand immediately in front of him. The passport checker stopped what she was doing, and without words passed Hud's passport to the security guard who took it and started inspecting it.

He looked several times from Hud's face to the passport and back again. Finally he spoke.

'Monsieur Hudson?' he questioned, dropping the 'n' from the end of Hud's surname.

'Oui, c'est moi.' Replied Hud.

The guard continued his conversation in English. It was clear that the passport checker could not understand, and she soon lost interest in the brief discussion that took place.

'Mister Hudson, Sir, I am sorry about your brother. A tragic loss for your country.'

'Yes, thank you for your concern. A tragic loss for his family also' Hud replied politely but with a hint of distance in his voice.

'I am sorry to have stopped you, Sir. The man that awaits you is immediately outside the terminal in a black Citroen C6 saloon. Step inside the rear door. The driver's name is Jean-Pierre. Have a good stay in Paris. Bonsoir.' He saluted with a click of his heels and a nod of his head as he waved the Englishman through.

Hud accepted the return of his passport and his instructions, returning the goodwill gesture to the guard. He walked through the main concourse of the terminal, a mishmash of steel and glass. Huge white pylons in nests of threes rose majestically from stone tiled floor to ceiling, where they met the glass roof that allowed the night sky to partially invade the artificially illuminated space below.

He came to the front of the terminal, where the black Citroen saloon was waiting as he had been told it would.

He opened the rear door, and poked his head in.

'Jean-Pierre?' he questioned the driver, reluctant to take his seat.

'Oui. Please Mr Hudson, we do not have much time. We have been waiting since your brother's death.

'This is Michel, also a friend.' The driver waved his hand at the man in the passenger seat, whom Hud had not seen till then.

Satisfied, Hud climbed in the rear seat of the car, after first throwing the holdall across to the spare seat behind the driver. Hud slammed the door tight behind him, relieved to be in the company of his brother's friends.

The car moved off with a start, throwing Hud spread-eagled across the rear bench seat. He made to sound his annoyance at this treatment as he clambered to an upright position.

That was when he saw the barrel of a pistol pointing directly in his face.

FOURTEEN

Judy held her gaze for the time it took Hud's cab to disappear out of the Green. It was just gone one in the afternoon so Hud had plenty of time to get to Heathrow airport in order to check in the obligatory two hours before departure.

She calculated the next time she would speak to Hud, going over the timetable several times in her head to cement it in her memory, even though Hud and her had spoken about their plans before he left. With the plane departing at five, and the flight lasting an hour and a quarter, Hud was due to land at six fifteen UK time. By the time he had made his way through the arrivals lounge and picked his bag up from baggage collection, Hud had estimated that he would be calling Judy at around eight o'clock European time.

Judy looked at her watch. She had six hours to wait before she would hear from Hud again: seven o'clock UK time, eight o'clock in France.

She glanced out of the window as she turned to make another coffee and quickly turned back again, her eyes straining against the glare of the sun. She looked hard, trying to avoid the yellow dot that was fixed in front of her as she adjusted to its dazzle.

She stared up the road, but if it had been there at all it was now gone. She continued to exam the vacant space at the side of the road, on the corner of Clerkenwell Green as it became occupied once more. She was sure that a silver BMW had recently sat there, moving away as she had turned from the window.

Sure but not certain.

She considered phoning Hud, but decided against it. She did not want to alarm him for an uncertainty. She continued to stare at the occupied space, striving to see around the corner she was sure the car had turned into.

Sure but not certain.

Eventually Judy persuaded herself that her sighting was just a mirage, caused by the brightness of the sun and the paranoia that Hud had partially transferred to her whilst he had been telling her of his trials since Jack's death. Judy knew that the mind could play weird tricks on a person, especially when in a state of anxiety.

Even so, she looked one last time to the end of the road before tearing herself from the window. She needed some air. And coffee. Proper coffee, not the instant grains that Hud had pumped into her upon her arrival.

She lifted the keys that Hud had left her from the coffee table where the file sat, and deadlocked the door from the outside before making her way to the Costa bar two doors down from the apartment.

Sitting at the window counter with a steaming espresso in front of her, Judy began to deliberate the rest of her day.

It had started badly with Hud not answering his phone the previous day. It had made her tense before her alarm had woken her, and the banging deep in the back of her head had forced her to take a couple of paracetemol before rushing out of the house to go to Hud's place. Her friend Amy had confirmed that he had been at Jack's most of the previous day, but she had been concerned when there had been no answer during the evening either.

Having spent time with Hud since, she understood what had delayed his arrival the preceding night.

It seemed to her that Jack had set his brother a mission, sending him to Paris after his death. Clearly Jack had been into something that had caused all of the cloak and dagger stuff, and whatever made Jack afraid enough to hide all that money, and procure a fake passport for Hud, was enough to make Judy afraid. If there was something going on in Jack's life that even his wife knew nothing about, then Hud was in danger.

She wondered if she had done the right thing in persuading Hud to take the trip to Paris. However she knew if she hadn't been there to do the persuading, then he would have done so anyway. He played their relationship as the lesser partner, making it seem as if she were making all the major decisions. If he had been strong - as decisive as he used to be before the Iraq incident - then perhaps they would never have split. But Iraq had changed all that, and he needed a rod to lean on that Judy just couldn't be twenty-four hours a day.

No, she knew that he would have gone to Paris anyway. He just wanted her to confirm that he was doing the right thing.

She turned her attention back to her coffee, which she had only sipped to half way. She finished the small cup in one further mouthful, the strong black liquid giving her the immediate caffeine burst that her body craved, and made her way back to Hud's apartment.

The streets were emptying from the midday lunch rush, and it only took a couple of minutes to go from coffee shop to front door. Judy again avoided the lift, taking the stairs two at a time. It was already gone two in the afternoon and she had files to read.

Her job was to make sense of the papers that Jack had left, to try to establish a thread that would lead to a natural conclusion, while Hud did what he was best at: fieldwork. Besides, Hud's brother had warned that the file must remain safe, and both Hud and Judy had agreed that the file was safer in the flat with Judy than on the road with Hud.

It was Hud that was being followed, not Judy.

Now Judy wanted to make some headway with the paperwork, so that when her ex husband called she would have something concrete to report.

She put the key in the door, turned the lock twice to release the deadbolts and made her way to the lounge, pushing the front door closed behind her.

Sitting at the coffee table she opened the file that lay in front of her. Although Hud had given her a good description of the first section, Judy wanted to read it for herself. She read it through once, and then a second time making notes on an A5 reporters pad as she went. By the time she had finished, she had made four pages of notes herself which she now reviewed, taking care not to split the pages through their rings as she turned each page back on itself.

To her it was as Hud had explained. Notes about an ex Nazi German, who had served his time in a British prison for crimes committed. Intriguing but no more than that. It seemed to pose more questions than give answers.

She looked at the wall clock. It was already nearly four in the afternoon, and she'd been working hard on the file for the best part of two hours already.

Her neck ached from being hunched over the coffee table for so long, and the light was beginning to fade. She stood, stretched the ache from her back and made a coffee. She'd have to make do with instant, but decided to make a large pot and put it on the ring of Hud's coffee machine to keep warm. She guessed that she had a long night ahead of her.

While the kettle was boiling, she pulled the blinds closed and turned on the lights. As she passed the bar she looked at the optics, particularly noting the half empty southern comfort and furthermore the empty bottle in the waste bin. She shook her head, quietly scolding Hud in her own mind for his excessive drinking. She hoped that one day he would realise that this was not the answer to any of his problems.

She put several spoons of coffee grains in the percolator pot and poured the boiling water over, the clear liquid turning dark brown as the infusion kicked up the smell of coffee. She poured a mug from the pot, and then walked it to the bedroom, where she placed it on the table in front of the window. She switched on the table lamp and drew the curtains tight. No light in, no light out.

She went through to the living room and returned with the file and her notes, extinguishing the lights as she went, and imagining Hud asleep on the plane before even taking off. She could never understand how he managed to fall so soundly asleep before leaving the ground, to awake as the plane was making ready for landing.

Placing the file and notes on the window table, she arranged them so that they were laid with her notepad on the right hand side with a blank page facing up.

She opened the file at the second section, denoted by having a black divider at the front, and began to read. She read slowly and methodically, digesting all the main facts. She found it necessary to read some paragraphs twice so she could be assured that she had not misinterpreted the printed word on first reading.

It was hard going, and to keep her mind focussed she had to take several breaks filling her coffee mug each time.

Finally she had finished the first read through. The coffee pot had long since been emptied, the last dregs boiling dry. It was only the acrid smell emanating from the kitchen that alerted Judy to turn the machine off and stop the pot from splitting into small pieces.

Having diminished her immediate reserves of coffee, and thirsting for something a little more palatable than the grains from Hud's jar, Judy decided on paying a quick visit to Costa's to catch a real coffee before they closed for the evening.

By the time she returned to the flat the clock had just turned six. Before tackling the pages for a second time, she decided to take a quick shower to freshen up so she would be fully alert for when Hud called in around an hour.

Leaving the file and her notepad open in readiness for her return, she collected a towel and made her way to the bathroom.

With the shower running, and enjoying the sensation of the warm water exploding over her body, she did not hear the crack of the front door being jemmied.

Once showered, Judy dried herself with the soft towel and slipped her arms into one of Hud's clean white shirts that she had retrieved from behind one of the mirror doors in the bedroom. She rolled the sleeves so that her hands came clean from the bottom of them, and did a couple of buttons up. The shirt fell to mid way down her thigh, the tailored cut hanging loosely around her waist. She stepped into her thong and pulled it up underneath the shirt before leaving the bedroom to pour herself a glass of water.

As she opened the door, the smell of a smouldering cigarette invaded her nostrils. She peered out to the darkness of the lounge, willing her eyes to become accustomed to the change in illumination. She felt the wall for the light switch, and as she flicked it to the on position was temporarily blinded by the first blaze from the bulb above.

All she was able to make out was a dark shape, swooping toward her from the darkness ahead. The thick set man hit her hard in the abdomen pushing her back into the bedroom as he rushed headlong at her.

She fell back, hitting the base of her spine on the floorboards, raising her arms in defence as a hand came hurtling. But the hand didn't hit, it grabbed both wrists in a vice like grip hauling her to her knees. The man's other hand pulled at the shirt, the buttons popping to reveal her naked breasts.

She heard him command her on to the bed, as again his strength overpowered her attempts to break free. She was lifted off the floor and flung backwards, landing on the mattress, her attacker following her, pinning her down with his weight.

Her shirt was now fully open, her nakedness on show to the man on top of her. His rancid breath made her want to choke, whilst sweat from his forehead dripped on her face. She lay diagonally across the bed struggling to break free, but her exertions to no avail. He was too strong, and too heavy, pinning her hands above her head in his hands and her legs together beneath his. He licked her face as he spoke.

'I was told there might be a little bonus for me. I'll just have my fun before I take what doesn't belong to you. If you're good, I'll let you live.' He hissed the words, like a cobra ready to strike at its prey.

He removed one hand from its grip, and placed it between her legs. Judy tried desperately to struggle free, but still his grip was too much for her. With a sudden jerk, her thong was ripped from her, the elasticated straps digging into her flesh.

Her attacker fell nearer, his tongue slobbering over her neck, his legs slowly prising hers apart, all the while keeping control of her.

Judy felt him undoing his fly, and struggled to break a hand free. She wriggled and tried kicking, and in his efforts to control her he allowed her right arm to break lose.

She continued to fight as hard as she could, all the while stretching out with her right arm, feeling for what she knew was there: perhaps the only thing that could save her now. As she felt the coldness against her fingertips so too did she feel the roughness of his hand against her vagina.

With one final effort Judy turned her head and bit into her would be rapist's neck on the point of a red and black tattoo in the shape of a St Andrew's cross, with arrowheads on each end. He yelped his grievance, and moved just enough for Judy to stretch her arm another couple of inches.

She wrapped her fingers around the neck of the bottle that Hud kept by his bed for his morning medication, and swiftly bought it crashing down on her attacker's head. It was enough to make him reel to one side, enough to give her the space to wriggle free.

She scrambled to clear the bed, but a hand grabbed her ankle.

'You bitch, you'll pay for that!' the voice behind her screamed.

She kicked backwards with her free leg striking the man's jaw, clawing at the boards in an effort to break free. She managed to get to her feet, lunging for the doorway, but somehow the beast appeared before her again, blocking her escape.

Judy backed off, as the man moved toward her his fists clenched. Blood dribbled from his neck, sweat poured from his brow, his yellowing teeth showed behind his evil grin. She warned him to stop, but still he came. He drove forward, his arms outstretched.

Instinctively, Judy hit the bottle against the frame of the bathroom door. Glass smashed and splinters flew. With one movement she pulled the jagged, broken neck of the bottle up between the man's flaying arms and urged the makeshift weapon into his neck.

She heard the crack of larynx as the glass dug deep, blood shot from the wound making splatter patterns on the wall. Still the man came, grabbing at Judy's shoulders and catching hold of her hair.

His mouth opened to spit more bile, but no noise came. His eyes bulged and his hand released Judy's locks. He sank to his knees, his hands now around his own throat. A few attempted breaths later and he fell forwards on to his face, his hands still tight around his neck. His body moved no longer. He was gone.

Judy backed away, too frightened to release her stare from the beast lest he suddenly came back from the dead. She fell to the floor, her back in the corner of the room, her legs clutched tightly to her chest.

Tears came as she began breathing. They streamed down her face, washing away the vile sweat that had dripped from the man that now lay dead before her. The remnants of the broken bottle fell from her grasp, spinning to a halt on the floor as lifeless as the creature it had struck moments earlier.

She cried, and tried to think if this was the feeling that Hud had each time he had killed.

Finally she rose, and skirted the body to enter the bathroom. She vomited before she showered, and kept the door wide so she could see the unmoving body, too scared to take her eyes away.

She took a long time, washing away the deeds of the violation that she felt. As the water drained, so her mind raced.

Hud.

The man now in her flat had said that he was to take what didn't belong to her. The files sat on the table, untouched. But there was no doubt in her mind that they were the real target.

She bounded over to the window, and pulled her cell phone from her jacket pocket that now laid strewn on the floor, flung there in the preceding melee.

She pushed a couple of buttons and waited for the ringing to be answered.

No answer.

She cut off and tried again.

Still no answer.

She looked at the time. It was gone half past seven, half past eight French time. Thoughts somersaulted through her mind. He should have phoned already. He was in danger, perhaps dead. She didn't know.

But she knew one thing: she had only one option available to her. She had to follow Hud. She had to get to Paris and find him.

FIFTEEN

As soon as his plane had landed, Mark Chatfield pushed the power button on his mobile. The mini screen shone brightly as he keyed in his security pin, and the phone sprang to life with the manufacturer's jingle alerting his travelling companion to its use. He tutted in disgust, the simultaneous shake of his head chastising Mark for giving his mobile phone life before the plane had come to a complete standstill.

Mark had contended with the fat man sitting next to him the whole flight. He wore just shirt sleeves with an open collar and, even in the cool of the air conditioned cabin, was sweating profusely.

Although the flight was of limited duration, the fat man had downed several vodka tonics without effect. Several times he had attempted to strike up a conversation with Mark, extolling the virtues of the new breed of super-jumbos or the light-bite options available with certain airlines. As he flicked through the free in-flight magazines available to him from the pocket by his knees, it seemed that every turn of a page would herald another subject upon which he was an expert. Eventually Mark had felt no option but to tell the fat man to shut up.

'Ah, a nervous air traveller. I used to be like that', he had retorted, going on to spend the next five minutes telling Mark how marvellously hypnosis had worked for him.

Finally Mark had plugged in a set of earphones and turned his head away half way through an explanation of the advantages and disadvantages of ice cubes versus ice balls. As Mark looked out the port hole the fat man had got the message, finishing his drink and ordering another from the overworked stewardess.

Now that the plane had landed the fat man was showing his dislike of the way his attempts to begin a friendship had been brushed aside, by showing contempt for Mark's lack of respect for airline rules.

Mark didn't care about the fat man and ignored his protestations. He was anxious to hear positive news from his colleagues both in Paris and in London.

The plane finally docked at the terminal, and the warning lights sounded its termination. A surge of seat belts snapping open ensued, and passengers crowded the aisle. Mark had to wait for the fat man to haul his hulking size out of the seat before he too could begin disembarkation.

Grabbing his hand luggage, Chatfield followed behind the throng and passed unhindered into the terminal. As he walked through the guards and toward the exit, his cell phone called to be answered. He took the phone from his inside top pocket and thumbed the device open, whipping it to his ear in one smooth movement.

It was Jean-Pierre confirming that they had Peter Hudson under their control. The operation had gone smoothly. They had easily managed to bribe a guard to look out for Hudson as he emerged from Arrivals, and the hundred Euros it cost for him to be pointed in the direction of their Citroen had been worth every penny. Now they sat with Hudson at gunpoint, making their way to their Paris headquarters.

Mark slipped the phone back into his pocket, satisfied that the operation was running well. He looked at his watch, which showed the time as seven thirty. He was still on UK time. He stopped and spun the dial to adjust for the hour forward in Europe.

He took out his phone again, and made to call Rogers in London. Half way through the dialling he stopped. He allowed himself a wry smile. He had no doubt that Frank Rogers would soon be in touch. He was probably busy with Judy.

Chatfield's smile almost turned to laughter as he thought of the horrors that Hudson's ex wife would be going through. He felt sure that he would hear from Rogers soon. He returned his phone once more to his pocket, and carried on through the terminal on his way to the waiting taxis at the front of the terminal building. His flight had made good time, and he now expected to be with Jean-Pierre in within 30 minutes.

He sat back in the cab, a Mercedes with cloth upholstery. He breathed deeply through his nose and held the breath for a few seconds before exhaling, keeping his eyes closed throughout.

The queue at the taxi rank had been longer than he supposed it might, and he had now fallen behind schedule. However, with his Glock 35 secreted in his hand luggage, he had not wanted to raise the suspicions of any guards on anti terrorist duty and so had been forced to impatiently wait his turn in the line.

Now he was relaxed in the rear, he pondered the reasons that Rogers had not yet called. He should have been finished by now, his orders had been concise. Mark had told him to silence Judy, and had given his permission for Rogers to do with her what he wanted once the file had been secured. It disturbed him that he had not yet received the call to confirm the file was safely in their hands.

He decided to call Rogers. He dialled the number and waited for a response.

The phone rang in Mark's ears, but there was no answer. It cut to message mode, and Mark cut off. They never left messages, in case the phone should fall in the wrong hands.

He looked at his watch once more: eight forty-five. Rogers was late, but not yet too late. Chatfield decided to wait until the end of his journey to try the number again, if he'd not had confirmation from Rogers himself by that time.

They had left the bright lights of the airport behind, and now travelled northbound through the outlying suburbs of Paris on the A6, the main route from the Aeroport de Paris-Orly. Cars flashed past, headlights a blur.

Paris is divided into twenty municipal districts, arrondissements spiralling outwards and clockwise from the 1st arrondissment on the right bank of the River Seine.

As his taxi drew closer to Paris, Chatfield could see the lights of the Tour Montparnasse, which stands like a watchtower guarding the surrounding artistic district of the 14th arrondissement Montparnasse.

They swung left to pass the Cimitiere d'Arcueil and were soon facing the campus of the Cite Internationale Universitaire. Here they headed West along the Rue Saint-Albin, cutting across at the Paris Expo so as to take the adjacent Boulevard Victor across the Seine.

After crossing the bridge, the driver took to the Voie Georges Pomopidou running parallel to the river. Lights from the Left Bank shimmered on the water as it was disturbed by the boats above, plying their trade to the tourist market of evening dinner whilst cruising the main artery of the city.

Before long the driver again headed north on the Avenue Des Nations-Unies through the Jardins du Trocadero. Cutting into the Avenue D'Iena, they headed for the Place de L'Arc de Triomphe. Locals walked side by side with tourists, and the restaurants and café's spilled their custom to the pavements outside, where waiters tried to cajole ever more passers by to become patrons for the next hour or so.

They negotiated the circular road around the attraction in the only way that any Parisian taxi driver could, loud blasts of the car's horn interjected by curses and furious hand signals to his compatriots. It always amazed Mark that there were not more fatalities on the roads of France's capital.

Finally they made their way south West down the Avenue Victor Hugo before turning into the Rue Paul Valery, where Chatfield's Paris headquarters lay. The driver had taken the tourist route rather than the more direct approach but Mark happily accepted the higher charge, the knowledge that Peter Hudson was in the organisation's hold giving him an unusually warm feeling.

The receptionist looked up from his desk as Mark entered the building and, recognising the suited intruder, raised his right hand to his brow in salute before looking down again to his crossword after Chatfield had passed. The lobby was panelled in dark oak, with high ceilings accentuating the space. A small table with international newspapers sat surrounded by four leather armchairs. It could, in fact, have been the foyer of any small financial boutique. For that's what it was: a niche trading house that made money for its clients by trading the up and downs of the markets, buying and selling shares around the globe, hedging and speculating with futures and options and taking bets on the direction of commodities such as gold and oil. All the while influencing the movement of the world's major currencies.

The only difference between this and many hundred's of other similar operations world wide was that this boutique operation served just one client.

That client was the one Mark Chatfield really worked for and was now one of the most powerful, yet secretive, on the continent. It had similar buildings in most of Europe's main capital cities.

Now Mark Chatfield sat at his desk in his office on the ground floor, awaiting the arrival of his guest from London. He looked around him, surveying the trappings of his loyalty.

His private room was the most opulent in the building. Carpeted in thick Axminster, from floor to ceiling his personal space oozed wealth and power. On the far wall there were six plasma screens showing the world's markets, and a further three with world news channels. He liked to keep up to date with world events when he spent time in Paris. He had soft leather furnishings, in a deep red to match the carpet, and his drinks cabinet was stocked with some of the finest spirits imaginable. The walls were finished in the finest oak and pure white marble. Behind the desk was a concealed door that led directly to the basement. At the far end of the underground chamber was a further door that exited upwards to the rear entrance of the building. This is where Peter Hudson would be bought.

The traders that sat in offices above merely knew Mark as the client's right hand man in Paris. They worked feverishly in pursuit of the wealth and power that had been bestowed upon Mark Chatfield. Each and every one of them wanted to own Chatfield's office. None of them realised that they, themselves, were owned by their one and only client. A client they simply knew as the organisation 'Schengen.'

To its loyal followers it was the organisation that would not only shape the future of Europe, but would *be* the future of Europe.

SIXTEEN

Peter Hudson had never been this close to the wrong end of a weapon before, at least not one over which he didn't have control. He looked up from the business end of the barrel to see Michel staring fixedly at him. Clearly he meant business.

Hud pushed his back into the seat, the pistol following his movement. He covertly tried the door release but it moved without engaging. The driver, the one that had introduced himself as Jean-Pierre, had control of the locks as well as the situation that Hud now found himself in. He castigated himself for not taking greater care before putting himself in this position.

'It is no use, Peter Hudson,' the driver said, noticing his captive's play to be free, 'the only way for you to get out, is for me to allow you out. You can not open the doors or the windows in the rear without my say.'

Michel smiled, exposing a missing tooth just behind his upper left incisor, and waved the gun menacingly.

Jean Pierre, clearly the senior of the partnership, continued the one sided conversation.

'Michel has orders to shoot if you try anything... how do you English say?...funny.'

Hud sat in the rear, trying to relax as much as possible. He knew that in high tension situations it was important to keep as calm as possible.

He counted his breathing, holding his inhalations for five seconds before exhaling gently, then waiting another five seconds before repeating the process. This was a method of relaxation that the Army shrink had taught him. It was about the only thing of any use that he had got from him before he had been honourably discharged.

He sat quietly while his kidnappers spoke in French between themselves. Hud had never been a good linguist, but did pick the thread of the interchange. It seemed that Jean-Pierre was bringing Michel up to speed with what he had said to their passenger. Perhaps the two were equals after all, the only seniority being the driver's ability to speak English.

Jean-Pierre lifted a cell phone from its pouch on the dash, and pressed a couple of buttons. Speed dial. It didn't take long before his call was answered.

Hud again picked out a few words, the most important being 'quarante cinq minutes': forty-five minutes.

He spied the clock dial through the steering wheel. Eight thirty. Wherever they were headed, they were due to arrive at around nine fifteen. It only gave him three quarters of an hour to think of a way out, and execute his escape.

Hud's phone chirupped inside his pocket. Instinctively he moved to answer, and Michel, equally instinctively, pushed the nozzle of his pistol closer.

'Arretez! Stop!' he commanded, followed by a garbled babbling to Jean-Pierre.

It was the driver who gave the next orders.

'Please, Mr Hudson, take the phone slowly from your pocket and place it on the seat next to you where my friend will be able to see it. Only use two fingers, Mr Hudson, or Michel will take your hand away with a bullet.'

The phone had stopped ringing by the time Jean-Pierre had spoken.

Hud did as he was told, carefully removing the phone from his inside pocket, before placing it face up on the seat next door. He held his hands palm forwards, fingers spread, and in front of his chest once he had completed his instructions, iterating to the gunman that he had nothing to hide.

Hud did not like the nervousness that the ringing cell phone had instilled in Michel, who now was talking excitedly in French to his friend.

Charles de Gaulle Airport had long since disappeared behind them, and Hud had felt the car turn southwest onto the main A1 bound toward Paris.

As Michel's voice seemed to become more excited, so the car's speed seemed to increase. Jean-Pierre shouted at his driving companion and Michel fell silent, but still with his eyes trained to the rear.

'Mr Hudson, please ensure your belt is fixed securely. We are running behind schedule and need to travel a little faster' ordered Jean-Pierre.

Hud looked at Michel, who waved the gun towards the rear seat belt, his actions endorsing the orders that Hud had just received. Hud reached with his left hand across his chest and slowly pulled the belt out and down, pushing it firmly in place. As he did so he managed to move his head so that he could see out of the passenger side wing mirror. A pair of lights followed closely behind, weaving through the traffic as the Citroen was now doing.

As they sped past Le Bourget Airport, Michel started snapping orders to Jean-Pierre once more. Gathering speed and the closeness of the car behind had confirmed that they were indeed being followed.

Jean-Pierre had to concentrate on the road ahead, and Hud could see that he was flashing his headlights in an attempt to clear the tarmac from traffic. Industrial buildings flashed past, and soon they were hurtling past the outer conurbation of Paris, still on the trunk road but Hud knew they would hit areas of higher population and narrower roads soon if they were indeed headed into Paris.

The wheels squeaked against the smoothness of the road as they sped south, the Stade de France rising high on their left, and high technology industrial units on their right. The National Research Centre too came and went, articulated lorries struggled to move over, and twice Jean-Pierre steered first one way and then the other undertaking and overtaking between long wheel base vehicles and the central reservation.

Still he could not shake his pursuer, the Citroen flipping from trunk road to single carriageway bumping over a weak curb and makeshift entrance. The car behind conducted the same manoeuvre, spitting sparks from its undercarriage as it leapt in the air and landed over the curb. They now ran parallel to the main trunk road before it disappeared below ground.

Both cars rushed headlong through a crossroads, the car behind pulling almost alongside the Citroen.

Hud looked across and saw that the pursuing flame red Renault was occupied by a lone driver, a determined look upon his face watching both his speeding prey and the road ahead. The two cars matched each other nearly neck and neck, before Jean-Pierre cut across to his left veering in front of the Renault, which in turn mounted the kerb before coming back down and losing its front bumper.

Jean-Pierre had crossed to the other side of the road, travelling contra-flow to the traffic heading toward him into the wild flashing of headlights.

Both cars now sped side by side, but separated by gardens and play areas between the two roads. Both twisted in and out of traffic, Hud's driver pushing his pursuer to the limit, each able to spy the other through intermittent gaps in the tree lined roads.

Before hitting the Porte de la Chapelle, where the main east-west artery interconnected with the end of the E19, and the exit roads to all corners of Paris, the Renault was suddenly lost.

Michelle looked across, and behind, but their follower was nowhere. He called his delight to Jean-Pierre. He in turn checked all his mirrors. Sweat beads had formed on both men's faces, yet throughout Michel had kept his pistol trained on Hud's chest.

Hud's heart sank. Jean-Pierre concentrated on the oncoming traffic. As he slowed to negotiate the entrance slipway, which was to be his exit, headlights behind flashed their alarm to the occupants of the Citroen, and once more Jean-Pierre put his foot hard to the metal.

Heading east and then spinning the wheel hard right, he rejoined the traffic going his way, burning rubber during the turn. Again they turned south now joining roads with no central reservation. The Renault followed their path, never far behind but never close enough to head them off the road.

Jean Pierre mounted the pavement, with his horn blaring and lights flashing. Pedestrians dived for cover from the two cars. The one followed the other as it dashed on and off the pavement between the double bank of elm trees.

Police sirens sounded from behind, as they were joined in their indiscretions. Still they travelled at speeds of up to ninety miles per hour through the dense avenues of outer Paris. The traffic got heavier, each car diving in and out. Cyclists fell away, knocking tourists and locals to one side.

Then a mistake, Jean-Pierre misjudged the speed of an oncoming van, clipping its rear wing as he passed.

Screeches of brakes followed as the van tried to steer clear from its spin. The driver overcompensated and the van toppled. The Renault swerved left and missed the upturned van, which now slid on its side, spinning toward the pavement opposite.

The driver of the police pursuit car was not so lucky, ploughing directly into the exposed belly of the van. The tank exploded upon impact, orange flames spiriting skywards. Shrapnel rained down on passers by. The van continued to move, spinning in a fireball like a Catherine Wheel, hurtling towards a roadside café. The pavement was mounted as the van careered into the seated diners. Screams of horror rang out from behind as the Renault continued to chase Hud's captors.

They negotiated the traffic at the Impasse Du Gue, cars from all directions screeching their pain as they were forced to abrupt standstill, metal scraping against metal, a melee of broken machines blocking the path of subsequent oncoming vehicles.

Behind, more sirens as the city's Gendarmerie joined the chase.

Across the intersection of Rue Marx Dormoy and Rue Riquet, Jean-Pierre called his car sharp right, the back end signalling its resistance with tyre smoke. Through the compressed back streets of Paris they raced, parked cars losing wing mirrors and gaining unwanted stripes as both the Citroen and Renault marked their route.

Pedestrians fled, leaving their hand baggage behind as the two cars ran close, just yards between them. Michel considered firing shots from the window to deter their hunter, but could not take his concentration away from their cargo.

Young children opened first floor windows as the chase spun twice around the Rue De Suez and Rue De Panama, police cars gaining ground and closing the net. They faced oncoming traffic as they hurtled through the Rue Leon, the chasing Renault wounded by a 2CV that was too slow in effecting its escape from the path of the second madman.

They rushed the wrong way through Rue Cave, the Citroen removing the wing of a parked vehicle on the corner of Rue Affre. Car alarms traced their progress, the sound and stroboscopic effect of flashing headlights proving a disco through the unlit streets.

Suddenly, directly ahead of Jean-Pierre, and without warning a car pulled from the kerb of the crowded rat-run. He tried desperately to avoid the collision, slamming brakes and spinning the wheel first one way and then the other. Michel's head hit the ceiling as the car took off, momentarily cruising on its passenger side tyres before violently meeting the rear bumper of a stationary Volvo.

The Volvo lurched with the sudden impact, the Citroen flipping skywards and rolling in mid-air before the windscreen shattered as the hunk of metal came crashing to earth bottom side up.

On landing, an explosion rang from inside the Citroen in the cool of the night air.

Hud grabbed violently at his left side as the heat of the bullet seared through him, the pain burning into his sinews. His left arm fell limp, yet his body stiffened in spasms. He could feel his heart thumping to a samba beat inside his head. He saw the contorted face of Michel staring wide eyed back at him. Outside the world sat upside down, house doors were opening and feet ran toward the mangled vehicle.

Then all was black and silent.

SEVENTEEN

Mark Chatfield sat in the plush surroundings of his Paris office, his fists clenched on the desk in front of him. He had recognised the Citroen on the live streaming news of the France 24 channel tuned in to one of his wall-mounted sets.

What he didn't yet understand was how the crash had occurred. The reporter spoke about a high speed chase through the Parisian streets, and witnesses claimed that there had been two cars involved. Police had arrived quickly on the scene, and the Channel was airing a live interview of a bystander who had apparently witnessed the crash. The reporter had positioned the bystander so that the remains of the Citroen were visible in the background of the shot.

'Two cars came round the corner very, very fast. The first, a black Citroen, hit a car as it was pulling out. I saw it from the top of the road. Over there' the teenage boy pointed behind the camera, which turned to pan the street and then returned to the witness as he continued.

'Then it turned over and there was a loud bang. The car that was following it - I think it was a Renault

- screeched to a halt behind. I saw a man get out of the second car, and that's when I ran to my house to get my brother to help. When we came back, the second car had gone, and there were people running all over the place trying to get the men out of the Citroen. I don't know if anyone is alive or not, but one of my friends said at least one person had died. I saw an ambulance take someone to hospital.'

The camera zoomed into the scene behind the boy.

An area had been cordoned off from the public by the use of blue and white scene of crime tape. The car sat upon its roof, partially on top of an old Volvo saloon. The front end of the Citroen was mangled almost beyond recognition: the bonnet had caved in, the windscreen smashed and the roof in a 'v' shape.

One of the rear doors hung by a single hinge, and the two front doors lay at the side of the road. Mark surmised that the authorities had removed these in order to take the driver and the front passenger out of the wreckage.

He could see also on the side of the road, partly concealed by a Gendarme trying to move the camera crew away from the scene, a bodybag.

He knew there had been three people in the car, and now wanted to know if Jean-Pierre and Michel had survived the crash. And what of Hudson: was he dead or alive? And who had been driving the second car? Where had it disappeared to?

There were too many questions unanswered for his liking. By now he should have had Peter Hudson under his charge. But he didn't. He should have received word that the file was on its way from London. But he hadn't.

He was still waiting on news from England, but guessed that it too was going to be bad.

His day was turning to crap, and he sensed it would get worse before it got better

The phone on his desk rang. He stared at it for a few moments before lifting the receiver: this was the call that he had been dreading, the call from London.

While he had awaited the arrival of Hudson from Charles de Gaulle, Chatfield had twice more tried to contact Rogers without success. He knew that Rogers could be a sadistic animal where women were concerned, preferring to mix business with pleasure as it were, but had never known him to be so late reporting his success. It was because of his reputation that Chatfield had chosen him to retrieve the important file. When he confronted Hudson, he wanted also to be able to crush his world. He wanted him to know that it was his friend Mark Chatfield who had murdered his brother, given the order for the mutilation of his ex wife – the only woman that had meant anything to Hudson – and now would squeeze the life from him. Slowly.

Chatfield had feared a mistake had been made in London, and so had sent another employee – one who was adept at twisting bad jobs to good - to investigate. While he waited patiently for the update from London, before his eyes the horror of the situation in Paris unfolded, courtesy of Channel 24 News.

Now he placed the telephone's earpiece to his ear, hoping - but not expecting - to hear good news. He listened with increasing apprehension, as the words coming to him described everything he hoped not to hear.

The flat had been broken into, but there was no sign of the woman, nor any files. The apartment was in pristine condition, except for the bedroom.

Rogers lay in a pool of blood, face down with his throat ripped. The weapon, a broken bottle, lay near, and blood stained the walls. A man's shirt with the buttons ripped away was strewn on the floor beside the bed.

Chatfield barked orders for the clear up man to stay put in the flat and make sure no one entered. He had to have time to think before he acted. And that was important at times like this. He needed to compose himself and act, not react.

He stood and turned away from the television screens. With his back to the mahogany desk, Mark pulled open the drinks cabinet. He fingered the bottles before deciding on a rare Cardhu 25 year old single malt scotch.

He poured a large slug in a glass, and took half in his mouth. He savoured the smoked oak taste before allowing the liquid to glide warmly southwards. He added a couple of ice cubes from the freezer compartment, spun them in the whiskey tumbler and took a seat on the sofa. He sank a little in the soft grain leather, and with his head resting on the flat surface of the low back closed his eyes as he contemplated his next move. He also considered how he could put a positive spin on his predicament when he reported to the Director, which he would have to do before the night was out.

He cleared his mind, and let the silence drift over him. All that invaded his peace was the chink of ice on glass and the soft murmur of the television set, meagre background noise for his cogitation. He lifted his head so that the scotch could once more play with his taste buds, giving his tongue first an alcoholic numbness and then after burst alive with the clean taste of the fine beverage.

He decided to put the London problem to one side. He had that partly under control, the flat having been made safe. Although both Judy and the file had vanished, he felt sure that they would be found together. That was a matter of time.

The events in Paris, however, were of priority concern. He did not know the status of Jean-Pierre or Michel, and nor did he know the whereabouts of Hudson. Two of his finest men and perhaps his greatest enigma, could be alive or dead. Or vanished into thin air. He needed also to find the mystery man in the Renault.

He considered his options, and decided to telephone a friend of his that would be able to help. A man that, like Chatfield, was loyal to the Schengen.

He took to his feet and moved once more to his desk, glancing at the screens on the far wall. Channel 24 had moved on to a story about the recent terrorist threats, with analysis of the counter measures that Europe had taken. It always surprised him how open the democratic governments of Europe were when it came to National Security. It was a question of 'we know that there is this threat or that threat, so we'll let you know how we propose to safeguard our people against such attacks. Then our enemies will know how to circumnavigate our defences.' He felt heartened to know that there would soon be a change of modus operandi in Europe, and that his power would grow because of it.

He dialled, and he waited for the familiar voice to answer. When it did, he would speak in French so as to offer his friend the respect he deserved and so that he in turn would know the need that he would place upon him.

A deep baritone thunder came back at him in reply to his call, announcing the respondent's name. The Department was obviously busy. But Chatfield knew that nothing was more important than the work of the organisation, especially at this time when it was so close to realising its destiny. He simply requested the favour he needed, and knew that his bidding would be done.

'Ah, Prefect Rousset. It's good to hear your voice. I need to know about the crash in Paris tonight, the one that is on all the major French news channels. I trust that you will have a full report for me. It is a matter of urgency' Chatfield did not even need to announce himself, he knew that Rousset would recognise his voice. Besides, there were few people who had Rousset's personal cell phone number.

Rousset acknowledged that the instructions would be carried out, and the report would be ready within minutes. He would call back when he had all the required information.

No matter what case he was working on, Rousset would always be available for Schengen business. The organisation had high-ranking officials across all of Europe's police forces, ready for the day when they were needed.

During the time he waited for Rousset's return call, Chatfield called England again. It did not take long for his lover to answer, and although they only had a few minutes it was always she that restored his faith in what he was doing. She confirmed that she would soon be joining him in France ready for the day when the whole of Europe would turn to Schengen for leadership and guidance. They made a good partnership, and the way was now clear for a more concrete alliance between them. They talked until his other phone chimed Rousset's report.

Rousset confirmed that there had indeed been a second car, the Renault as reported by the Channel 24 bystander. Tracking it would take a little longer, but the Department were now making it's detection top priority.

He also confirmed that there had been only two men in the car when the police had arrived, and no sign of the pursuing Renault. Those two men were the dead man, Michel; and the driver Jean-Pierre, who had sustained cuts, bruises and a broken leg, and had been taken to the Hopital Lariboisiere where there were officers in readiness to question and charge him. He also confirmed that the police were currently searching for a third man that had been suspected of travelling in the rear of the Citroen. Forensics had found a bullet buried in the upholstery of the rear bench seat, and bloodstains gave credence to the theory that the man had been shot.

Chatfield requested that the officers waiting at the Hospital to speak to Jean-Pierre bring him in to Rousset, and that Rousset would then order his release. He also requested that when the third man in the car was found, that he be bought to the organisation's headquarters. Rousset agreed all of these points.

Chatfield gave praise to Rousset for his sterling efforts and rapid response, telling him that he would be well rewarded, and then cut off.

He fixed himself a second scotch, and sat considering his next move. The report of the car chase had reappeared on the television, now shown on a video loop.

He sat and watched, waiting for inspiration to hit. He took another swig of whiskey, again holding it in his mouth in readiness for the aroma to bounce of his tongue. As he swallowed he had the notion of what needed to be done.

He placed another call to the clean up man in Hudson's flat, and a further call to Rousset.

Then he made one final call to the Director, explaining the night's events and the actions that would now be taken to rectify the situation.

Whilst he was maddened by the loss of both Hudson and his ex wife, and particularly the missing file, the Director was pleased with the plans now put in motion.

Neither of them yet knew, but both Judy and Peter Hudson would soon be in the hands of Schengen.

EIGHTEEN

Judy had taken the underground to Waterloo Station. It had been a nervous journey and, to keep her from dwelling too long on the devastation that she had left behind her, she had paced the train furiously.

She had run from the flat to Kings Cross Station, and travelled without an overnight bag. She had considered returning to her house to pick up a change of clothes and toiletries, but had decided against doing so. Her priority was to get to Paris as quickly as possible, to find Hud and help him.

She carried a large handbag over her shoulder, into which she had hurriedly stuffed Jack's file and her notes. She had zipped the top and now clung tightly to the bag under her arm, clinging to the straps with both hands. She was thankful that she always carried her passport with her, a habit that infuriated Hud. He would always remind her how easy it was to steal someone's identity, and that she was only making a criminal's job even easier. Now she did not have to travel home to retrieve it, and she was happy to be on her way rather than have to cross London and back.

She had taken the Piccadilly Line the four stops to Leicester Square where she changed to the Northern Line to travel the three remaining stops to Waterloo.

Her nerves jangled at each stop, relieved as people got off and suspicious of all that embarked at each tube station. Passengers eyed her as she moved back and forth along the coaches, anxiously avoiding their stares. Her hair was dishevelled, and she had washed away her makeup with the tears she had shed at Hud's flat less than a half hour earlier.

Twice she had feared being stalked, and twice she had alighted to return to the carriage via the next open door. Both times her suspected follower had remained unmoved.

And so it was that she had finally arrived at Waterloo, rushing up the escalator and away from the underground terminus. She now stood on the concourse of the mainline station.

The rush hour had died away, and passenger numbers were now waning. A Japanese couple were busying themselves taking photos of each other on their latest, state-of–the-art digital camera, posing in front of the Victorian outer shell of the station. There were a group of city types whiling away the last few minutes, laughing and joking over their last pints of the evening in Bonapartes, the on station bar franchise. The Costa and Burger King kiosks were busy with small queues of commuters getting their supplies for the journey home.

All around her, commuters, business men, holidaymakers, tourists, and railway employees were oblivious to the woman who now stood in their midst. The woman who had that very evening been subjected to the most brutal attack, and had consequently killed a man. No one paid her any attention, no one suspected. Provided she could keep her nerve, she could move unhindered amongst the clean and the pure.

A policeman walked toward her, and for a second she stood rooted to the ground, convinced that she was to be arrested. But the officer simply nodded at her as he passed, and carried on to exit the station toward the South Bank and the London Eye.

She walked to the Bureau de Change and changed two hundred pounds into Euros, using her Visa card. After receiving her cash and receipt, Judy walked back toward Platform 19 and travelled the escalator to the Eurostar terminal. She looked up at the Departures Board and saw the next train was due to depart in a quarter of an hour.

She hurried to the ticketing kiosk where a portly employee advised that she required a business class ticket to take advantage of the next available train. She handed over her Visa and punched in her pin when requested to do so. She rushed to the entrance machine and inserted her ticket, panic swept over her as she waited for the barrier to swing open. She glanced all around her, but could not spy anyone in her pursuit.

She scooted down the platform and finally decided on Coach seven, taking a single seat facing toward the front of the train and benefiting from a half table onto which she placed her handbag so as to deter any fellow passenger from sitting opposite. The carriage was almost deserted, except for a few businessmen who had already settled into sleep mode having exerted themselves fully during their respective meetings in London and now returning to their native Paris.

Once underway, Judy lifted her bag and made her way to the toilet where she freshened up, washing her face and hands. She applied some make up from her purse, and brushed her hair. She pulled her hair through a band to hold it in a pony-tail, and exited her powder room. She looked into her coach through the glass door, before requesting a strong black coffee from the bar.

Settling back into her seat, she took the file from its hiding place and began to read through once more, this time making notes as she went. She needed to keep busy to hold back the terrible memories of that evening that kept invading her.

When they stopped at Ashford, her thoughts once more strayed to Hud as she strained to see the scaffolded building which had nearly taken his life a day earlier. She thought of his car, still parked there and tried to imagine Hud still alive and well in Paris. She attempted to call him on her cell phone once more, but still there was no answer. She had to remain hopeful, but her optimism for his well being was fading.

She considered getting off the train then and there, taking the file and her knowledge to the authorities, but Jack's written words haunted her: 'Do not let the file fall into anyone's hands.'

As the locomotive resumed its journey, so Judy resumed her work reading and making notes as she went. The train continued its rocking, as page by page Judy started to build a picture of a similar rocky journey taken through the last sixty years.

As they entered the tunnel that would take them under the Channel and through to the high speed link to Paris, Judy reviewed her notes carefully, cross referencing to the file now and again and ensuring that she had correctly collated all the relevant details. If her understanding was correct, she was beginning to realise the dreadful danger that Jack had put Hud into.

She folded the file and her notes, placed them in her bag and walked through once more to the buffet. She needed another coffee, and to take a breather from the concentrated note making she had been undertaking. As England started to disappear behind her, so did the picture of Hud's flat as she had left it. Thoughts of Hud in Paris were getting stronger and she longed to see him, to know he was alive.

She felt the speed of the train pick up, and at the same time the sensation of standing still. The journey at high speed was smoother on the French side than the rickety slow progress through the Kent countryside. Rural France sped past in a blur as she sipped the hot black liquid.

She knew that she needed to return to her reading, but also knew the value of regular breaks to keep the mind alert. She decided that she would continue her work once settled into her hotel, and took another coffee at the bar. This time she added cream, no longer requiring further shock treatment that black coffee gave her senses.

Holding the cup in her hands, she started to remember Hud as he used to be. The way he could command a room of people just with his eyes, the authority in his voice and the decisiveness of his actions. She thought of the plans they had made together, of a time when they had their future mapped out in front of them.

And she thought about how all those plans had crumbled when he had returned from Iraq, a broken man.

How she had been unable to understand the torture that he went through night after night. How she could never understand why he sought refuge from his demons with a bottle, and not with her. She also thought that perhaps now, now that she too had killed, she might be able to empathise with him in his darkest moments.

She was still deep in thought when the announcement of their arrival in Paris interrupted. As the train pulled into the Gare du Nord, Judy made her way to the front of the train, moving through the Standard Class Carriages.

The station crackled with the atmosphere of Europe's largest railway station, even at this late hour. Orbs of amber light cut through the darkness of the night, and great green iron columns held the roof aloft. The grey and cream floor tiles shimmered in the glow, like sun bouncing from puddles after a sudden downpour.

Judy made her way to the exit, where taxis were waiting by the dozen.

She took her seat in one, and gave the driver instructions. He clicked his meter on, and pulled away driving the length of the station before heading south-west. She marvelled at the ornate decoration of the station, with its clockface at the centre and above statues depicting all the cities that its lines serviced, including the international destinations of London, Warsaw, Amsterdam, Vienna and Brussels.

Soon they were headed up the tree-lined Champs Elysees toward the Arc de Triomphe, and then turning left into the Avenue George V.

Judy had always stayed at the George V Hotel whenever in Paris. The first time that she had visited had been on their honeymoon, and she had fallen in love with the Hotel. She never stayed anywhere else whenever in the City of Light.

Each time she entered by the main foyer, the opulence of the place took her breath away. From a humble concrete façade, she walked into a lobby that exuded light and space.

Marbled floors shone in shades of grey, green, and gold under the sparkle of oversize chandeliers, vases of two and three dozen red roses marking every table. Fine works of art adorned the walls, and beautifully restored marble and alabaster statues of pure white looked down upon antique oak and deep red mahogany furniture. The entrance of guests was announced by identical floral displays of lillies held in a twinned pair of three foot vases standing upon heavy set brown marble table tops held by gilded legs. Behind the concierge hung a twenty foot tapestry depicting a Greek scene in blues, reds and golds.

She had phoned ahead and booked a room for two nights and then left a message on Hud's cell phone, simply saying that she had travelled to Paris. She knew that he would know where to find her.

The concierge called for a porter to show her to her room, and at her request he escorted her via the stairs to the second floor. She left the porter at the door, and thanked him for his kindness with a small tip.

The room was furnished in greens and golds. A kingsize double bed was draped with a silken gold duvet, two sumptuous pillows sitting atop. The furniture was cedar, with the detail picked out in goldleaf. By the window, which overlooked the Hotel's central Marble Courtyard, stood a desk with two oval back chairs, behind which was the door to the bathroom. There were white porcelain lamps either side of the bed, and a thick padded armchair sat in the opposite corner from the desk matched by an equally sumptuous footrest. Limited edition prints that depicted the city's main tourist sights floated on the walls underneath picture lights. A chandelier underneath a ceiling rose bathed the whole room in light.

Judy drew the heavy velvet curtains and placed her bag on the desk. She looked at her phone.

No missed calls.

She went and threw the safety chain across the door, kicked off her shoes and looked over at the file sitting patiently on the desk. She walked over to take it in her hand, and returned to slump on the bed. She rested her head on the pillow, and allowed the file to slip softly from her fingers.

Her eyes welled, and tears started to roll down her cheeks. She had to return to the arduous task of deciphering Jack's work. But not yet, not at that moment. That very moment was for her to let out her fears and anguish.

Still crying, for Hud and for herself, she fell asleep knowing that - for the time being at least - she was safe.

NINETEEN

The walls were pristine white, like mountain top snow. Rays of sunlight streamed through the windows diffusing into a haze before rebounding first off one wall then another, dust particles creating a rainbow prism. The brightness made Hud's eyes water as they adjusted from the darkness of his unconsciousness.

His head felt heavy inside, throbbing to the chime of his heart, and his neck stiff from the contortion of his pillow. The bed he lay on had no give in the mattress, so that it felt as if he were lying on floorboards.

A jug of water rested next to the cot, and an empty high back chair sat to the side facing toward him. White sheets bestowed a modicum of modesty, wires and tubes fed from him into a machine that beeped an even rhythm. Above him perched a bright red button that he now reached for, but the exertion was too much to bear.

The beeping of the machine first quickened, and then returned to its steady pace as Hud fell once more into his unknowing state, his eyes closing involuntarily.

The next time Hud's eyes opened, it was to the violent shaking by the man that now stood over him. The stranger supplemented the violent jarring of Hud's shoulders by equally agitated speech. But the man was not shouting, rather he was whispering close and loud into Hud's ear. The man's hands on him caused Hud to wince as pain shot through his left shoulder. He could feel his assailant's hot breath on him, and tried feverishly to push him back.

It was then that Hud realised he only had one arm free, his left strung tight to his right shoulder in a sling. The man backed off as he spoke in English.

'Mister Hudson, we must get you out of here. Now. It is no longer safe for you. I have clothes here in a bag. You must get up and put them on.' He spoke quickly, but precisely, enunciating every vowel as foreigners do.

Hud looked at him suspiciously, the memory of the night before - the car chase and being shot - flooding back and calling him to his senses.

The man who had bought Hud out of his state of slumber stood upright and in silhouette against the backdrop of the hospital window. Hud strained to see him.

'Mister Hudson,' he continued, 'I am Claude Duval. I knew Jack very well, he asked me to meet you at Charles de Gaulle should anything happen to him. You were taken from me at the airport, which necessitated my following your captors. I stole you from the wreck of their car and bought you here, but now the police are searching the hospitals for you. We must go.'

With that the man who had announced himself as Claude Duval moved away from the window and round the bed to block the doorway. He parted the blind as he looked anxiously along the corridor outside the room, first one way then the other.

As he stood next to the door, Hud took note of Duval's appearance.

He was a short stocky man with slightly hunched, but broad, shoulders. He was balding to the top and front, but other than that had black unruly hair that hung over the large lobes of his ears. When he spoke he showed the yellowing of teeth typical of a heavy cigarette smoker. He wore a loosened tie around an open collared plain white shirt, over which hung the jacket of a dark grey suit. His paunch belly forced the jacket to hang free which emphasised the shortness of his legs.

Looking back and forth, Duval made expansive hand gestures to Hudson urging him to dress hastily.

'Why should I trust you?' Hudson quizzed.

Duval stopped his furtive glancing and stared directly into Hud's eyes. He answered simply.

'Because Jack trusted me, as he trusted you. And because I risked my life to save you from death last night, as I do now. If you do not come with me you are a condemned man. Now please, get your trousers on. It will not look natural for you to walk around Paris in your underpants.'

He smiled, and Hud trusted him.

They made their way through the corridors of the Hopital de la Salpetriere in silence, Hud following his knowledgeable companion like a dog following its master. Hud had taken his left arm from its sling and now held it limp at his side with his hand in his trouser pocket. It ached to move, but had been well bandaged against the bullet wound in his upper arm.

Duval had told Hud that he had taken him to the hospital to the South East of central Paris after dragging him from the Citroen, after it had crashed at the bottom end of the Rue Affre. While the hospital was not the closest to the scene of the accident, Duval had friends who worked the night shift.

Hud had been booked into the hospital under the name of his brother's false passport, and he had smiled at the lack of originality when told his name for the evening had been John Smith. Now, however, events had necessitated his rude escape from the hospital. Duval did not know the day shift, and nor did he know how long it would be before John Smith was recognised as Peter Hudson.

They had not spoken any more about this until they had arrived at Duval's home. They travelled the whole journey not speaking, nor hardly acknowledging each other. As the humdrum of the city whirled around them, through the rush of the commuter traffic, they had travelled in silence, Hud playing follow my leader along the Paris Metro and through the crowds of pedestrians. Just another Parisian making his way to the office for a normal day's work.

Duval carried Hud through the streets of Paris in this manner to the door of his ground floor apartment, where he ushered Hudson first. It was the first acknowledgement that he had shown to his refugee since absconding him from the Hospital.

Once inside and with the door safely closed behind them Duval began to speak again, this time less hurriedly and with a less desperate tone.

'We are safe here. I am not known to the organisation. Please, come and sit down.'

Duval led Hud through to his lounge and offered him a chair. The floorboards creaked under their steps, and the curtains sounded their resistance as Duval drew them together to extinguish the outside world. He walked back across the room and flipped the light switch, the room coming back to life in the dim glow of the unshaded ceiling bulb.

It could not be said that Duval lived in luxury.

The armchair that Hud sat on had long since seen better days, the faded upholstery wearing thin where the head rests and at the end of the arms, threads hanging like dismembered cobwebs.

There were a further two soft furnishings in the room, a two seat sofa and another armchair, and both in a similar state of repair to Hud's. None of the three would go with any of its partners to make a matching pair.

A low table took centre stage in the room, dust marks outlining the rings left by the bottoms of coffee soaked mugs.

Discoloured striped paper clung to the walls under a discoloured whitewash ceiling, both telling the tale of smoke filled nights. The hearth was filled with the ashes from a prior fire, and an ashtray sat friendless on top of the cedar mantle above.

Duval went to the cabinet that sat in the corner of the room and took out a bottle and two glasses, holding the glasses in one hand and with a finger in each. He walked them over and placed them on the coffee table around which the armchairs and sofa were anchored, splitting the glasses apart as he slid one toward Hud.

He poured the drink as he spoke.

'Jack told me to have a bottle of southern comfort in my drinks collection in case we had the misfortune to meet.' He successfully skirted the reason for Hud's arrival in Paris.

Before taking a seat on the chair next to Hud, Duval picked the ashtray from the mantle and emptied its contents in the hearth. A cloud of ash billowed like a small volcano, and spread to settle in a little circle around the point of impact.

Duval set the ashtray on the table between the glasses and raised his to toast his visitor. Taking a gulp quickly, he grimaced as he swallowed and held the glass quizzically in front of him at arms length.

'I don't know how you can drink this,' he said, his tongue trying to expel the taste from his lips.

'Usually by the bottle' Hud replied with a smile, and raising his glass firstly toward Duval before bringing to his lips and downing the contents in one mouthful.

Duval took a pack of cigarettes from his pocket and lit one before offering to Hud. He took a Gaulloise from the pack, placed the filter between his lips and drew deeply as Duval held a lighter in place. He savoured the first rush of nicotine, but did not care for the aftertaste of the Gallic tobacco. Duval replenished Hud's glass before taking command of the conversation.

'Hud...may I call you Hud?' he asked without waiting for a reply,'your brother was a fine politician. A man that knew the difference between right and wrong, good and evil. That is why I approached him with the knowledge that I am going to impart upon you now.' He paused to take a sip of his drink, the grimace less pronounced than before, and then continued, choosing his words purposefully.

'Some time ago I came across a cadet in the Gendarmes by the name of Rousset. He was a fine young policeman, and quickly rose through the ranks. He soon became a detective in the Paris Prefecture, and was attached to the division that was responsible for investigating all crime associated with objets d'art.

'We in France pride ourselves on our heritage, and our knowledge of art. During the Second World War the Nazis plundered our galleries and private collections. Many of these treasures have been recovered since the war, so much so that we – that is the French government - have opened our books on the art that we still have that is, perhaps, not legally ours. Rousset was credited with the detection of several pieces of work that now sit in some of our major galleries – the Louvre, Orsay, Pompidou, for example – and was considered by some as a genius for all his hard work.

'When the Prefect of the Paris Police died in a car accident a couple of years ago, it was only natural that Rousset should take his place. The rapid promotion of such a talented individual was applauded in high places, even though it is unusual in France for one so young to achieve such high rank.'

He paused again as he lit another cigarette. Hud declined the offer of a second Gaulloise, but accepted a further tumbler of southern comfort. After settling back into his chair, Duval restarted his tale from where he had broken.

'Personally I had never trusted Rousset, and I took a keen interest in his career. It puzzled me greatly how such a young detective could uncover so many works of art that had remained hidden from the rest of us for so long.

'I did some... how do you say?...digging... and came to the conclusion that Monsieur Rousset is not all that he seems to be. Many of the pieces that he found were in private art collections and had been recently acquired by their owners, sometimes for millions of Francs. In each case the owner could not – or perhaps would not – say who the seller was. The piece was simply confiscated from the owner, who also had to pay fines. These were wealthy people more than able to pay rather than go to jail.

'I managed to speak with one of these collectors, and he told me the name of the agent who had negotiated his purchase of a painting by Manet that had been missing since 1940.

'By the time I went to see the agent, which was just a day or two later, he had died in a car crash on the outskirts of Paris. Some witnesses said that they had heard a gunshot before the car fell out of control and ploughed head-first into a juggernaut driving in the opposite direction, but that was never proved.

'A week later, the art collector was also dead, having suffered a severe heart attack at his home.'

He broke again as he stubbed his cigarette butt in the ashtray.

'Within a year of Rousset becoming Prefect, I had been transferred to Calais. The sea air did not suit me and so I resigned my post and moved back to Paris, taking a job as a government administrator.

'I met Jack at the Headquarters of the European Union in Brussels, when I was translating for one of our Ministers. That is when he and I struck our friendship, and when I first told him what I am telling you now.'

'I don't really follow', said Hud. 'What has any of this got to do with Jack's death?'

'I had built up a file on Rousset, which I handed to your brother. Jacques Rousset has connections with many people in positions of power, and your brother was particularly interested in a man named Pierre Donat. When he bought the file back to me, we spent a long while discussing this man.'

'So who is he? Why was my brother so interested in him?' Hud asked, agitation showing in his voice.

'There is not a great deal known about him, but what I can tell you is this: He is the Head of a financial trading company called Schengen. It is what is called a hedge fund, and is financed by some of the wealthiest entrepreneurs around Europe. These are all secretive people, but none more so than Monsieur Donat.

'There are certain other connections that we can make', he looked at Hud, who shrugged as if to say 'carry on.' Given his guests approval, Duval proceeded.

'Every art collector that Rousset apprehended in his early years is a contributor, an investor if you will, of Schengen. The agent that conducted the art deal, of which I told you, had previously been visited by a Schengen salesman.

'Do you also not find it curious that Rousset's predecessor, and the agent to the art sale, both died in road accidents? Also that the collector died from a massive, and unexpected, heart attack so soon afterwards?'

'Your brother phoned me a week ago, to arrange that we meet. He said that he had new information about Schengen, and also about Pierre Donat. He seemed very agitated, very nervous. That is when he told me also that were anything to happen to him then you would arrive in Paris, and that I was to help you all I could.

'And then your brother dies of a massive and unexpected heart attack. Exactly the same as the art collector I spoke about.'

Hudson let the words hang in the air. Duval was talking about high finance, murders, accidents, a chief of police.

It was too much to take in without help. He poured another drink, and helped himself to a Gaulloise from the pack that lay on the table. He took a long slug of his drink and an equally long lug of the cigarette. The smoke and alcohol mixed in his mouth as he leaned his head back. Finally he spoke.

'I need to phone someone. She has something that we need.'

'I have your phone here. Before you call anyone, there is something that you must see.'

Duval looked at his watch and strode to the drinks cabinet where he switched on the portable television that sat on top. After adjusting the picture by spinning the aerial round, he stood back so that Peter Hudson could see the screen.

Hud sat in silence, staring at a picture of himself.

TWENTY

It was now mid morning, and Mark Chatfield had not left his office all night. He had been able to continue his work for Schengen in spite of the problems that both Peter Hudson and Judy were causing him.

Now he stood in his office, perched on the edge of his desk watching the Channel 24 news, with a self-congratulatory smile. The previous evening, with the catastrophes that Frank Rogers and Jean-Pierre had produced in turn, meant that Chatfield had needed to react quickly. And react quickly he did.

The clean up man in London had done his job more than adequately. The door had been fixed so that it no longer looked like the flat had been broken into, and surfaces diligently wiped to ensure that Chatflied's prints could not be found. Ashtrays had been emptied and crockery and glasses washed. The bedroom had been straightened so that no signs of a fight existed. Anyone walking into the place now would see what Mark Chatfield wanted them to see: a cold blooded murder.

As usual Rousset had performed well in Paris. But then his friend Jaques Rousset understood the depth of gratitude that he owed to Chatfield and Schengen.

Chatfield wondered sometimes if Rousset realised that he would never finish paying back the organisation, and Chatfield in particular, for the generosity it had shown him and the faith it placed in him. The Director had been instrumental in Rousset's rise to the top of his profession, and Chatfield instrumental in keeping him there on more than one occasion. There had only been one time that Mark had been forced to remind Rousset what would happen if he ever failed in his duty to Schengen.

Rousset had once questioned Chatfield's authority to request 'favours' of him, and had refused to co-operate with the release of a suspected murderer who had been on Schengen business. He had said that there were no possible grounds for release of the man, and he could not tamper with the evidence that the arresting officers had accumulated. Also that he felt the services that he had performed for Schengen far outweighed any carried out in return.

Within the hour Rousset's car had been blown apart under the very noses of his police officers. Chatfield had then phoned to remind Rousset how easy it was to remove his predecessor and replace with a loyal servant. The following day Chatfield's employee had been released from arrest for murder, and another suspect had taken his place.

Rousset had taken charge of the investigation of the murder of Michel Pignon, shot whilst driving a Citroen the previous evening. The shooting had by now been linked to a man that the British Police were hunting for, and whom they suspected had travelled to France. That man was Peter Hudson.

Rousset's orders were easy. Find Hudson and deliver him to Chatfield.

Mark took the remote control in his hand and tweaked the sound so that he could hear fully the report. A photo of Peter Hudson was static on the screen as the reporter spoke.

'Police in Britain are searching for this highly dangerous man, Peter Hudson, and have reason to believe that he has recently travelled to Paris.

'Peter Hudson's brother, Jack, is the recently deceased Foreign Secretary of Britain. It was at first thought that Jack Hudson had died from a massive heart attack on Monday night, but his death is now being treated as suspicious.'

The camera cut to video of Jack's country farmhouse as the reporter spoke.

'A police spokesman has said they are now investigating the possibility that Jack Hudson was murdered at his home near Ashford in Kent. Guard dogs have been found dead in the grounds of his house, and there was no sign of a break in.'

The shot on screen then changed to show the exterior of Hudson's apartment block. There were a couple of police officers on guard at the main entrance to the block, and a squad car stood nearby. Police cones had stopped any other cars parking in the immediate vicinity.

'Meanwhile, a body has been found in Peter Hudson's home, here in Clerkenwell Green in London. Whilst the Police have not yet issued any concrete details, the spokesman has said that the dead person had been brutally stabbed through the throat with a broken bottle. There is no sign of any struggle, and police believe that the dead person was killed in cold blood. The same spokesman has told us that, upon a search of the flat in which Hudson lives, there is no sign of his passport.'

The picture on the television set changed once more to show an aerial view of Hudson's Lotus Exige. It had been cordoned off by blue and white police tape, and there were forensics officers dressed in white from head to toe examining the vehicle inside and out.

'Hudson's car - shown on screen now - has recently been found near to Ashford International Rail Station, leading to the theory that he may have boarded a train headed for Paris. CCTV tapes have been confiscated, and are currently being examined for evidence of Hudson's movements.

'Jack Hudson's wife has confirmed that her brother-in-law spent time with her on Tuesday, the day after her husband was found dead in his office.

'Jack Hudson had been due to attend the European Union Conference in Brussels today, at which he was expected to sign the ratification of the new European Treaty. It is known that Peter Hudson did not share the same political views of his brother, and it is thought that the police are considering this to be a possible motive for Jack Hudson's murder.'

The screen cut back to show the still of Hud once more as the reporter gave further details about him.

'Peter Hudson was a war hero, but was honourably discharged a couple of years after serving in Iraq during the first conflict. According to the military Psychiatrist who treated him for several years, the war affected him dramatically leaving Hudson with, and we are quoting here, an 'unstable nature: a man who would be prone to violent outbursts. Clinically he suffers from post-traumatic stress disorder, however he has developed into a manic-depressive who is reliant on alcohol.'

'It is stressed that this man is potentially very dangerous, and police do not know whether he is armed or not. The public are advised not to approach him.'

The reporter finished his piece by giving details of an emergency hotline number in Paris to call if Hudson was sighted, the number appearing too under the still on the screen.

Mark Chatfield was happy with the result of the work that he had instigated after the debacle of the previous night. Any sightings would be reported to the phone number on the screen, and then reported directly to Rousset who had taken personal charge of the investigation in Paris.

The police in the UK would be left chasing shadows, any sightings on that side of the channel being investigated by them. Meanwhile Rousset would sift through potential sightings in Paris, and report directly to Chatfield. If the police got to Hudson before Chatfield did, then Rousset would ensure his delivery to Schengen.

Mark thought it more likely, however, that Hudson would see the report on the screen and be panicked into showing himself. He was now a fugitive, on the run from the police both in Paris and in Britain. He had nowhere to hide, and no-one to turn to, and would need a friend. Mark Chatfield would be that friend.

He switched the television sets to silent.

He had work to do before he called Hudson's cell phone, and needed the room to be silent so that he could concentrate.

He looked at his watch, and saw that he had a little over an hour in which to prepare for his next meeting.

He started by spreading a map of Europe across his desk. Outlined in Black was the vast area that constitutes the member countries of the European Union and in thick red marker pen, the larger area that had signed up to the abolition of border controls: this area included Iceland, Norway, and Switzerland but excluded the United Kingdom and Ireland. It was no coincidence that this area, and the agreement for free movement, had been recognised internationally as the Schengen agreement: the Director even had the power to make this happen.

He surveyed the map. All this would soon be under the control of Schengen, an area the size of the USA and with the industrial muscle to rival any economic area of the world. An alliance with Russia would soon follow, and Europe would become self sufficient in all natural resources.

Most importantly of all, Chatfield would be given the responsibility for security of the new European Empire.

But first, the governments of Europe would need persuading. The plan had taken decades to come to fruition, and the time for the culmination of all those plans was nearly upon them. The Director had given Chatfield the responsibility for ensuring that the final act of persuading the nations of Europe to unite under the flag of Schengen would be successful. Everything leading up to the momentous events of the next few days had been orchestrated by the Schengen, and now the final honour would be Mark Chatfield's.

He moved his right hand to his collar, and gently rubbed his neck beneath with his index finger. Europe would soon fly the flag of Schengen.

He looked at his watch once more, and cast an eye around his office. He replaced the bottles of alcohol in the cabinet, and removed the used glasses from view. On his coffee table he placed a jug of fresh iced water, and one of orange juice with a handful of crystal tumblers. He lifted the phone and gave instructions for coffee to be served upon the arrival of his guests.

Finally, when he was satisfied with his preparations, he moved back to the desk and began fingering each capital city of the European Union countries. These had been highlighted by the use of small circular black 'stickies.' With every major governmental building in Europe out of action, persuasion to accept the new leadership would be easy: the people of Europe would have no choice.

The door rapped and, upon Chatfield's acceptance, the concierge showed in the three men that had been expected. They were, as ever, a little tardy being their customary ten minutes late and after placing his hand on his heart and bowing slightly, Chatfield shook hands with the men before they all took seats around the coffee table. The man seated in the middle of the three would do all the talking, being the senior.

Omar Ali bin Akhbar wore the traditional white dishdasha, reaching down to his ankles and secured round the waist by a hajj belt. On his feet he had black sandals, and atop his head he wore a black turban which flowed over the shoulder of his dishdasha. His compatriots wore dark blue, western, business attire, suitable for hiding the handguns concealed beneath their jackets and held in place by shoulder holsters.

Before turning to business bin Akhbar discussed trivialities, and the three guests partook of the refreshment provided. Their host had served morsels of dark pita breads with Hallal meats, and had offered Arabic coffee as accompaniment.

Soon Chatfield and bin Akhbar were hunched over the map laid open on the desk and illuminated by the harsh whiteness of the lamp. Chatfield was pointing at the capital cities in turn, and bin Akhbar was talking in a low voice.

'My friend, we have been over this before many, many times. You must learn to trust the word of Omar Ali bin Akhbar' he said, gesticulating his words with open palms.

Afraid that he had offended, Chatfield replied in similar respectful low tones.

'Please, I mean no offence to you or your people. I merely wish to convey our thanks to you, and to ascertain that all is in hand. If there is any further assistance we may offer please feel free to request of us.'

'Mr Chatfield, we have shown lately that we are able to infiltrate even the highest level of security. The Towers of democracy in New York, the bombings in London, the destruction of a passenger train in Spain: all attributable to the power of al-Qaeda.

'The Western World will take us seriously, and we, of course, are happy to assist you and your organisation in return for that which you promise. We will deliver Europe into your hands, and when that is complete, you will deliver America into ours by withdrawing all your troops from the Middle East region. When we have crushed their aggression in our region, and we have Israel under Allah's control, then oil will flow freely once more to our friends in Europe.'

The two men eyed each other, mutual in their respect. They were both men that held the lives of others in the palms of their hands, both men not to be trifled with. Chatfield recognised the cold steel of confidence within bin Akhbar that he held himself. He was happy to deal with such a man, a man of war and a man of honour.

'We are in agreement, Omar Ali bin Akhbar. Once we have received confirmation from Brussels that the Treaty which will give the European Parliament its full legal rights has been ratified and signed as agreed, then we - in our turn - will make our donation as a sign of faith that Allah will deliver what you promise' Chatfield bowed his head again, and the two men shook hands and hugged.

As the triumvirate of terrorists departed, Chatfield could not help but to think a down-payment of twenty five million US dollars was a large amount for the services of al-Queda. But he knew that Schengen would make billions from the fallout that such widescale terrorist attacks across the whole of Europe would cause.

He picked up the phone to call the Director and tell him the good news, before calling Hudson on his mobile.

Despite the trials of the last couple of days, Mark Chatfield felt good. He felt strong.

Invincible.

He took the bottle of Cardhu from the cabinet and poured a double measure. This time he would be drinking in self-congratulation: the web was drawing closer around Europe, and Peter Hudson. Within days Hudson would be history, and Europe would be under the control of Schengen.

Chatfield afforded himself a smile as he savoured thoughts of the power and wealth to come, the thoughts deepening as the warmth of the whiskey moved deeper within him.

TWENTY ONE

Hud paced Duval's small living room, a mixture of anger and curiosity giving purpose to his steps. He talked at speed, more to himself than his companion, as his thoughts streamed as an audible deluge from his mouth. Ringlets of smoke abandoned his lips after each puff of the cigarette that he held in his right hand, and which now was in danger of burning his fingers.

The floorboards creaked their disapproval of their harsh treatment under Hud's heels, and Duval was now standing imploring the Englishman to sit and think rationally. On more than one occasion Duval was nearly Knocked off his feet by Hud, whose eyes were fixed on the small television screen which now flickered in stroboscopic fashion each time he passed.

Suddenly the fury that had exploded within him subsided, just as quickly as it had burst forth, and standing in front of the television Hud stretched an arm to twist the power off. The screen flickered, and the set hissed, punctuating the abruptness of the silence that now engulfed the room.

Hud turned and moved forward to stand underneath the unshaded bulb, his face cast half in shadow and half in light. He threw the stub of the Gaulloise in the fireplace, adding to the small mountain of cigarette ends there, and immediately lit another. He looked down upon the balding pate of Duval who had returned to his seat when the worst of the storm of Hud's rage had ended.

He did not need to put voice to his request but simply held a hand outstretched toward Duval, who pushed inside his jacket and salvaged Hud's phone for him. He took it and tapped the buttons, bluish light emanating from the hand held device as Hud's keying bought it to life.

Then he stood there, staring at the keypad, knowing that he must dial but scared his call would go unanswered. The word's of the news reporter repeated themselves over and over in his head, "..a body has been found in Peter Hudson's home…". No mention whether a man or a woman, just "a body". In those few moments he feared for Judy's life more than he had ever done so before. It had been he who had left her there alone, unprotected.

He should have known better. How could he be so stupid, what had he been thinking? Someone had got to Judy, in the flat alone. Maybe they had suspected it would be Hud there. Thoughts spun in his head, as the words of the reporter repeated over and over. He needed to know, but at the same time didn't want to know.

The phone vibrated in his hand, it's shrill ring bringing Hud crashing back from his subconscious. He looked for a few seconds, seconds that seemed to him like hours, before he pressed the green "accept call" button and raised the phone to his ear.

He heard her voice, heard her telling him that she was travelling to Paris, and relief swept through him. A weight lifted from him, the darkness that he had descended into moments earlier lifted. She was safe, and for those precious seconds nothing else mattered. He let the phone fall to the floor, and let out an audible sigh as the relief washed over him, closing his eyes and facing skyward. He looked again at Duval, then he spoke.

'Duval, I need to go to the George V Hotel. I've got to go now!'

Duval, who had been watching Hud all the while, did not question his reasoning. Slowly he rose from his seat, stooping to pick Hud's phone from the floor where it had fallen and burst open upon impact.

'Monsieur, if this is important then we will go there. But first we must take some simple precautions' Duval said, holding the two pieces of Hudson's phone in his hand for Hud to see. 'We do not want you to break in two so easily?' Duval raised his eyebrows as he spoke, turning his statement into a question.

Hud, snapping the two halves of his phone together, realised that the question needed no answer and followed Duval through to the kitchen, which on the whole was brighter and less worn than the room they had just left.

There were no wall-mounted units in the long narrow space and the bare plaster was painted a primrose yellow. Hud negotiated the small dining table and two chairs that sat near the doorway from the hall, and walked past the veneered cupboards to his left that each housed a draw at the top and red ceramic tiles under their feet. Gleaming steel pots hung from their own dedicated hooks that were posted at regular intervals each side of the hob. The opposite wall was almost entirely taken by a large white French dresser that housed a full set of blue and white crockery upon its open shelves.

Duval led Hud to the porcelain sink at the far end of the space, above which perched a sash window that allowed light to flood into the cramped space. Turning the taps on and filling the bowl beneath, Duval told Hud to remove his shirt whilst he hunted in the cupboard below taking bottles of cleaning fluids out and replacing them until he had found the substance he was searching for.

'Please, I need your hair wet,' Duval requested as he signalled an instruction for Hud to place his head in the bowl. Water ran down his face and neck when he resurfaced, and Duval hurriedly placed a towel around Hud's shoulders. Hud noticed that Duval was now wearing thin rubber gloves, the type that paramedics use on blood victims. He closed his eyes when asked to do so, and felt the coolness of some solution being poured on his head before the gloved hands were massaging his hair.

After a few minutes and a rinse with warm water later, Hud was led back to the living room where he viewed himself in the mirror.

Where once he had blonde hair now it was dark, almost the shade of a raven's down, and he was astonished what a difference it made to his appearance. To Hud, the difference in tone seemed to reshape the contour of his face, softening his jowls and decreasing the length of his forehead.

'People will be looking for a blonde Peter Hudson. This way you will have a chance of walking the streets of Paris without being detected' explained Duval.

Hud nodded his satisfaction, and his agreement with Duval's logic, whilst replacing his shirt leaving the collar unbuttoned. He turned to Duval to discuss their next moves, wanting desperately to see Judy at the George V.

They sat and discussed what needed to be done, Duval once more taking Hud through the details that he had pieced together about Schengen and their operations and the connections that Rousset had with them. In return Hud told Duval all he knew about the file that Jack had left for him, about being followed in England by car and on the train, and about Judy and how she was helping.

Duval asked several times if Hud's brother had spoken of Schengen and Pierre Donat, and each time Hud had replied the same:

'Jack and I didn't see eye to eye on political issues, and if he were working on something like this, I'm not surprised that he kept the details to himself. I've got no doubt that the file he left will explain more. Otherwise, why send me to Paris? That's why I've got to get to Judy.'

They had been talking some time when the chirrup of Hud's cell phone cut into their conversation. Without thinking, Hud answered immediately hoping that it would be Judy calling.

He was both dismayed and elated at the same time when he heard Mark Chatfield. Although it wasn't Judy, at least it was a friendly voice.

'Hud. Hud, is that you?'

It took a second or two for Hud to register whom it was talking to him through the airwaves before he replied.

'Chatters, thank God its someone I know!'

'Hud, I've seen all sorts of tripe about you on the television. Are you ok?'

'Yeah, I'm ok. That is, I've been shot in the arm, but I'm fine. I never realised how much it hurts to be shot. Don't believe everything they're saying about me on the television. Its all bullshit' Hud said.

Chatfield had to bite his lip before speaking again, to stop himself from telling Hud that he was lucky, that he wishes his brother had been so lucky in Iraq.

'I know that Hud. But someone's out to get you for some reason. Look I'm in Paris for a couple of day on business, if you want somewhere to stay?' Chatfield hoped that his friend would take the bait.

'No, Chatters, that's ok. I've got somewhere to sleep. I don't much like being on the run for something I haven't done, though.'

Chatfield's heart sank when Hud spoke though he tried not to show it in his voice.

'Well look, the offer's there if you want to take me up on it. Where are you staying? Perhaps I can come over, help to figure a way out of this mess?'

Hud looked at his watch: in the dimness of Duval's living room he had lost track of time. It was three o'clock in the afternoon.

'Tell you what, Mark. I'll meet you at the steps of the Sacre Coeur at seven. There maybe something you can help me with.'

With that the friends said their goodbyes and hung up.

Duval looked at Hud in an enquiring manner.

'He's a friend, Claude. A good friend. He's in Paris on business and he's got connections. He may be able to help us.'

'Ok, Hud. I trust you. But be careful, for you the City of Light might be your City of Death.'

'I'll be fine. I need to see Judy first. Once I've spoken to her then we'll have a much better handle on what we're dealing with here. Besides, who's going to be looking for a dark haired Peter Hudson? I'm just another tourist.'

With that Hud slipped his arms through the sleeves of a coat that Duval had lent him and popped a trilby hat on his head.

As he left Duval's place and headed toward the Champs Elysees Hud looked up to the gathering clouds above. Spats of rain dotted his cheeks, but he had fresh hope in his heart: he was going to see Judy, and then after his friend Mark Chatfield. With Duval also on his side he would soon unlock the secrets of his brother's death, and then he would be able to walk a free man again.

TWENTY TWO

The darkness of the sky accompanied by the sporadic pitter-patter of rain made native Parisians, and tourists alike, neglect their surroundings as they went about their business. Heads were bowed against the falling droplets, and a number of umbrellas popped up as protection: businessmen picked out by their long handled black umbrellas, whilst the ordinary folk - the mothers and their children, and day visitors to the city - held aloft umbrellas in a multitude of colours, mostly of the 'pop-up' variety.

Small lakes of rainwater started to form underfoot, distorted reflections of the city above spiralling out as leather clad feet stepped in and out. Pavement cafes emptied as diners sought sanctuary from the growing precipitation, waiters and waitresses hurriedly moving their clientele to the crowded interior of their establishments. Window shoppers went about their business from within, feigning interest as they mauled the haute couture displayed on neatly positioned hangers on racks in neatly positioned rows in the city's high class boutiques.

The street artists in the Place du Tertre huddled together under their canvas awnings, exchanging views on the works of their predecessors, the likes of Picasso, Dali, and Utrillo, as the bulk of their tourist trade evaporated in the inclement weather.

Agitated sounding of car horns seemed to increase in ferocity, no quarter given through the gridlocked traffic, frustration and impatience surfacing in the screwed up faces of the occupants of each unmoving vehicle.

Heads remained bowed whilst the gloom of the mid-afternoon downpour was only occasionally punctured by the merest patches of blue sky poking their head through the greys and blacks of the heavy clouds below.

Hud too kept his head down, as he made his way to the Hotel George V, but not in protection against the rain. Nor because of melancholy forced upon him by the bleakness of the afternoon. He had no screaming children to worry him, nor was he concerned with the disappearance of the afternoon trade. Indeed, Hud felt elated inside. Judy was safe. Nothing else seemed to matter to him as he pressed on against the rain and the incessant ebb and flow of the pedestrian traffic.

His only concern was being marked by a keen amateur sleuth, an anonymous passer by with a desire to become famous as the one who caught the murderer from London. Even though he had hardly recognised himself with his newly coiffured black hair, he could not trust that his new look would shield him from such a fate.

Even though he travelled at marching pace, the walk from Duval's place to the Hotel seemed to take forever. He arrived in the marbled lobby sodden from the rain, and kept his head bowed as he requested the Concierge to call Judy's room on the house phone and announce his presence. He had decided to keep the name that his brother had chosen for him, and listened to the one sided conversation as he waited at the reception desk.

'Ah, 'ello Madame. There is a Mister John Smith 'ere to see you.

'Oui, as you wish, I will send 'im straight up.'

As he replaced the receiver, the Concierge gave directions to the lift and asked if Hud would like an escort. Politely declining the offer, Hud made his way through the lobby and then to Judy's room.

It was only as he knocked upon the door that he realised what a mess he must look, and wished that he'd had the benefit of an umbrella upon his journey through Paris.

Judy opened the door, and for a split second looked upon Hud in incredulity. He stood there, steam rising from his damp clothes, water dribbling down his face from under his hat and dripping from his chin. His trousers stuck to his thighs where they touched.

'Hud, you look awful. And what have you done to your hair?' asked Judy and, not waiting for a reply, she pulled him through the open doorway.

'You better get out of those wet clothes, I'll get you a bath robe.'

Judy turned and headed for the bathroom, with Hud following closely behind. She left him in the bathroom to change out of his wet clothes, and told him to hang them on the heated towel rails.

Hud took the opportunity to freshen up a little before emerging a few minutes later wrapped snugly in an oversize plain white robe with the hotel emblem embroidered in blue on the left breast. He rolled each sleeve so that his hands were unencumbered by the cuffs, and gratefully accepted the coffee that Judy had prepared.

As he looked into her blue eyes he wanted to take her in his arms, and suspected that Judy had given him a coffee to prevent him from doing so. She looked at him perhaps a second too long, before slumping into one of the chairs next to the desk upon which she had the file opened. Placing her forehead into one of her hands she began to weep, her tears coming uncontrollably. She didn't know if it was the relief that she was alive, or the guilt of what she had done in London, or the feeling of dread of the situation that they were in that made her cry so.

Hud knelt in front of her and placed his hand at the back of her neck. He wanted to hold her, but there was something stopping him. He wanted to comfort her, but could not find the words. He just let her cry, and when she had finished she told him about London, about the intruder in Hud's flat, about killing a man.

'I never knew, Hud. I never knew that's how it felt. The terror! The guilt! Yet at the same time the joy of being free. It's horrible. I never knew I was capable of such a thing.'

'You did the right thing, the only thing you could have. Thank God you did. If he had… I mean if… Judy, I don't know what I would have done if anything had happened to you. I…'

Judy put her index finger to his lips, and for a moment Hud felt the world stand still, before Judy broke the silence.

'Hud, we've got to find what it was that your brother had discovered. We need to look through this file and try to make sense of it all. But first, tell me what's happened to you. Why the dark hair?' she asked, a feint smile creeping to her lips.

'Yeah, not really me, is it? But needs must. You obviously haven't seen the news' and with that Hud started to recount the time that they had been apart. The car chase, awoken in a hospital bed by a stranger, being rushed through the streets of Paris, and about Duval, his benefactor. He finished with the television reports and the necessity for him changing his appearance.

Upon finishing he stood up from the desk where they sat, and walked to the mini bar. Not being stocked with southern comfort, he opened a miniature whiskey and drank from the bottle.

'Hud, I do wish...' Judy stopped mid sentence and, remembering the recounting of Hud's trials to date in Paris, decided better of castigating him for his drinking on this occasion.

'...you would use a glass' she finished.

'How far have you got with Jack's file?' Hud asked, ignoring her pleas for a little etiquette.

Judy pulled the folder across and opened her notebook at the beginning. She skimmed her notes, before asking if Hud wanted the fuller version as described by Jack in the printed page or the potted version from her notes.

Hud looked at Jack's file and then at the reporter's notebook that Judy was still flipping back and forth through. To him there seemed very little difference in thickness, which was not surprising to him given Judy's regard for detailed note making, however he chose the more diplomatic answer.

'Give me what you make of it,' he said.

'Ok, well you've read through the first section, but it's probably worth us just reacquainting ourselves with the pertinent facts,' she looked at Hud for agreement, and when he didn't argue she continued.

'It all seems to start with this Nazi Admiral, Karl Doenitz. Well respected by Hitler, promoted through his career. My guess is that one reason Hitler thought so highly of him was that he had been in prison the same as he had: albeit a PoW camp after the First World War, rather than a domestic jail.

'Doenitz is pretty much in awe of Hitler, sees him as the way forward for Germany, as did many of his compatriots at that time. He doted on his two sons (Klaus and Peter), born to him by his wife who died in 1962.

'When Hitler committed suicide in his bunker, he expressly made Doenitz his successor through his will. By this time, of course, the war was all but over, the German military in disarray and being pushed back on both fronts. Realistically Hitler had left Doenitz to broker peace with the Allies, which he did. He got two others, Alfred Jodl and Wilhelm Keitel – there's more about them later - to sign the treaties.

'Doenitz lost his second son during the war, and took his first, Klaus, out of active duty. However, and this is the strange thing that your brother picked up on, he apparently allowed him on a fast boat that was to attack Britain as a 24th birthday treat,' Judy paused and looked at Hud expectantly.

'And?' Hud shrugged his shoulders, emphasising that he saw no abnormality.

'Hud, why would he send his son back into active service, at a time when Germany was losing the war, and on a mission that was probably doomed to failure? It says in your brother's report that all hands went down with the fast ship that Klaus was on' she left the thought hanging for a while before carrying on.

'That's a big question that your brother has asked, he's actually written it in himself' she flicked through the folder, locating Jack's hand written question and emphasising by pointing it out. 'I think your brother may have something there. But let's carry on.'

Again she looked at Hud for his permission to proceed: she didn't want to lose him while she had the bit between her teeth. Hud kept quiet and so she began to talk again, turning the pages of her notepad back and forth as she did so.

'Ok, so now we come to the bits that you haven't read before. Tell me if I'm going too fast for you,' she instructed, and without looking up from her notes kept a rapid rate.

'Keitel: he was a high ranking General, a "Greneralfeldmarshall", and stood up to Hitler on several occasions. However each time he backed down, eventually earning himself the nickname of "Little Lackey". He signed many orders from Hitler that would be considered by others as illegal, for instance the Commissar Order that stated any Soviet political officer captured was to be shot immediately. He allowed Himmler a free hand with racial controls in Russia.

'Keitel signed the second part of the unconditional surrender in Berlin, having been asked by Doenitz to do so.

'Then we come to Jodl,' said Judy, wetting her finger and placing it on the corner of each page as she moved them backwards and forwards.

'Ah, here we are!' she said, locating the position with the tip of her index finger.

'Alfred Jodl: another General, key to military operations and gave advice directly to Hitler. His first wife died in April 1944, and he married his secretary and mistress, Luise Katharina von Benda in 1945. He acted as deputy to Keitel and signed the unconditional surrender in Reims in France as Doenitz's representative.

'He had no children, devoting his life to his military career. Reported to have signed the Commissar order with Keitel, and also abetted the deportation and execution of Jews in concentration camps.

'So we have three Generals, all of whom were close to Hitler during his reign, instrumental in the signing of the surrender documents that ended the war.'

'I don't really understand what is so earth shattering about that. What in that would cause my brother's murder and all that's happened to you and I since?' Hud remarked with more than a hint of cynicism.

'It's not the facts that are important, although you need to know them to assess the questions that your brother raises' answered Judy.

'And it's those questions that are the perhaps the key to everything that we are now going through.

'At the end of the second section, there is some commentary on the selection of the three Generals to be representative at the signing of the surrender documents. Many historical commentators believe that the Allied leaders, even though the war had been clearly won and Germany crushed, wanted to ensure that it was high ranking officials that they could trust that would sign the documents. The Allies wanted a show of strength, and Eisenhower in particular wanted these three to sign.

'Some historians believed that a deal had been struck that would see all three Generals survive any trial. But that didn't happen' she concluded, waiting for the question that came almost immediately from Hud.

'So what happened to Jodl and Keitel?' he asked.

'Both hanged after the Nuremburg trials for war crimes committed. It took Keitel twenty seven minutes to die!

'Keitel's last words were, hold on I've written it down here' she said struggling to locate her notes.

'His last words were "I call on God Almighty to have mercy on the German people. More than two million German soldiers went to their death for the fatherland before me. I follow now my sons—all for Germany", and Jodl's were "My greetings to you, my Germany".'

'So we have a story of three Nazi Generals, two of whom hanged at the end of the second World War, one imprisoned for ten years, and died of a heart attack in 1980' Hud paused for a second or two, his right hand rubbing his chin.

'I don't see what this has to do with us today, here and now. This all happened, what sixty years ago?'

'Hud, that's the point. Your brother has uncovered something big. We just don't know what yet. Perhaps there's something in the General's last words that we are missing. We need to concentrate on finishing this file, and then we can move forward. Perhaps even put this nightmare behind us.

'There must be information in here that is worth killing for. We just have to uncover it' she finished, holding the file up to reiterate her words.

Hud stared at her hand held aloft, as if she were holding a trophy that she had won. A world of Nazis, trials, hangings, murders and treaties from decades previously were swimming in his head, and colliding furiously with the present. He looked at his watch: five in the afternoon. He had an hour to spend before he would have to leave to meet up with Chatfield.

'Let's get cracking, then' he said, picking up a stray pen.

TWENTY THREE

Hud never relished the idea of copious paperwork, and so was relieved when an hour had passed and he had to make his excuses to leave.

Judy was not sure that it was a good move for Hud to be meeting with his friend, but understood why Hud felt Mark might be able to help. Their friendship went back a long way, and apart from Duval – whom he had known for less than a day – Hud only had Judy on his side at this time. He was a hunted man, and Judy had argued about the wisdom of meeting in such an open place as the Sacre Coeur. She had been somewhat placated when Hud explained the place would be mostly occupied by tourists who would have other things on their mind rather than reading newspapers or watching the news on television, and so his logic ran that he would be less likely to be spotted there than elsewhere.

'Of course, I could phone him and ask him to meet me here instead: we could work through all this paperwork together' Hud said, devilishly rounding off his argument.

'No, Hud, you know what I think of him. But he's your friend, and I respect that. Besides, I would prefer to work through this myself. And I don't think you should mention too much of this to him, either. Just be careful out there' she advised, and Hud noted the angst in her voice.

Hud's clothes were not completely dry and so Judy turned the hotel's hair dryer to them, running the hot air up and down the legs of his trousers before throwing them at Hud to put on. They were still a little damp when he exited the room, leaving Judy to sift through the final few pages of his brother's work. He hoped that Judy would be able to make sense of it all, and had arranged to return the following morning.

As he left the hotel, the cool air of the early evening hit him. He felt uncomfortable in his slightly damp clothes, and so walked at a brisk pace. The rain had stopped, although the mustiness of the atmosphere, along with the residue of rainwater that lay in puddles dotted here and there, told the story of the heavy downpour that had preceded the now clear skies.

Along the way, restaurant staff were busying themselves for the night trade that would soon start, relaying tables and changing menus. The remnants of office workers were leaving for the evening, street lamps starting to burn as windows turned to black beyond.

The big high street stores had long since closed their doors but still the boutiques plied their trade, striving to extract every last ounce of value from the dwindling footfall.

The city centre was entering the lull between day and night, when the bistros and cafes would come alive once more with the hubbub of the Parisian population, some temporary, some permanent.

Hudson kept his pace up, not acknowledging the draw of the passing bars, intent only on reaching the Sacre Coeur at the allotted hour.

As he walked through the narrow streets, the Quartier Pigalle was just coming to life. The Moulin Rouge shone out its global notoriety in a tumult of reds and yellows, well dressed patrons queuing to be shown their seats for dinner before the risque show began. The sails on the famous windmill dazzled against the now deep blue sky.

Along the Avenue de Clichy he strode, avoiding the fervent salutations of the district's bar "introducers". Twice he had to pull himself free of the men who ply the trade of the local brothels, begging passers by to enter their "bar" to see a show. Once in, of course, the naive customer would be duped into paying for drinks and unwanted girls at inflated prices, the penalty for non-compliance being "special treatment" from two or three thickset bouncers.

The openness and brash exterior of the theatres, sex shops, and brothels was enough to corrupt an innocent visitor into believing the area to be something other than a front for the seedy businesses that operate within. The reflected imagery of the neon lit facades on the wet pavement below lent an air of magic, stroboscopic illuminations exploding throughout like multi coloured fireworks.

On through the Rue St Denis, where the prostitutes and their night owls were beginning their own working day, and finally to the foot of the hill upon which the Sacre Coeur sits like a priest overlooking the sins of his flock below, and waiting for the inevitable confessions.

The Sacre Coeur: the gleaming white jewel in the crown of Paris. The Basilica stood lit against the navy backdrop a monument to a bygone century, the Byzantine domes representing the three of the father, son and holy ghost, and mirrored by the three arches of the portico that form the entrance. Above the arches and cast in bronze sit the national saints, Joan of Arc and Louis IX, riding horseback. Ornate stonework, carved out of the travertine stone by hand a century or more earlier, gives emphasis to the proud monument.

From its vantage point, the church could see Paris in its entirety to the south. And at the foot of the steps that led to the grassed area immediately below, where tourists would picnic in the heat of the summer sun, Joan and Louis could now watch the meeting of Peter Hudson and his friend Mark Chatfield.

The two men shook hands - the meeting looking no more than a chance encounter between two acquaintances to a young couple descending arm in arm down the steep steps - before deciding to make their way to a nearby bar where they could talk discretely but in comfort, hidden from the chill evening breeze.

They made their way south along the Rue Foyatier then cutting west into the Rue Gabrielle, and walking another couple hundred yards before taking a seat at a table at a bar named, aptly, "Le Rendez-vous des Amis" ("Friends Meeting").

They chose to sit on a bench outside, away from a small group of twenty-somethings. Hud took his hat off, exposing his black hair to Mark for the first time. Chatfield raised his eyebrows, realising why Rousset had not reported a positive sighting.

'I had to do something, and this is the best that Duval could come up with,' he said leaning forward to keep his voice low.

'Duval? Who's Duval?' asked Mark.

Their conversation was interrupted by the appearance of the garcon who wiped the chrome table clean and removed an empty glass before accepting Mark's order. After the waiter had returned with fresh place mats and the two white beers in iced glasses, Hud answered his friend's question.

'He's a man who was to meet me at Charles de Gaulle, but I got waylaid by a couple of oafs who picked me up instead. Chatters, whoever is doing all this seems to know my every move.'

The two men sat talking, silhouetted against the whitewashed walls of the bar and half hidden by the red awning above, one sitting upright and concentrated on the other's voice, who sat with his head bowed the whole time spinning his tall glass in his fingers and watching the pattern that the beer made as he spoke.

The bar was filling up inside with the young chic clientele that enjoyed the ambience of the place, decorated in traditional style with decor in beiges and reds, music of the day playing from wall mounted speakers. The garcon was starting to get busy, and neglecting his clientele outside, so Mark went inside to order fresh drinks, reappearing a few minutes later and apologising for the delay.

'No problems, where were we?' Hud asked.

'Christ, Hud, I don't know. What with all this talk about Nazis and murders, you being kidnapped from the airport...well, its all gone over my head a bit. How's Judy coping?' he enquired casually, not wanting to appear over eager to find where she was in hiding.

'She's fine, Chatters. As fine as can be, anyhow. It's all been a bit of a nightmare for her, but she's strong, you know' he replied.

'Where is she now Hud? If these people, whoever they are, are able to keep pace with you – and have gone for her once already – don't you think it would be wise to stay close?' he hoped the caution he sounded in his voice would prompt Hud to spill the information that he wanted.

Hud sat silent for a second or two, contemplating whether he should tell his friend where Judy was staying, and the sum of the part she played.

'No, I think they've lost sight of her for the time being. When she left my place in London, she left behind a dead man. I don't think they expected that to happen… her overpower him, I mean… and were too intent on catching up with me. All their efforts have been directed toward me since I left London. I'm sure Judy's safe, for the moment at least.'

Chatfield was annoyed, but didn't show it. From what Hud had told him, Judy was the one working on the paperwork, and he had not given any clue as to where she was, whether in England or nearer, perhaps even in Paris. All he had told been told by his friend was that Hud could call her at any time.

The waiter appeared from the crowded doorway, carrying a tray with two more beers and a plate of hot cheese tarts that he placed on the table in front of the two men. As the night sky had darkened, so too had the nip in the air grown more bracing and Hud now felt the chill in his bones. He shivered a little before lifting one of the tarts from its plate.

'Thanks, Chatters, thoughtful of you. Time's ticking, I ought to be getting back.'

'Yeah, me too, I've got work to do. We'll just finish our drinks and these snacks before we go,' confirming to Hud's relief that this would be the last drink: he was getting a little concerned about the number of people drinking now, and was anxious that he would be spotted as the fugitive from London.

Chatters looked at his watch; it had been ten minutes since he ordered their last drinks. He did some mental arithmetic: another ten minutes to finish and then the walk back, say another fifteen minutes. Perhaps not quite time enough. He called the waiter over and leaned toward him. After he had gone back inside, he faced Hud once more.

'Just ordered a short for us - one for the road. He'll bring them out when we've finished our beers' he told Hud, still running the minutes through his head and hoping that the extra drink would take long enough.

"Forty five minutes total, more than enough time" he thought to himself.

They spent the next few minutes engaged in small talk, and consuming the 'tartes au frommage' that the waiter had left. The second beer had tasted better than the first to Hud, but he was not used to the gas and felt a little bloated. He appreciated the heat of the southern comfort as it hit the back of his throat, setting a furnace within him against the easterly wind that was whipping through the back streets of the city.

When they had clapped their glasses together one last time, and thrown their heads back to drain the last drops from their tumblers, Mark placed a twenty Euro note with the cheque on the small round silver tray that the garcon had left behind. The two men stood and shook hands before departing. Just two friends having enjoyed an evening drink before going about their business.

When Chatfield had walked a few paces, he turned to watch Hud turn the corner of the Rue Gabrielle and move out of sight. His cell phone signalled a message received which he read with a smile, now certain that before the night was through Hudson would be in need of his help again.

TWENTY FOUR

Rousset rapped his knuckle against the weathered blue paint peeling from the heat blistered wooden door. He looked up and down the narrow street, checking for onlookers. Both kerbs were littered with cars parked higgledy piggledy, their daytime colours changed under the eerie radiance of the street lamps that shone down on them. A stray dog, all skin and bones from the lack of ownership, stood sniffing one of the lampposts halfway along the street on his side, before cocking its leg to mark its territory and then crossing the road swiftly to the next.

As his eyes followed the mongrel in and out of the shadows and beyond the iridescence of the half lit and unkempt road, Rousset could see no sign that any of street's inhabitants were paying any more attention to him than the dog that was going about his routine business. There was no twitching of curtains, no opening of doors, the community oblivious to its latest visitor.

He knocked again, impatience sounding upon his fist beating down on the door.

The wind continued to signal its intent, blowing cold and easterly. The rain had long since passed, but the storm had not yet come.

The dog once more darted in and out of the darkness, and further along the street unseen screeches alerted it to the presence of a pair of the neighbourhood's alley cats. The orphan stopped short, lifting its nose from the open trashcan it was investigating and pricking its ears to hear more clearly. It stood a few seconds, then decided against the chase, and resumed nosing through the debris of someone's supper, taking the easy option and feeding from another's plate.

Footsteps sounded from behind the door as the occupant approached, and illumination appeared through the small half circle of stained glass that sat above the broken brass knocker. The two bolts, one high and one low, slid across with a dull clang and then the door half opened flooding Rousset's face with the white of the light beyond.

The Chief of Police was ready for the incumbent's reaction, had already placed a foot on the doorstep and had gained momentum from his violent push on the door using all his bodyweight to gain entrance, before the occupant could force the door closed.

He closed the door behind him as he stepped through, not removing his eyes from the man that lay in a heap on the floor of the hallway. Rousset stood over as his victim scrambled back, using his heels and elbows to haul himself away and pushing himself to his feet with his hands grasping at the rope twisted newels that held the stair handrail in place.

'Good evening, Duval' Rousset said calmly to the smaller man who had now begun to compose himself.

Duval looked at the man standing in front of him. It had been some years since they had last been together and Duval thought those years had not been kind to Rousset. His hair was greying rapidly, and the crows' feet around his eyes told of a man who had seen many sleepless nights.

For a second Duval thought about rushing Rousset, but the idea quickly evaporated when he saw that his assailant was waving a pistol indicating for him to move through the house.

'Let's retreat to somewhere a little more comfortable, shall we?' Rousset ordered, following a couple of paces behind as Duval led the way through to the lounge.

The unshaded bulb was lit, and the room reverberated to the flickering luminescence of the television standing ablaze on the cabinet.

Rousset indicated for Duval to sit in the armchair that had earlier been occupied by Hudson, and crossed the room to switch the television set off, not removing his eyes - nor the loaded gun - from Duval. Returning, he sat opposite his enemy, blocking any attempted escape, the coffee table in between with the half-finished bottle of southern comfort still atop. Rousset's eyes dropped and spied the two empty tumblers surrounded by dust.

'Had a visitor today, Duval?' Rousset enquired.

Duval kept quiet, his eyes trying to pierce through to Rousset's inner thoughts, desperate to find what he knew.

Rousset lent forward a little, and poured himself a small shot from the opened bottle. He raised the glass to his nose and sniffed, unwavering from his guarding of Duval.

'I've just had a call from a friend of mine. He is meeting with someone at this very moment who is partial to this beverage. I don't suppose you know him do you?' Rousset taunted. Still Duval was unmoved, waiting his opportunity. Rousset ploughed on.

'The man's name is Hudson. Peter Hudson. Very dangerous: fled here from England. I'm sure you must have seen the news. On the television' he nodded his head toward the now silent set, which had been tuned in to the news channel.

'What do you want, Rousset?' Duval broke, hoping to buy some time, preparing to pounce.

'That's better. I just want to talk. It's been such a long time since we last had a chance to chat. When was that, I can't remember?'

'You know when it was, Rousset. When you had me transferred to that hell hole in Calais, you bastard' Duval spat the words. 'But that's not what you want to talk about, is it?'

'Always so perceptive. You really would have been able to make a name for yourself in Calais. Personally I thought it was a wonderful position, and just right for you. I was disappointed when you decided to return to Paris. And to take a job in administration…' Rousset tutted mock sadness, his grin telling a different story.

'You seem to know a lot about me. Tell me, do you consider all your ex-employees such a threat?' he retorted.

Rousset sat unblinking. He would not let his hostage steal the upper hand. He would not let the anger within him surface and give itself away. He needed to stay in control, and bring the conversation to its inevitable conclusion.

'At one time, Duval, I will admit that you were a threat to me. But that time is long gone. Now you are an annoyance, a little cockroach that scurries around. A parasite, nothing more. But I have waited for you to step out of line so that I can step on you, and crush you under my boot.

'And finally you have done so.

'Harbouring a known criminal, a man on the run. You have gone too far this time' he said, again shaking his head with sarcasm.

Duval sat, his arms stretched along the length of the rests of the chair he occupied. He said nothing.

'Please, Claude, let us be pleasant to one another. After all we go back a long way. We should be friendly. Pour yourself a drink' Rousset tried to change the tone a little, all the time not diverting his eyes from Duval.

'Move slowly, though. I would hate for an accident to occur' Rousset commanded as Duval lifted the bottle off the table between them.

Duval did as he was told, and took a half tumbler measure before reverting to his position pressed back into the chair. He took a mouthful before he spoke.

'What is it you want, Rousset?'

'That's a good question. Let me fill you in with what I know. Please feel free to interrupt if I miss anything out' he began.

'You were to meet Hudson at the Charles de Gaulle, but he was apprehended before you got to him. You followed, at high speed might I add – very dangerous through Paris – and this ended in an accident in the Rue Affre. One man dead, another injured, and Peter Hudson shot in his upper left arm.

'However, you were able to rescue Monsieur Hudson from the wreckage, and took him to the Hopital de la Salpietre where he was tended to overnight by people friendly toward you. However, with the news breaking that he is a murderer on the run, you had to steal him away from the hospital and bought him here for safekeeping.

'Late this afternoon he left here to go and see a friend of his at the Sacre Coeur, and is due back here very shortly.

'Have I missed anything out, Claude?' he concluded.

Duval sat in silence, thinking. He realised that Rousset believed Hudson had left Duval's in order to meet Chatfield. He needed to find out if Duval knew about Judy being in Paris.

'So his friend, Mark Chatfield at the Sacre Coeur is behind all this then?' he asked of Rousset.

Rousset did not answer, but instead asked another question. He looked a little uneasy, as if he had revealed a secret that he should not have. His mood changed from first name to surname again, and he spoke impatiently taking note of the time.

'Duval, I want to know if Peter Hudson left anything here. Something that might be deemed to be important?'

'A few clothes, that is all. Why, what is it that you and Chatfield fear so much?' he asked, knowing that he would not get an answer.

Rousset surveyed Duval for a moment -hoping to read his eyes, hoping that they would give the truth away, if indeed he were lying - before responding.

'Go turn the television on, let's see if your Peter Hudson has been arrested yet.'

Duval did as he was told, placing his glass on the coffee table before stepping over to the corner of the room.

'Don't try anything funny, remember I'm the one with the power here. I'm the one with the gun,' Rousset called to the back of Duval.

Claude Duval stood for a moment with his finger pressed against the television's power button. He released and the set burst to life, the sound exploding from the corner of the room.

He heard the shot, but doubted that anyone else in the street would have done so. Within the wink of an eye Duval was dead, the bullet neatly piercing the back of his head. He slumped forward on to the cabinet and as he fell to the floor so too did the television, erupting in a shower of glass and splinters. All was silent in the room as Rousset re-holstered his pistol.

He moved quickly through the rooms, coming across Hudson's bag. A few clothes, a little cash, and his passport, but nothing else. Not what Chatfield needed. No file. But he had done his job, and he was satisfied.

He returned to the lounge, where Duval now lay in a small pool of his own blood. He took a handkerchief from his pocket and wiped the glass that had been his.

Then he flipped open his cell phone and typed a simple message, knowing that he would not receive a reply.

"File not here. When the homing pigeon returns, he will find his keeper unable to be of further assistance."

On his way out Rousset left the lounge light on, but extinguished all others. He left the front door on the latch and made his way to his car.

As he pulled round the corner and away from the scene of his crime, Rousset noticed a man walking hurriedly toward Duval's home. The pedestrian wore a trilby and kept his head bowed, and paid no attention to the car that passed him.

TWENTY FIVE

Mark Chatfield arrived at the main entrance to Schengen's Paris Headquarters in high spirits.

It had been but a few minutes since he and Hudson had gone their separate ways, and since the kill that would finally tip the scales in his direction had been confirmed by Rousset. Chatfield knew the hate that Rousset had held for Duval, and knew that he would have found it an easy and enjoyable kill. It would surely not be long before Hudson would find the body, and being alone in Paris he would have no other option than to call on his friend to help.

And, of course, Chatfield would be only too pleased to oblige.

As he relaxed in the soft leather of his desk chair, he bought to life the plethora of screens in front of him and played with the remote - moving excitedly through the various pre-programmed channels. Finally he settled on the one that was confirming the news that he had been expecting to hear: after a long day of intense negotiations, all European Union member countries had ratified the European Treaty.

The European Parliament now had the authority to rule the whole of Europe in exceptional circumstances, such as declaration of war by a foreign nation or the inability of member states to govern themselves.

He looked at the map of Europe that remained spread upon his desk from his earlier meeting with bin Akhbar and spoke openly to himself.

'Now we have the power! Now we can move!'

He fingered each black circle that picked out all of Europe's major capital cities. He knew that the Al Queda were capable of producing the destruction and mayhem that they said they would.

The plans were flawless, and several attacks on transport hubs had been carried out in previous weeks. Each unsuccessful, of course, just as bin Akhbar had said they would be. But each securing the idiotic notion that near term terrorist attacks would be concentrated on Europe's ports, airports, and railway termini. Each securing a little more focus on such potential targets, and distracting attention away from the real targets.

Mark Chatfield knew better: he knew where those attacks would come, and he knew how. He had helped to plan the razing of each country's governmental home.

Within a week Europe would be torn apart by the destructive power of Al Queda, the independent political power would be ripped from each of Europe's democracies.

All of Europe's governments would disappear in one day of bloodshed that would shape the destiny of the continent forever. Every President and Prime Minister would be wiped from the face of the earth; the majority of senators, congressmen and members of parliaments would be blown to smithereens; and the people of Europe would turn to the unscathed European Parliament to protect them from the lawlessness that would follow.

And Schengen controlled most of the Parliament's members.

At last Schengen would control Europe, and the prophecy of so many years before would be fulfilled.

Chatfield clenched his fists, bringing them down as one on his desk in celebration. He turned and took the bottle of Cardhu from his drinks cabinet, and poured a large measure into a tumbler with ice. He placed his cell phone on the desk in front of him, and waited for the call that he knew would come.

He had not finished the scotch when the phone rang, causing the map underneath to vibrate as it did so and making Chatfield think of the effect that the following Tuesday would have. He looked at the screen on his phone: Hudson, exactly on cue.

'Hud, what's wrong? We only just left each other. You don't have to phone me to thank me for the drink, you know' he said cheerfully, masking any knowledge that he might have.

'Chatters. Something bad has ha...I need help. Its Duval! He... he's dead' he finished, speaking quietly but clearly in a panic.

'Dead? What do you mean? I mean, how? What's happened? When?' replied Chatfield, feigning concern.

'Now. I mean, recently: he's still warm. He's lying in a pool of blood. He's been shot, Mark. Through the head.'

'Ok, calm down! Keep calm, you know the routine, breath slowly' Mark took control over the phone. He knew that the fear of being caught in a house with a dead body would be the final nail in Hudson's coffin, especially when that dead body happened to be a man who had helped him to escape from the hospital earlier that day.

'Right, look Hud, have you got anywhere you can go now. Get right away from there as soon as possible? I'm a little tied up now' he asked more in hope than expectation.

The phone went dead for a moment or two, and then Hud answered.

'The hotel. I can go to the George V, where Judy is!'

Bingo, thought Chatfield.

'Judy?' he asked, and without waiting for a response, 'Never mind. Go now. Make sure you take everything that might belong to you. Get out of there, fast. Don't leave anything behind. Use the back roads and side streets, it will be easier to see if you're being followed. Call me when you get there and we'll plan our next move' he finished.

Hud agreed and hung up.

Chatfield felt good: he was now in complete control. Hud had confirmed that Judy was here in Paris. The nervous tension that Hud would be feeling as he plotted his way through Paris to the hotel, wherever that was, would weigh heavy on him the following morning. Chatfield knew that Hud would not be followed, but Hud didn't.

When he got to the hotel, Hud would panic Judy as well then Mark would have them both. He would make them sweat, of course. They would become tired remaining awake, expecting Mark to arrive at any moment. And when tired they would be more disorientated, and easier to control. He didn't want any further hiccups.

He finished the glass and poured a second. The warmth inside felt good. He turned the screens off and went to the sofa, where earlier the three merchants of death had sat.

He kicked his shoes off and laid back against the arm of the settee, throwing his feet to the opposite end, still with his drink in his hand, and now resting on his chest.

The room now sat silent again, being protected from the outside world by all round sound-proofing. It was something that he had insisted upon when Schengen had acquired the building.

All ceiling and floor edges had been caulked, and the cavity walls had been packed tight with jute fibre wadding. Air conditioning vents had been removed, being replaced by large floor standing fans and dehumidifiers. Under the carpet lay a specially prepared inch thick matting, and the ceiling above had been lowered by a foot with the addition of a false gypsum board ceiling, the void created filled with foam mat blanket. The doors were extra thick solid core, and any gaps had been filled with specially prepared gaskets.

He was thinking about retiring to the basement room, when his phone sounded Hud's second call.

He reassured Hud that he would be safe in the George V for a short time, and that he would drive over to collect them as soon as he was able. He said that he was involved in a late night security meeting at one of the offices that his firm had franchise on in Paris, that an emergency had blown up while he had been out with Hud, but that he should soon be through.

Before saying goodbye, he told Hud to make sure that he and Judy were ready to leave as soon as he arrived.

Hud had said that they would be awake and ready to leave at a moment's notice.

Closing the phone, Mark Chatfield afforded himself another wry smile and looked once more at his watch. It was nearly midnight.

Once more he thought about taking himself to the basement room, but decided against it. He was comfortable where he was, and the special space below had been prepared for his very special guests. It would, perhaps, be a little small - and certainly rather too hot and stuffy for two - but he was sure that overall it would prove to be the perfect accommodation. Besides, it would only be for a short while.

He fixed himself a final self-congratulatory drink, this time without the ice, and replaced the bottle in its cabinet. He made a mental note to ensure that there was a bottle of southern comfort available in the 'guest room' in the morning.

Again he surveyed the map of Europe on his desk as he made a whirlpool of the scotch, the thought of power sending a shiver up his spine. His eyes sunk deep into the rings of the alcohol as he sunk into a deep trance, the exhilaration of the following day already giving him the rush of adrenaline that he felt when he killed.

It had been a hard day and Chatfield needed to rest, but he was still too pumped up to put his thoughts away immediately. He needed to tell someone the good news, to revel in his triumph and share the hopelessness of Hudson's predicament. He knew just the person, and dialled her number on his cell phone.

When she answered, she responded to his good fortune the way that he knew she would. She praised his dedication and his intelligence, and congratulated him on the way that he had handled adversity. Then she spoke softly to him, as only she could. He was a cold hearted killer, but just the sound of her voice could melt him. What had started, for him at least, as an affair of convenience had grown into something far more serious. He had never missed a woman when apart as he did her. He was pleased she would soon finally be with him, and that their partnership would no longer have to remain a secret.

Lying back on the sumptuous leather sofa, he closed his eyes and fell asleep: a luxury that he knew Hud would deprive both himself and Judy of. In the early hours of the morning they would be easy prey.

TWENTY SIX

Peter Hudson must have looked like a man possessed as he made his way from the corpse he had left behind. With straps in hand he slung the holdall over his back, his brisk walking pace verging on a sprint from the scene of the crime. Constantly looking left and right, and even resorting to walking backwards for yards at a time so that he would be able to spot any pursuer, by the time that he had arrived at the George V he was positive that he had not been followed.

He kept his head low as he walked past the reception desk, and could feel the eyes of the Concierge piercing from behind as he made his way to the elevator. He did not have to wait long before the lift arrived, and feverishly punched the buttons to get the doors to close and take him the two floors to Judy's room.

As he travelled upwards, he viewed himself in the mirror that rested on the rear wall of the elevator cabin. He still wore the clothes that Duval had given him and that he had been attired in all day, less the hat which had flown off during his return to the hotel and which he had not wanted to pause to retrieve. His hair was dark and wet, beads of sweat upon his forehead. A shadow was beginning to appear round his chin where he had neglected to shave for the last few days, and dark rings were manifesting themselves around his eyes from lack of sleep.

The elevator rang out its arrival, and Hud turned right to stride half the corridor to Judy's room, his shoes padding silently on the carpeted floor. Once there he looked both left and right along the narrow passage before tapping lightly on the panelled door. He had to repeat the knock another two times before receiving an answer.

He heard footsteps from within approaching and then the door opened only a few inches, just enough for Judy to peer round and identify her caller, before being flung fully open for her to welcome him back; surprised but not disappointed.

Before she could speak he raised his fingers and held them vertically in front of his lips, signalling that she should make no noise. She complied, and shut the door behind him before they faced each other. He dropped the holdall from his grip and seeing his distress she hugged him tightly.

Where he had earlier been soaked to the skin from the downpour of the afternoon, now it was the perspiration of his run to the hotel, the nervous energy that he had used, which made Hud's clothes stick to him. It felt good to him to be in the cool of the air conditioned room, and good to see that Judy was safe just as Chatfield had said she would be. His journey to this point had been littered with death and murder, and he was thankful that Judy had not been added to the list.

He was grateful for the coffee that Judy made for him, and they ordered a couple of rounds of sandwiches from room service. While they waited, Hud told her about the scene that had met him when he had returned to Duval's.

Judy listened intently, hanging on Hud's every word and only speaking when Hud had finished the sorry tale.

'Bloody hell, Hud! It could have been you, perhaps whoever it was made a mistake and thinks that you're dead. What the hell's going on?'

Hud moved so that he was under the blow of the air conditioning unit and then answered, having considered the notion on his journey from Duval's house.

'I don't know what's going on, I was hoping that you had made some progress on that front. But never mind that for now. As far as Duval's murder is concerned...well, I don't think it was a mistake' he looked at Judy who raised her eyebrows. Without waiting for the next question, Hud answered.

'He was shot in the back, and it looked as if he knocked the television on to the floor when he fell.'

'Yes, but that doesn't mean whoever shot him didn't think it was you! Maybe they shot him as he was trying to escape?' she struggled to make the method fit her hypothesis.

'No, Judy, I don't think so' Hud answered. 'For a start, where the television was positioned: if Duval had been trying to escape, and had run toward it, then he was running into a blind corner, away from the door and window. No, I think that he spoke to his murderer, and then he was executed: in cold blood.'

'Shit, Hud, that can't be right...no...I mean.... Hud, we've got to get out of here' she said hysterically, and collecting things together for their exit.

Hud grabbed her by the shoulders and held her firmly, looking into her eyes as he spoke, trying to calm her.

'And go where, Judy?' he asked rhetorically. 'I'm a hunted man. Police here and in England are looking for me for the murder of two men, my brother included, and when Duval is found they will make that three. No, our only hope lies in that file,' he said pointing to the desk, 'and on finding what it is that my brother had discovered.'

'But we can't stay here, Hud. It won't be long before the authorities start looking for me, and then they'll find I'm in Paris. Hud - we'll be found here, sooner or later!' she said struggling to break free of Hud's grip.

'Calm down, Judy!' he yelled. It had been a long time since he had shouted so at her, and immediately he did so he was sorry he had. He stopped and waited for her verbal retort, but it never came. She just stood, rooted to the spot, looking into his eyes. When the reply didn't come he continued, firstly relinquishing control of her shoulders.

'We've got help coming: Mark's going to pick us up as soon as he can. He's in a meeting, and as soon as he's through then he'll be here. He said we're to wait for his call, and be ready to go at a moment's notice.'

Hud saw the look of horror in her eyes at the very mention of his friend's name. It was always the same, and she had never explained why she disliked him so. Whenever he asked her, she skirted round the issue, avoiding answering with phrases like "its just something about him" or "call it women's intuition".

'We have no choice, Judy. I know you don't like him. God only knows why: I sure as hell don't' he saw the look of distrust for his friend in her eyes again, and took her hands in his. Drawing her close he made his final plea.

'Trust me on this one, Judy. It's our only hope.'

Looking at him, she realised that he had made this choice for them. It had been his decision and, although she didn't like it, he was right. There was no other option for them. In a strange way it felt good that he had taken control, and there was something about him that she hadn't seen for many years. Something she liked.

'Ok, Hud. I'm with you one hundred percent. I'm pretty much ready, but I think you could do with freshening up' she said, and as he made his way to the bathroom she smiled, but inside was thinking of a moment in time years before. A time when Hud had gone missing in Iraq and Mark had offered her his support. An incident about which she had vowed to herself that she would never tell.

Hud and Mark had been real close back then, almost like brothers. And as such she too had become close to Mark. As a friend: nothing more.

Regularly, Mark would spend a Saturday evening with them, watching a video or perhaps playing snooker at the club where Hud was a member. Very often it would lead to Mark crashing at their house, and having a hearty Sunday breakfast before returning to his digs on barracks.

She had often felt sorry for him being alone, and could not understand why he had never hooked up with a girl, although he'd had plenty of girlfriends: all of them casual.

It had been Mark who had knocked on the front door of their three-bed semi to break the news that

Hud was missing in action. As soon as she had seen him standing in the porch, she had known that it was bad. He had come in and they had sat, talking and crying, for a long while. She'd asked him to stay for dinner, not wanting to be alone, and he'd agreed.

He suggested that they have a bottle of wine, and had gone to the local off-licence to buy it. When he returned their dinner was on the table, and he had bought two bottles of red with him.

They ate, and talked, and before she knew it they had finished both bottles. He had helped her get through the toughest hours of her life, and when she got up to do the dishes she bent to kiss him on the cheek to say thank you. And that's when it had happened.

He grabbed her, placing one arm round her waist and with the other hand turned her face to his. He had forced her mouth open and penetrated her with his tongue. She had pulled away, and looked at him in horror, and disgust. She felt violated, as if a trust had been irreparably broken. For his part he had said that he knew she wanted him, and that Hud need never find out.

He had left when she'd told him to, but she had ended up crying herself to sleep. From that moment she had never wanted to be near Mark Chatfield again, but had never been able to tell Hud why.

Her train of thought was broken by Hud's return from the bathroom. He had washed and brushed up, and had attempted to shave with one of the hotel's complimentary razors, covering the nicks in his cheek with little squares of toilet tissue. He still wore Duval's shirt - which had turned to an off grey from pristine white -and trousers, having nothing clean to change in to.

He headed straight for the mini bar, and before he opened it he looked back at Judy who nodded.

'I'll have one as well' she called.

He came back across the room with a miniature whisky for him, and a one glass bottle of red wine for her. She took it, but didn't open it.

'Do you want something else instead?' he enquired, as he poured his scotch in a tumbler.

Judy picked the bottle up and held it in the palm of her hand, pretending to read the label, and then answered.

'No, I've changed my mind. Thanks all the same' she said, and then asking when Mark was likely to arrive.

'I really don't know. As soon as he can get away, he'll call. Don't fret, he won't let us down.'

'It's not that, Hud. I'm tired, that's all.'

'We ought to stay awake, Judy. Alert, for when we've got to leave. That could be anytime.

'Come on, let's have another look at this file. How far did you get when I left?' he asked spryly, trying to enthuse her for the paperwork that they had to get through.

Judy opened her notes and began to flick through, but not a lot of it made sense to her. At least, not that could be tied together to read like a story. She began to go through her scribblings methodically, cross referencing with the file where she wasn't certain that she had noted the pertinent facts correctly. It took perhaps twenty minutes to fully complete.

When finally she had finished, Hud repeated back what she had told him but in a summarised fashion, so that he could be sure he had retained the knowledge she imparted.

'Ok, so what we've got is this: a present made to Russia by Germany in 1716 called the Amber Room. This was basically a room that was lined with amber and other semi-precious stones, and was embellished during the reign of Catherine the Great. Now it would be worth hundreds of millions of dollars, but it is believed to have been lost at the beginning of 1945. The Germans had dismantled it and moved it to Konigsberg in 27 crates after Hitler had invaded the Soviet Union in 1941, and its believed that the Allies blew it to bits when they conducted air raids on the area. A part of the old room was found in 1997, when a lawyer in Bremen tried to sell a mosaic on behalf of a client who was the son of a German Officer who had accompanied the wartime convoy on its way to Konigsberg.

'Konigsberg is now called Kaliningrad, and is a port on the Baltic Sea. It was very important to the Germans in World War II.

'Russia controlled the Baltic Sea towards the end of the war, and its believed that they sank a lot German shipping in the straits.

'After the war ended, the leaders of Europe were determined to find a solution to the war mongering that had blighted the continent for centuries. To this end the Treaty of Rome was signed in 1957. This treaty created the blueprint for today's European Union.

'In 1997, in a documentary about the Amber Room that was never broadcast, an old man claimed that he witnessed a U-boat surfacing in the port of Stralsund in the May or June of 1944. He claimed it was met by two military trucks, and unloaded a consignment of armaments packed in crates. The elderly eyewitness died in his home of a heart attack one week after being filmed.

'It doesn't make a lot of sense to me, either, Judy' he finished.

'Yeah, its weird. A lot of it seems to be unconnected ramblings' she said, before adding, 'there's just a few pages that I haven't had the chance to go through. They were tucked right at the back. Strange really, because your brother seems to have put everything in separate sections and then there's these few pages at the end that aren't categorised.'

'What? We've spent half an hour going through this stuff, and you only now tell me there's more?' Hud questioned, his face screwed in anguish.

'Hud, I'm sorry: it's not my fault. I've been stuck here worried out of my skin about you, hardly able to concentrate, and then you come in telling me about finding Duval in his own blood…'

Hud butted in before her screams woke the entire floor.

'Sorry! Sorry, Judy! I wasn't thinking. Let's…' before he could say "keep calm" Judy had started again.

'That's the problem, Hud! You never do think! Just leave me on my own to go and see your mate Mark, and think that when you come back the little woman will have done all the hard grind for you.'

'Judy, I'm sorry. I really am. But there's no use in us arguing. Look Mark will be here soon. We can look at this later. If it's only a few pages then it won't take us long. Why don't you get a little sleep?'

He realised that their arguing was a symptom of sleep deprivation, and that Judy would feel it most. She was a woman who needed her sleep, and the last few days had been particularly traumatising for her. She looked at him quizzically.

'What about you? What about Mark phoning?' she asked.

'Don't worry about me. I'll do a bit of reading, see if the last pages tie anything up for us. If you stay dressed, then we can be gone as soon as Mark calls. Go lay down.'

She looked at him and smiled.

"Thanks, Hud' and with that she went and lay on the bed, leaving Hud to continue by the light of the desk lamp.

After an hour of reading, he had finished his brother's work. He looked over to where Judy lay sleeping. She looked beautiful, peaceful. He was pleased that she had not had a chance to read the last few pages.

He now realised why his brother had been murdered. He now knew how close Duval had been to the truth, without realising it. And in his hand he held the reasons for the mess that he now found himself in, and had dragged Judy into. But still he felt that there was a piece of the jigsaw missing, something that he couldn't quite put his finger on.

His cell phone chirruped on the desk in front of him, and he lifted it off Judy's notebook. It was Chatfield.

Time to move.

TWENTY SEVEN

Hud had hoped to bring Judy up to date with his brother's findings before Chatfield arrived, but the call had curtailed his wish.

For her part, the ring of the phone had not woken Judy. She had always been a deep sleeper, and Hud was envious of her ability to ignore any volume of commotion around her and drift in to the land of nod. There had been many occasions, during military operations or on the battlefield, upon which Hud had needed to sleep but been unable to. He knew what damage lack of sleep could do to a soldier, blunting their reflexes and giving the enemy a split second advantage.

Now Hud went to the bed and, sitting half facing her and with his legs hanging off the side of the bed, gently shook Judy with his left hand on her right shoulder. She let out a low groan, but nothing more. Hud thought how peaceful she looked in the tranquillity of her slumber, and reluctantly tried to wake her a second time. He leant near whispering her name as he shook.

Judy opened her eyes and, seeing the silhouette of Hud's face near hers, sat bolt upright with a start. She stared at him a few seconds and then the realisation of their situation returned, her face changing from unwelcome surprise to acceptance of being woken by her ex-husband. She rubbed her eyes with the tips of her fingers before cupping her face in the palms of her hands and asking Hud the time. He looked at the dial of his watch glowing phosphorus yellow in the shadow he cast, and then answered.

'Its gone four in the morning. Mark just called: he's on his way. We need to meet him outside' he instructed, getting up from the edge of the bed and flicking the switch on the bedside lamp. The room burst into light, Judy screwing her eyelids against the unwelcome and temporarily blinding intrusion.

'We can't take any luggage, or else we'll be stopped downstairs by the night Concierge,' he continued. 'We're not checking out; we just can't sleep and need a walk, if we're asked. Hopefully he'll be half-asleep and not take too much notice. We've got to try and act as natural as possible.'

'Natural? Walking out of a hotel at four in the morning as if it's a regular occurrence? I'll do my best, Hud, but don't you think we'll look just a little bit odd? I suppose we could say that we're trying to get the rush on the tourist hotspots!'

He knew that she had a point, but there was no easy solution. They had to move and this was the only way. Then he had a thought, and turned to Judy to give more commands.

'I've got money stashed round my middle. We don't need any spare clothes. Not that we've got any; I'm certain that Mark will get us some replacements when he sees the state of us. Make sure you've got your passport. Oh, and the file - stick it in the waistband of your skirt.

'Right are we ready? We mustn't have left anything behind that we might need. Nothing that gives away the fact that it was I here with you.' He was talking to himself as much as to Judy as the pair rushed through the room ensuring that all the items they needed were in stuffed in pockets, in Judy's handbag, or secreted about their person somehow.

After a minute or two they were ready to make their exit, Judy now alert and not looking the least as if she had just been disturbed from her rest – Hud never understood how she was able to do that. Hud clutched the shirt that carried the deep crimson evidence of his shooting on its sleeve, and before opening the door told Judy to stay put with the door ajar.

'I'll be back in a moment. Don't move' he said.

'What are you doing? Where are you goi...'Judy started to ask, Hud interrupting with a "sshh" as he slipped the lock on the room door.

Hud glanced both ways down the corridor and then left the room, turning back and nodding at Judy to confirm that she would hold the door for his return. He moved swiftly and silently, Judy's eyes following him as far as they could before he turned the corner toward the lift.

He came to a laundry basket that he remembered had been sitting near the escalator doors when he had arrived earlier that night. He lifted the lid, and holding it high above his head dug deep with the hand that held his blood stained shirt, secreting it between the bundle of white sheets, gowns, and towels within, all the while looking eagerly around him to ensure that he was not being spied upon.

Having ridded himself of the incriminating evidence, he walked the few feet to the escalator and stood in front of the mirrored doors examining the walls for what he knew he could use to aid their leaving the hotel without being noticed. Spotting the little red box, he pinched the cuff of his jacket between finger and thumb and pulled the sleeve down so that it stretched tight. He raised his arm and bought the point of his elbow into the glass front of the box with a crack.

The hotel erupted to a cacophony of bells, the dimmed corridor lights suddenly ablaze. Hud turned and headed back to Judy's room able to move more quickly now, the sound of his footsteps masked by the electronic ringing throughout the hotel. Within seconds he was back, and closed the door behind him. Without a word he moved across the room to the window overlooking the inner courtyard and parted the curtains a couple of inches, just enough to see across to the windows opposite.

Judy stood there incredulous, the deafening fire alarm resonating in her ears. She wanted to shout at Hud and tell him what a fool he was, but knew it would do no good to do so. There was nothing she could do about the fire alarm now, and she knew that he wouldn't take any notice of her even if he could have heard over the noise.

Within moments lights started appearing from the rooms that Hud could see around the courtyard. He dropped his grip on the drapes and came over to stand with his ear pressed hard against the door. Judy stood statue like, still dumbfounded by his actions.

The bells were sounding intermittently now, and between rings Hud could hear that all was at first quiet through the corridor. Slowly the inevitable exit of guests began, staff could be heard running the corridors shouting instructions and rapping their knuckles against the heavy wooden doors to alert those that had not emerged from their rooms. Only when the knock came at Judy's door did he open it to a night porter who seemed to be panicking more than the patrons he had already evicted. Hud grabbed the man's arm and spoke slowly.

'What's happening? What do we need to do?' he enquired.

The porter spoke rapidly, his breathing shallow and fast.

'Sir, the alarms… you must vacate your room… down the stairs… not the lift… follow the others, please.'

'What is it, a fire?' asked Hud, refusing to release his grip on the member of staff who was struggling to break free.

'We think it is a false alarm, Sir. But we cannot afford to take the chance. You must go, please. Follow everyone else and wait outside the building. Thank you' he said with more control, wrenching himself from his interrogator and disappearing down the corridor, banging on each door and shouting instructions in French and English as he went.

Along the passageway people were emerging in various states of dress. Some had thrown on the clothes that they had taken off the night before, creases in their attire giving them away, whilst others walked in striped pyjamas. An elderly couple, clearly startled by the panic of the porter, were making their way through the corridor dressed only in George V bathrobes and holding each other tightly for moral support. Mothers' carried babies, whilst Fathers' stopped the older children from running with excitement.

Hud took hold of Judy's hand and pulled her through the door.

'Come on,' he said 'we've got to get out of here. You heard the man!' He had a look of boyish mischief in his eyes, a glint that Judy had not seen for years. She liked it. And she complied without question.

Hud made sure that they weren't at the head of the flow through the corridors and down the stairs, nor at the rear. The stairway arched downwards, the thick brown and gold carpeting underneath cushioning their march as they mingled with the crowd. As they approached the lobby, through which they would complete their departure, Judy realised the genius of Hud's plan. The hotel's clients kept the night staff busy, enquiring what the problem was, and how long they would have to stand in the morning dew.

Children escaped from their parents and ran about the place. One particularly active red-haired boy colliding into a table by the entrance and nearly knocking its arrangement of Lillies from their perch, the ensuing rumpus only being avoided by an eagle eyed middle aged woman who managed to catch the toppling vase just in time.

Amongst the throng, Hud and Judy went unnoticed and once outside moved away from the melee and slipped quietly up the road towards where Hud knew Mark would be waiting. As they approached his black BMW he flashed his headlights signalling his position.

Hud opened the rear door nearest the kerb, and they settled next to each other as the car pulled from its parking space, turning a 'u' in the road and heading away from the George V Hotel. Behind them the hotel was filling up once more, as disgruntled clients were being informed of the false alarm and the broken glass on the second floor.

Mark drove at a steady pace, not wanting to draw any unwanted attention, and the centre of Paris slipped gently away. They were quiet as they drove through the back streets of Paris, a short journey to the Rue Paul Valery.

Although cool outside, the car seemed remarkably hot to Hud and he could see by the orange light of the instrument panel that the car's heating was up full. Judy began to doze almost immediately, and Hud decided to wait until they had reached safety before discussing his brother's findings. He let his friend talk as he drove.

'Sorry I'm so late, Hud. It's been a nightmare couple of days for me, but I think I've got it sorted now. I'm going to take you to the office, we've got a room there in the basement that will be safe. No one will find you, I promise. You can stay there until we decide what to do.'

'Chatters, that's great! Thanks! I owe you one' Hud replied, thankful that Mark had been in Paris.

'What was all that at the hotel?' Chatfield asked his passenger. 'I thought World War Three had started!'

'Oh, you know: get out under the cover of maximum confusion. I guessed that they would have to be safe rather than sorry, and so I set the fire alarm off. I feel a little guilty: the management is going to have a lot of disgruntled customers in the morning. But needs must: we couldn't take the chance of being stopped in an empty lobby by an over zealous concierge.'

'That's good thinking, Hud. Nice one!' Chatfield

realised that his old army pal was regaining his composure under stress. He would have to deal with him quickly when they reached their destination. He decided to plug him for information.

'Have you found what the hell is going on? Why there's someone after you, I mean?' he enquired.

'Yeah, I think so. It's deep shit, Mark. Real deep. When we're sitting more comfortably I'll go over it with you, and Judy. I haven't had a chance to speak to her about it yet. She's got Jack's file stuffed in the back of her skirt!' Hud told him.

Chatfield left the conversation there, and drove in silence the rest of the journey, taking a slightly longer route than necessary as he thought. The chestnut trees cast long shadows across the wide Avenue Foch as the sun rose above the rooftops of the expensive mansions and apartment blocks beyond. Chatfield marvelled at the bourgeois opulence of the residences before turning south to drive along the eastern perimeter of the Bois de Boulogne, where he had on occasions employed the services of prostitutes to while away his lonely existence. That was before he had taken a lover, and he thought once more about the time – soon – when she would be with him and they could become a 'proper' couple.

After driving five more minutes he had decided how to handle the couple that had caused him such problems, and doubled back toward the city.

He manoeuvred his journey so that the front of the building, with its 'Schengen' emblem, was hidden from view, and pulled the car to a halt outside the rear door that led directly to the basement, to which only he had a key.

Both Judy and Hud were drowsy, Chatfield's plan - to exhaust them and then add to the feeling by overheating the car - having worked. He opened the rear door of the office before returning to usher his car's occupants across the pavement and into the dark and steep stairway, ensuring that Judy descended first with Hud immediately ahead of Mark bringing up the rear. As they entered, Chatfield tugged a chord that gave light to the room below.

Once they were out of view of the outside world, Chatfield withdrew his Glock from its holster and bought the butt end crashing to the nape of Hud's neck.

Hud fell limp instantly, his legs buckling beneath him and falling the few steps that remained, taking Judy with him. She struggled from under his weight, her knees grazed and bleeding, and looked up to where Chatfield stood over them, the barrel of his gun pointed directly at her.

'I think you have something that I want' he said with menace in his voice.

And that was when Judy spotted a tattoo poking from beneath Chatfield's collar: an emblem that she had last seen in London on the neck of another man.

She froze as horror struck deep within her, and the only man that could save her lay unconscious at her feet.

TWENTY EIGHT

Judy sat with her hands tied behind her back and her feet tied together. Her face was streaked where she had been crying for Hud, whom lay similarly tied. Mark Chatfield had forced her to drag Hud across the floor by his feet, his head scraping against the rough stone as she did so.

After tying the pair, and then securing them with cable ties to either end of the single bed, their captor had taken the file from Judy and left them. That was more than an hour ago, and still Hud hadn't opened his eyes. Judy looked round the room that was dimly lit by one bulb high on the ceiling.

It could not have been much larger than ten feet square, and it had a slightly musty smell to it. But at least it was cool.

There was no window, and the walls were grey stone like the floor. There was a white enamel basin that stood on its own stand in one corner of the room underneath a single tap that sprouted from the wall. Above the tap was a small wooden shelf that was home to a half used bar of carbolic soap and a face mirror on its own rest.

Underneath the sink was a drain hole with an earthenware grid where dirty water from the bowl could be discarded. A white towel, stained grey where it had been used and unwashed, hung from a wire loop crudely screwed to the wall next to the makeshift sink.

Against one wall, in the middle of which were the stairs that had been their entry, was a small rickety table with a kettle, a jar of instant coffee, and a single enamel mug. A metal chair with a green canvas cover sat next door.

Hud and Judy were tied hard and fast to each end of the tubular steel bed that had been bolted to the floor opposite the coffee table. Atop the bed was a thin green mattress, a plain white sheet and a hessian blanket laid military style with the corners neatly folded in and under so that the bedding was hard as a board.

A television monitor was screwed to the wall so that it could be viewed from the bed, but it appeared not to have any controls or tuning mechanism. Next to the monitor's home was a second set of stairs, and it was up these that Chatfield had disappeared. Judy had tried shouting for help but the noise seemed to merely reverberate around the walls.

She looked at Hud. Traces of dried blood clung to the back of his neck where his head had bounced off the scabrous surface as she had hauled him across from the steps. His head hung to one side, and the bullet wound in his left arm had opened slightly leaving a crimson trail that ran the length of his sleeve, finishing with a dry pool where his fingers felt the floor. She wished him awake, as she had been for the past hour, and he groaned lightly. His leg shook violently before his lids shot apart, eyes staring into space. Sweat poured from his head, wetting his hair, and he screamed like a banshee whilst struggling violently against his ties. She wanted to hold him, console him, but there was nothing she could do apart from watch helplessly until the fit had faded.

She fell in and out of semi-consciousness for some hours in the noiseless room, constantly wary of Hud's condition and waiting for the man that held them like this to reappear. She was beginning to wish that he would re-enter their prison, if only so she could have some water. Her mouth was dry, and she had long since been unable to salivate.

Her wrists were sore from her struggling to break free of her ropes, but with every movement they had just become tighter still until the chaffing had been too unbearable to continue. Even though the room was cool and dry, her exertions had caused her to sweat. The saltiness had run down her forehead and into her eyes, making them sting and redden where she had twisted to rub them against the harsh bed covering. Her blonde hair lay in matted locks, having surrendered the bouncy ringlets that it was accustomed to.

As she slipped once more into her periodic daze, at the far end of the cot Hud groaned ever so lightly. His head rolled, his chin pivoting on his chest. Garbled words began to run from his mouth in a slur as if he'd been drinking. The change in him bought Judy back from the edge of her own insensibility, and she watched with her eyes wide as Hud struggled to lift his head.

Slowly his eyes opened, pupils rapidly dilating as they became accustomed to the surroundings. Judy spoke words of encouragement softly, almost in a whisper, even though she was sure no one outside the room could have heard her. He moved his head from side to side in lazy gyration, each time falling to his chest an effort to bring up again. Gradually he woke, his listlessness ebbing, until finally he was looking into Judy's bloodshot eyes.

He made to caress her, and saw that they were both unable to move. He started to remember, fighting the throbbing inside his head and the pain screaming at him from every part of his body. He remembered the hotel, the bells, and being in Chatfield's car. Then he remembered the stairs and the thump on his neck, and falling, taking Judy with him. Then he remembered everything turning black.

No, not Mark! Not his friend!

He looked at Judy, hoping that this was some kind of bad dream, a nightmare that she would wake him from. She just looked, a tear forming in the corner of her eye.

'Thank God you're alright Hud!' she said, the quiver in her voice caused by the lump in the back of her throat.

'I don't understand. What's happening,' he asked of her.

'Its Mark. He's no friend, Hud. He's done this to us. He's part of it. Whatever it is. He's got a tattoo like the one on the man in London: the one that tried to ra...' she couldn't bring herself to say the word, the terror that she had felt flooding back to her.

'I don't believe it. He wouldn't. I mean...it's not possible!' he exclaimed, the throb in his head increasing in its ferocity.

Judy spent the next few minutes telling Hud what had happened to them after they had stood at the top of the stairs down to their cell. How Mark had held a gun pointed to her, had forced her to drag Hud across the floor – she apologised for his injuries that she had caused – and had tied both of them to the legs of the bed. She said that she had tried to break free, but her binds had become stronger with each effort.

'He can't be doing this. Surely any reward...' he said, unable to finish as Judy broke in.

'Hud, you're not listening! He's part of it. The tattoo!' she shouted, and all went quiet, Hud stunned by his friend's betrayal.

He was thinking. Thinking about the file, about what he had read, that Judy hadn't. Finally he spoke.

'Judy, I need to tell you about Schengen. What I think my brother had found he paused before adding. 'What led to his murder.'

Judy sat still, concentrating on Hud's word's as he spoke. Several times he had to stop and think hard about the words to use, and how to connect the strands of his brother's report to a coherent conclusion.

'Karl Doenitz was freed from jail in October 1956. He retired to live in Aumuhle, just east of Hamburg and about one hundred miles west of Stralsund. He was still revered by many as the last of the great Germans, and received many visitors, including politicians and people in positions of power.

'Strangely, he took particular interest in a little known Frenchman called Pierre Donat, who had come to him with a business idea shortly after he had been released from the prison in Spandau. After the release of Doenitz's first book, "Ten Years and Twenty Days" in 1958, Doenitz became a major investor in an investment fund run by the Frenchman.

'Barely a year after Doenitz's release from jail, the Treaty of Rome - which set the basis for today's European Union - was signed.'

He stopped to catch his breath, trying to visualise the printed words on the pages that he had read but Judy had missed. Soon he started where he had left off.

'After the European Union was set up – in those days it was, of course, called the European Community – it continued to expand, drawing in more and more countries including, most recently, many of the old Eastern Bloc countries. It started with just a handful of countries but now it covers practically all of Europe, right up to the border with Russia.

'In 1985, there was an agreement signed that basically gets rid of all internal borders across Europe. It was signed at a place called Remerschen on the borders of France, Germany, and Luxembourg. Free flow of people, goods, agricultural produce, and so on.

'On top of that, there was the introduction of the Euro in 1999. Most countries have taken that, or will be in the next two or three years.

'Britain is the one major country that has declined the currency and completely free borders internal borders.'

Judy interjected, with a little concern in her voice.

'Hud, that means Europe's effectively one massive country – apart from the different laws and Governments.'

'Exactly!' he said.'And we'll talk about the different laws in a minute.

'Ok. Then my brother seems to have dug something up about this documentary you mentioned. The one that was about the Amber Room – remember that – in 1997. The documentary was buried, panned. It was never shown.

'There have been various theories about what happened to the treasures of the room. Some say it was destroyed by Allied bombing, others that it was taken and hidden in a mine in Thuringia, or perhaps attempted to be moved and sent to the bottom of the Baltic Sea in a torpedoed steamer.

'In 1997, a piece of the Amber Room was found being touted for sale in Germany. That created quite a bit of press at the time, and a TV station decided to do a documentary on it. They dug up this real old guy that became the eyewitness, the one that died a week after he was filmed.

'Jack managed to get hold of a copy of that documentary. In it the witness says that he was sleeping rough in the dock area of the port of Stralsund in the middle of 1944 - it could have been May or June, he wasn't sure – when he saw this German submarine dock.

'The docks had been declared out of bounds to all civilians, so he had to hide. But from his hiding place he could see lots of crates being unloaded, and a young officer who was directing the loading of the crates onto two army trucks. This officer didn't re-board the submarine when it left, he stayed with the trucks. The trucks immediately left as soon as they'd been loaded.' He stopped when he saw that Judy was keen to question him.

'Hud, I don't see the connection?' she queried.

'Get this,' he said excitedly 'this old guy swore blind that the young officer had been addressed as Doenitz: Klaus Doenitz!' he left the statement in the air and waited for the question that he knew would come. He didn't have to wait too long for Judy to click.

'Klaus Doenitz was killed on a Fast Boat in the English Channel, Hud. May 1944. I remember that: I remember thinking "poor guy" about the father, losing both his sons during the war.'

'But what if he didn't, Judy?' Hud asked her. 'Klaus's body was never recovered, and this old guy was adamant that it was Klaus Doenitz that he saw.

'My brother believed him. He thinks Klaus Doenitz and Pierre Donat are one and the same. Do you remember the black and white photograph of old man Doenitz's funeral?'

Judy nodded, but said nothing. She knew that adrenaline was pumping fast through Hud's veins, and she didn't want to break his rhythm. He carried on upon her nodded signal.

'The man circled in red, I'm sure that Jack believed it was Pierre Donat, aka Klaus Doenitz.

'Do you see Judy? Do you see what my brother saw? What we've got to stop?'

She looked blankly at him, before speaking without conviction.

'There's some madman called Pierre Donat that's been corrupting Europe somehow?'

Hud smiled, the sort of smile that says, "I know something you don't". Judy was not in the mood for mind games.

'What is it, Hud? Tell me' she said agitatedly.

'Ok, here goes. There are a couple of facts I've left out.

'The town where the agreement for a free Europe was signed – Remerschen – was renamed Schengen, after the name of the agreement.

'The investment fund run by Pierre Donat is called Schengen. By the way, its now one of the world's largest investment funds, with a great many wealthy and very secretive investors.

'Pierre Donat – or Klaus Doenitz, if indeed that's his real name – lives in Schengen, an elderly recluse.

'There's one final thing. Eisenhower was concerned that the Germans who signed the surrender were fine upstanding military types. He called them the "Fair Generals", people whom he could trust. He asked Doenitz how he would say it in German. When he repeated the words, he couldn't pronounce them properly and so he shortened it to a Yankee style nickname. The words were "Das Schon Generals". The nickname he gave them was "The Schengen".

'Judy, it's not a madman that's corrupting Europe which my brother's uncovered, it's a whole fucking movement. It's like the Nazis have never really been away. They've always been there, in the background, controlling Europe and waiting for the opportunity to pounce.

'And yesterday, every nation in the European Union signed up to the new European Treaty. It gives the European Parliament absolute control of its member states under certain circumstances. The British Cabinet had accepted to sign, and my brother was the representative who was going to put pen to paper.

'I think he was going to refuse and scupper the whole deal: on his own, without the remit of the Cabinet.

'I think Schengen, somehow, found out what his plans were.

'And that's why they killed Jack. He would have taken away the last piece of the jigsaw that they needed.

They are creating the Fourth Reich, a European Empire, controlled by the far right, the Nazis.'

He looked hard and long at Judy before concluding. Judy could see the fire in his eyes, the hunger for battle had returned.

'We're Europe's only hope, Judy. You and I.'

From an unseen place behind Judy, a slow handclap rang out.

Judy turned her head, and Hud looked to where the sound came from.

It was Chatfield.

He had appeared unnoticed and had listened to the entire conversation.

'Very good!' he said, with his hands now clasped together.

'But there's nothing that either of you can do about it now. Within days Europe will be the Fourth Reich. We will at last be a super power to rival America, and take on the might of China when it comes.

But there are a couple of facts your brother seems to have missed. Let me fill you in while you're both sitting so comfortably.'

He descended the steep steps and took the chair that sat next to the coffee table. He spoke with the confidence and authority that his position afforded him. When he was finished he stood and gave his hostages a Nazi salute before ascending the stairs to his office.

'As you now know, I have work to do.

'I will allow you to watch on the screen.

'And then when my work is finished I'll bring you some water before I decide what to do with you.

'I'm sure the Director would like to meet you, Hud - the man who has caused us so many last minute problems - before you die.'

After a couple of minutes, the screen fixed to the wall fizzed to life and upon the screen the picture of a well-appointed office. On the desk in the foreground, Hud could make out a map of Europe. In the middle of the office was a coffee table with various delicacies arranged on plates, and a kettle of coffee.

Into view came four men, entering the office from the far end. One of them Hud recognised as Chatfield, who was clearly the lead in the conversation that took place.

The other three, he did not recognise. They took their seats together, the one with the Arab dress in the middle.

The final battle plans were being drawn.

TWENTY NINE

Hud and Judy sat in silence, eyes glued to the crystal clear images that they were forced to watch. What Mark Chatfield had told them minutes earlier would have been unbelievable had it not been for the events of the previous few days, but now it seemed to Hud that his one time best friend was gloating. It was almost as if everything to that point had been planned in meticulous detail. And not just recently, but for the last sixty years or more.

Now they were entering the end game, and there was nothing that Hud could do to stop the plans for the annihilation that was being finalised in front of them.

Even if they could break free, Hud was a fugitive. Schengen had made him a man on the run; had taken away his liberty even without the ropes that now held him. As far as the world was concerned he was a bloodthirsty killer: an insane murderer on the loose.

But not as insane as the men that now controlled him. He had to hold that thought and hope that the Schengen would make a mistake. That they would somehow slip up. If they didn't he knew that both he and Judy would be dead and that there would be no hope for a free Europe.

As he watched the meeting taking place next door, he thought about what Mark had told them. He thought about whom his friend really was, and about the power that Schengen held.

Power built on murder, corruption, and greed.

Power that had ended up being the cause of his brother's death, and that would now mean the same fate for Hud and Judy.

He looked at her as she watched Mark plotting the downfall of a continent, her eyes transfixed on the screen, her ears concentrated on every word. He wished that he had not drawn her into this. That he had been strong enough to push her away when she had offered her help.

Now she would die too.

And it was his fault.

As Chatfield spoke, Hudson's blood boiled. Their entire friendship had been built on a lie.

This was not the man that he had known during his military years. But then he had never been that man. Mark Chatfield's life had been an act, a pretence that had led to this point. And it had been Karl Doenitz, and later his son Klaus, that had given Mark the life he now had.

All the years of fighting for Queen and Country had meant nothing to him, other than a way to learn to kill. A way to learn to control men through fear.

From the moment that Chatfield had been told of his real identity, and the reason for his life, he had lived for this time.

It had been easy for him to see the family resemblance when shown the pictures of his Grandfather and his Father side by side. He had never known either, but still he knew it was so.

And it had been Karl Doenitz that had told him the truth about his origins.

Alfred Jodl had sired an illegitimate son by his mistress, Luise Katharina von Benda, in 1941. She had given birth in secret, and the boy had been moved to an orphanage so as to avoid the prejudice and scandal that would surely have followed. There were few that knew about the pregnancy, Doenitz among them. Before the Nuremburg Trials, Jodl forced Doenitz to promise that he would look after the boy if Jodl did not make it and was executed.

When he was freed from prison, Doenitz hunted the boy down and found him. He sponsored his move to Britain, and his assimilation in that country. He met a young woman, and they planned to marry. However, she became pregnant and gave birth to a son.

By this time, the young Jodl had become disillusioned with the political ramblings of Doenitz and his right hand, Pierre Donat, and threatened to tell all. For this he was murdered, and his son grew up the illegitimate son of Mary Chatfield.

When he was eighteen, and a couple of years before Karl Doenitz died, Pierre told Chatfield everything, and took him under his wing.

Now the two were the leaders of the Schengen. They protected its secrets, and promoted its political philosophy. Together they controlled vast wealth that could corrupt almost anyone.

They had the backing of many of Europe's wealthiest individuals: Businessmen, Religious Leaders, Politicians, and aristocrats. Those that were approached and didn't join were dealt with ruthlessly.

The movement's wealth had been built from the looted riches that were stolen away during the Second World War. The greatest of these had been the Amber Room. These riches had been multiplied many hundreds of times. They sold their artefacts to wealthy 'investors' and then invested the proceeds in the financial markets of the world.

The Schengen had orchestrated the so-called "Black Wednesday", when the British currency had collapsed. The press of the World had stated that George Soros, a world renowned investor, had made a billion dollars by backing against the currency. Schengen had made nearly three times that amount, in a single day.

Now they were soon to be all-powerful, ruling a new European Empire: the prophecy of the thousand years Reich coming true under the guidance of two madmen who would stop at nothing.

Donat and Chatfield.

The Cardinals of Schengen.

And the weapon that would bring their ultimate power was sitting with Chatfield in his office.

Terror.

Hud now watched, concentrating his efforts against the pain from what felt like every inch of his body. His heart beat its tune inside his head, and stabbing pains came in waves from the injury to his arm. His wrists and ankles were sore from the ropes tied around them, and his legs ached from their forced inactivity.

As the men in Chatfield's office spouted their horrific plans, Hud's mouth dried. The air that he breathed went cold, as cold as the voices and hearts next door.

'There are bombs planted in all of the Parliament buildings across Europe, as you wanted' Omar Ali bin Akhbar was informing his host.

'They are contained within the legs of furniture, under the floorboards and in the shafts of the air conditioning systems. Explosives are held within the space of cavity walling, and underneath generators and gas tanks that house emergency fuels. Where there are false ceilings it is the same.

'The main detonators will be in place on Monday. I will personally arm the controlling detonator at midnight on the same day. You will have the pleasure of beginning the tidal wave of destruction that Allah has blessed.'

Akhbar pushed a silver cased cell phone across the table and towards Chatfield. He picked it up and played with it in the palm of his right hand.

'What's the number I need to dial?' he asked.

'The number is programmed into the phone already. It is the only contact on the SIM card. The SIM card will be activated at nine in the morning on Tuesday. From then you can choose the allotted hour that you will take power.

'As each blast completes, it will trigger the next hundreds of miles away.'

'You have done well, bin Akhbar' Chatfield praised.

'For which you will pay well. Our service is not cheap.'

Chatfield arose from his seat and went to the computer on his desk. He put the cell phone in his jacket pocket as he went, and once sitting fingered the keyboard sitting in front of its monitor.

Hud and Judy could see that a financial transaction was being electronically executed. When a blue bar had run across the bottom of the monitor's screen, and a window had appeared saying "transaction complete", Chatfield spoke once more.

'As we agreed, twenty five million dollars into the Swiss account of your choice.'

'And the balance?' bin Akhbar asked.

'The balance will be paid after the explosives have done their job. And when the European Parliament has control of Europe, we will complete on our promises.'

'Good. I look forward to the withdrawal of all European troops from Allah's lands. We will then be able to crush the American infidels' bin Akhbar finished, as he stood to leave.

'And we in turn look forward to unlimited oil, and an increasing friendship with Allah's people' Mark replied, bringing his right hand to his forehand then down in a circular motion to his chest and bowing his head slightly.

Soon after the three terrorists had left the office, the screen that Hud and Judy had been watching went blank and the door at the top of the stairs to the office opened. In the doorway Chatfield stood erect, his feet shoulder width apart and his Glock in his right hand.

Hud could see the maniacal grin on his face.

'Your brother could have been part of the greatest Empire the World has ever seen. But he declined our invitation.

'I killed him, Hud. And I took pleasure in doing so.

'Soon it will be your turn. And that will be my most pleasurable kill. I have waited years to repay you for the deaths of my brother and my mother. I will enjoy watching your face as you die slowly at my hands.

'But not yet. The Director wants to see you, and I don't want you here. Tonight you go to Schengen. And next Tuesday you will witness the awesome power that we hold. And afterwards you will die.'

Hud held the stare of his captor, not giving a quarter.

Judy eyed first Chatfield and then Hud. She saw hate in each man's eyes, but in Hud's she also saw something else. She saw the determination of a fighter backed in to a corner, and the pride within him that would see him battle to the death.

THIRTY

Chatfield kept them locked up in the bowel of the building for what seemed like hours. He deprived them of water and food, and with each passing moment they grew weaker. Tiredness overtook them, and they both drifted in and out of periods of involuntary unconsciousness. Neither wanted to sleep, but were unable to resist.

Hud knew that Mark was treating them in this way deliberately, forcing them to stay awake by interrupting their sleep, entering the room and kicking whichever had closed their eyes within moments of doing so.

He was watching them suffer under the solitary bulb that had become their sun. He was ensuring that they would be pliable for when he needed them to be, when he needed them to be compliant. When he needed to move them.

The underfloor heating would come and go, adding to their discomfort. Their lips were dry, cracking in the drought of their prison cell. Their tongues were numb, their mouths drained of saliva.

The only moisture they had was the sweat that the fire underneath them caused, seeping from their heads and running blindly into their eyes, the pain of the salt biting under their lashes.

They did not struggle to break free. There was no point. If they had been able to loosen their ties, there was nowhere for them to run.

The door that led directly to the outside world had been bolted and padlocked by Chatfield.

And through the other door their captor waited. Armed. And if he were watching them, as Hud suspected, then they would have no element of surprise. They would be lambs to the slaughter.

And so they stayed, bound and unmoving, talking about the past. About better times that they had experienced. Not mentioning the present. Not daring to contemplate the future.

Hud tried to apologise to Judy. She should not have been there. This was Hud's fight, not hers.

Each time she batted the apology away. She told him that he could not face this alone, that she would not have wanted him to. That he had to be strong for the both of them.

He craved a drink. His body was telling him that it needed a shot of the alcohol that he fed it at regular intervals, and that he had been forced to deprive it of, and had started to rebel. He sweated more, and was becoming more irritable than his military training would have allowed.

He had felt the pain of being forced to stay awake before, the way it could eat at a man's ability to think and behave rationally. Survival under that type of duress had formed part of the preparation for active duty of an SAS Officer.

But he had never before had to make do without his regular fix of alcohol, and it had started chewing at him, unravelling him from inside out.

And still Chatfield would appear, taunting them. Heightening their pain. Hud would fall deep into despair when Chatfield had left the room, begging for Judy's forgiveness. But he wouldn't give sway to Chatfield, he wouldn't give him that pleasure. He wouldn't allow him to see that he was broken. Not face to face.

Chatfield would step deliberately down the stairs, and cross the room to the makeshift sink. He would run the tap into the bowl, and pour the cool clear water away. And then he would disappear to where he had come from, laughing as he passed his pair of prisoners.

Hud and Judy tried to keep each other optimistic, and they used Mark's mind games to work against him. Yet more regularly they slipped into unconsciousness, until Mark was satisfied that they could do no harm.

It was Hud that was bundled into the back of Renault Box van first.

Mark had appeared at Hud's feet, kicking him awake as he had done several times before. This time, however, there was another man with him: a hulk of a man, standing well over six feet tall, and just as wide. He was bald with a scar running the length of his left cheek, and a tooth missing on his bottom set. He was dressed all in black, and Hud could see the outline of a pistol strapped to his waist beneath his pullover.

The hired muscle lent down and grabbed Hud by his lapels, as Mark cut through the cable tie behind. With one movement Hud was off his feet and over the shoulder of the bald man. He walked him up the stone steps and into the cool breeze in the side street where Chatfield had delivered them earlier that day.

Where the sun had been breaking when they had arrived, the sky above was now the deep blue of night. No lights lit the dead end road, and there were no passers by to be alerted.

The doors of the van were wide open and gently swinging in the wind, as Hud was thrown in the back like a piece of butchered meat. He landed with a thud, wincing with the pain that shot through his arm as it hit the steel floor first. Then he heard Chatfield give further instructions, before footsteps told him that he had returned to the cellar with the bald man to collect Judy.

The van's engine turned over with the thump of a diesel as he waited for Judy to be bought up the stairs.

She came quietly, the bald man treating her a little more gently as he placed her in the back of the van. For meting out this easier treatment Mark castigated him, before turning to the pair lying tied on the floor of the transporter.

'Enjoy your trip. Make the most of your time together. It is not long before you both shall pay the price for your interference.'

With that the rear doors were shut tight, and they were left in the pitch black to await their fate.

Hud slid across to be close to Judy as they felt the van move and turn left, taking them away - for the time being at least - from their torturer. Hud moved to find Judy's ear next to his mouth, and spoke quietly. He could feel the panic in her, and remembered well her fear of enclosed places.

'Judy, are you ok?'

'Yes, I think so, Hud' she said, her voice soft but strong.

'I've got an idea. Can you move your hands?' he asked of her.

'I don't know. I think so, but the ropes are so tight where I tried to get free before' she said, as she wiggled her fingers a little.

'I need you to undo the buckle of my belt, and hold it in your hands. Do you think you could do that?'

'I'll try' she said trying to feel the leather of his belt.

Each time she was close, the van would hit a pothole or turn a corner and slide Hud away. They would have to inch closer to each other, Hud bouncing along the cold floor and coming down on his injured arm at every twist.

After several attempts, and having failed each time, they found themselves wedged in the corner furthest from the doors. They could hear the bald man talking to another as Judy struggled with the buckle once more. This time when the van lurched Hud stayed still, and Judy was able to prise the leather through the loops of his waistband until finally she had the whole belt in her hands.

'Now what?' she asked in a whisper, fearful that the men in the driver's cabin would be able to hear them.

'Stay still, I need to roll over so my back's to you' Hud replied in an equally hushed voice, before using the side of the van to lever his body up and round so that he lay back to back with Judy.

Hud took his belt from Judy's clammy hands and passed it inch by inch through his fingers until he felt the cold metal of his buckle between the thumb and index finger of his right hand. He started working the tine of his belt buckle into the fibres of the rope that held his hands together, whilst at the same time listening to the sound of the road roaring beneath them.

The busy noise of the city had been left behind, and the start stop journey through the lit streets of Paris had become a constant drone of rubber against tarmac. No longer were there the sharp turns and rough potholes to throw Hud's tired body against the van's walls, which was a relief to his aching body. It also made working the rope easier, and he was able to separate the strands between his wrists. Once separated, Hud used a sawing motion to try to cut through the thin fibres. It was hard work, and each time he moved his buckle up and down the rope around his wrist tightened a little more.

Several times he dropped the belt, the buckle landing on the steel floor of their prison and clanging like a dulled bell. Each time he had to retrieve his makeshift tool, and blindly feel his way to the clasp before once more starting to saw away at the frayed cords.

He constantly listened to the sound of the engine and the conversation between his jailers for signs of a break in their journey, twice having to stop as the van pulled to a halt. Each time he had heard the men talking before the large bald man had exited the driver's cockpit to walk to the rear of the van and flung one of the doors open. He would then shine a flashlight into the back, checking that the cargo was under control. He held a pistol in his right hand as he did so, and the door was only open a few seconds so that he could be satisfied that his precious goods were still intact before he returned to his colleague in the cabin.

Hud had been able to work his ropes to the point of breaking when he felt the van begin to slow again. Feverishly he worked harder, pulling his wrists apart in rapid jerks with all the force that he could muster. He could feel blood beginning to meld in with the rope where his exertions had begun to chafe the skin on his wrists. Finally, with one last effort, his hands were free, the rasping pain from his arm subsiding as he pushed himself away from the side of the van.

He told Judy to keep quiet as he hauled himself to his feet, which were still tightly bound and clasped the handle of the rear door. As he did so the opposite door crashed open as it had done before, revealing the silhouette of the bald man as the cold night air swept in though the opening.

Hud saw the look of surprise on the scarred face of his guard just before being thrown back by the force of the blow. Using the handle as a pivot, Hud had swung round aiming his feet at the chin of the oversized Frenchman. The impact had been like a hammer coming at full pelt from below and sweeping the large man off his feet, his head whiplashing backwards as Hud followed through the doorway and fell on top of the limp body.

The man's pistol fell with a clatter on the concrete of the hard shoulder that the van occupied on the dark highway, and Hud scrambled away from the unconscious guard and toward the point where he had heard it fall. Behind him he could hear the sound of the driver calling to his friend, and the cabin door slamming shut. The beam of a second flashlight broke through the darkness, as footsteps fell on the tarmac, the driver approaching. Hud searched with his hands, desperately willing the fallen pistol to come to him, his fingers outstretched as he arced his arms back and forth clawing the concrete in front of him.

The light from the driver's torch grew stronger as the second man came closer to the rear of the van, calling his colleague. Hud knew that he must find the gun before he was spotted. He strained his eyes against the blackness beyond darting his gaze first this way then that, hoping for sight of the gun. Suddenly the ground in front of him was bathed in light as the driver rounded the corner of the van.

The driver saw Hud half-tied and stooped on all fours a short distance from his compatriot who lay prostrate on the cold tarmac. The split second of shock was just enough time for Hud to see the mislaid pistol to his right, and he made a grab for it as he rolled close to the floor and away.

A shot rang out from the direction of the torchlight, narrowly missing his left side as it ricocheted off the road and away to the trees beyond. As Hud fell down the grassy slope of the embankment he fired two rounds at the source of the light that had followed his fall. He heard the hiss of expelled air as the shadowy figure fell after him, rolling without meaning down the slope in Hud's direction.

Hud too was still sliding, on his stomach now and watching the driver somersault toward him. He followed the fall with his pistol, and released another round as the body came over him. He heard the bullet hit its mark once more as a trailing leg thumped hard into Hud's forehead, throwing him back to land in the water in the bottom of the roadside ditch. Beside him lay the dead driver, eyes wide and unmoving.

For a second the world stood still and silent, before the sound of Judy's voice spilt into the quietness, the screams following the path of Hud's fall to where he now lay. He called back, breaking into Judy's anxiety with his own, as he pulled free from his bonds around his ankles.

Pushing the pistol in his waistband, he used his hands to drag himself up the bank from the driver's watery grave. The surface was slippery from recent rains and he had to claw himself away, grabbing at handfuls of grass to pull himself whilst his feet slid up and down the sodden bankside.

When he eventually reached the roadside again, the large guard still lay unconscious. Hud dropped to his knees and rolled him down the slope to be with his friend. He knew that he should have killed him - that he should have put a bullet through his head - but did not want to be the cause of any more bloodshed. He knew it might pass that the large guard might drown next to his dead friend: but Hud felt that to die in such a way would not be his doing.

And so he left him.

To live or die would be the Frenchman's choice. Hud had other choices to make, other priorities. Someone was going to pay for the hell that Hud was in, and he knew who that someone was.

First, though, Hud had to get Judy to safety.

THIRTY ONE

Judy sat in the seat next to Hud as he drove the van that had been their prison around the winding country lanes to the north of Paris. She held her knees tight to her chest, with her feet resting on the dash in front of her. Heated air blew from little grills on the dash and underneath warming the driver's cabin that the two fugitives now occupied.

Once Hud had freed Judy from her incarceration, they had driven from the scene of their escape and exited at the next junction. Hud had spent twenty minutes travelling through back roads before able to marry the few direction signs they crossed with the map they had found in the glove compartment of the Renault Van they had commandeered. They were now heading back toward the outskirts of Paris, but keeping to a route that would avoid the main roads as far as possible.

The French countryside was dark and quiet, and Hud drove stealthily with just his sidelights on. Ahead of them on the horizon they could be see the dome of light that was Paris, gradually increasing in size across the open fields that extended before them.

They were both tired, but at least they were now warm, and Hud's clothes had begun to dry from the rain water they had absorbed back in the roadside ditch where he had left one dead and one unconscious guard. He felt some guilt at the way he had left the second guard, possibly to die, and had to remind himself that the fate of the guard was not in his hands. All that had happened was down to one man, a man that Hud had once counted as his greatest friend: Mark Chatfield.

They now sat driving in silence, Hud concentrating his efforts on remaining on the road and yet at the same time his mind wandering formulating his plans.

Hud knew that he needed to act quickly to stop Europe from becoming embroiled in a Schengen induced spiral of racial hatred and civil war, an anarchy that would allow Schengen and its followers to assume control of the continent. The takeover had been planned to perfection, but Hud needed proof of even the existence of such a movement. He needed to expose the history of the last six decades and make people believe that the Nazis were still a viable force. Then that they would somehow use Al Queda to seize power in Europe, and that there were dozens - maybe even hundreds - of high ranking officials and politicians involved and corrupted by Schengen.

He needed a weak link and needed to hit that link hard within days, before the destruction of Europe's democracies was started with the bombings of all the parliamentary buildings of its member states.

He had discussed this with Judy while driving, and although she agreed with his plans – and the logic behind them – she didn't like it. She thought it was too big a risk, that they should go to the authorities with what they knew, and let the police, or Interpol, or the military, deal with it. Hud pointed out that they didn't know who was involved, that there could be any number of police and politicians in the pay of Schengen. He told her what she already knew: that they had to find a way of busting the whole thing wide open. And that's when he had told her what he intended to do.

And so now they were not talking.

Hud felt alone, isolated.

It was Saturday night. He had until Tuesday to change the course of Europe's future, and to take his revenge on Mark Chatfield. The one person who would make it all worthwhile was next to him, but he felt now more than ever a great distance lay between them.

And so he drove back to Paris, to where Judy would be safe and he might be able to give himself a fighting chance.

Paris was drawing close now, and the outskirts were dotted with small semi-rural residential areas where the city was spreading. Purpose built houses for wealthy commuters sprang from the earth as a prologue to the concrete jungle that was fast approaching. The tentacles of Paris were attenuating ever outwards, just as every city in Europe was with the economic growth that a continent at peace promoted.

Hud turned his headlights on, so as to draw little attention to himself. He passed a police patrol vehicle and looked in the wing mirrors, expecting to see the car start up and follow, but it didn't. Either he hadn't been seen, or they weren't interested. If only the police inside had known it was Peter Hudson driving the Renault Box Van then they could have been the most famous gendarmes in the whole of France, the ones who had captured the escaped murderer from Britain.

They followed the road a further mile or so, and then took a right turn which led them to a clutch of a dozen houses in a dead end. As he entered the close, Hud extinguished the headlights once more. He killed the engine and sat with Judy, observing the house that sat on its own at the far end of the cul-de-sac.

Elms lined the street, like small watchtowers keeping undesirables at bay. Each house was similar, but at the same time different also. They all stood back from the road, with individual arced drives allowing cars to come and go in their own little one way systems. Some houses had large garages, and some had just a single car port attached to the side. All had shutters at the windows in French country style, and every second residence had palatial columns either side of the main entrance. Roofs were of dark slate, and some of the houses were built in red brick while others had a stone façade.

The two-storey mansion at the far end was the most grandiose of all, with a long drive curling around a central grassed area that housed a fountain in its middle. The angel with her toe in the water was still, as was its want when the house's occupants were away. The shutters were closed upstairs but open on the ground floor, which seemed odd to Hud. The house was in darkness, lit only by the half moon that was now poking through the clouds.

As he fired up the engine and pulled toward the house, swinging silently through the gated entrance, Hud could see why his brother had liked his French hideaway so much. Now Jack would never see it again, but Hud knew his brother would approve of its use as a safe house for Judy while Hud was in Paris.

He drove along the gravel drive and past the detached double garage to the back of the house, parking the van so that it would not be spied by the house's neighbours. As they pushed the doors closed behind them, Judy spoke for the first time since they had argued.

'I wish you'd let me come with you, Hud. I know what you say is true, but I can't bear the thought of you going through this on your own. Besides, I'll be lonely in this big house on my own' she protested as he neared her.

He took hold of her arm and spoke softly as he led her to the door at the rear of the building.

'Judy, you know I have to do this. It's the only way that I'm going to have a chance to clear my name. And you know what's going to happen on Tuesday. You saw it: every government in Europe will be wiped out. We've gone over this already' he finished with a tone that told Judy not to pursue the argument any further.

Kneeling down, Hud traced his hand over the low wall that formed the outer skin of the flower border and removed the third stone from the door. There in the cavity was the key.

'I can't believe that Jack kept the key to this place there. What about burglars?' Judy remarked.

'It's one thing getting in, its entirely another not being caught' Jack said, slipping the key in the lock and pushing the door open.

He raced across the utility room that they had entered and knelt down by a rack that was laden with shoes and boots. Placing his hand on the rack, he pushed it to one side and revealed an alarm box upon which a red light was flashing. He flipped a cover open to reveal a numerical keypad, and punched five numbers in which illuminated in orange on an LED panel above. Immediately he had done so the flashing red light was replaced by a steady green.

Hud replaced the cover and pushed the shoe rack into place.

'How do you know all of Jack's passwords?' Judy asked as she stood beside him in bemusement.

'It's easy. Jack once told me that he could never remember passwords, so he always used the same one. Dates of birth, marriage and so on would be too easy to decipher.

So he always used the size of his first majority that got him his seat in parliament: eleven thousand and twenty two.'

They walked to the kitchen and Hud pulled the blinds closed before putting the light on. He looked at Judy.

She had smudges of dirt from the floor of the van upon her face, and her makeup had run in tracks with her tears. Her usually immaculate hair was dishevelled and had begun to mat. She looked tired, and her eyes were bloodshot from lack of sleep.

She stood scruffy, her clothes dusty and her shoes had lost a heel.

And yet Hud could not think of a time that she looked more beautiful to him. He smiled at her and she blushed a little, as if bashful at the state that she was in.

He made coffee while Judy went upstairs to the master bedroom.

While he waited for the water to run through the filter Hud surveyed his brother's house, getting his bearings and trying to think of anything he might need to take with him.

There were pictures of Amy in every room. Some on her own, and others in a variety of poses with Jack. Pictures taken on holiday, skiing or shooting, or in Jack's office and one particularly large frame on the mantle in the lounge of Jack and Amy outside Number Ten on the day that Jack was awarded the job of Foreign Secretary.

Hud lifted this picture from its resting place and looked at it fondly. Already he missed his brother, and for a second or two he was lost within his thoughts of happier times before the realisation of the present came upon him like a great weight. With cold determination he replaced the frame on the mantle.

'I'll get the bastard for you, Jack' he whispered as he turned and headed back to the kitchen to find the coffee brewed in its pot. He poured two mugs and put powdered creamer in each before returning to the lounge.

Judy was already sitting down, and wearing one of Amy's dressing gowns. She had showered and was warming herself by the gas fire that she had lit. The shoulders of the dressing gown were streaked where her hair damp hair lay. She smiled as Hud handed her a coffee, apologising immediately for there being no real cream to whiten with.

'Maybe we should have phoned ahead, and let Amy know we would be staying here?' she jested.

'Listen, we'll have a few hours and then when I've gone in the morning you had better call her. Let her know you're here' said Hud.

Judy nodded, and they sat close drinking their coffee and staring at the flames of the fire before either spoke again. It was Judy who broke the silence.

'Hud?' she whispered.

He looked at her, staring deep into the blue of her eyes.

'What is it?' he asked, seeing the trouble she felt.

'Tomorrow, Hud. I mean, tonight. I mean...well, I don't really know what I mean' she said, not being able to put her fear for his safety into words.

'I'll be fine. It's going to be ok' he tried reassuring her but could see that it wasn't working.

Judy cupped her empty mug in her hands and stared at the fire once more. She looked at the ticking clock on the mantle, and then stood up.

'Hud, it's already tomorrow. Soon you'll be gone. Now might be the last time I see you.'

She held her hand out and led him upstairs, where they laid together while he held her in his arms and she drifted to sleep.

In time Hud too closed his eyes. When the sun rose he would have work to do.

Before then he needed to rest.

THIRTY TWO

Hud took the keys to Jack's Citroen C6 saloon from the drawer of the desk in his dead brother's study and tucked them into the pocket of his trousers. He looked around at the memories with which Jack had surrounded himself.

Black and white photographs of the two brothers as young boys adorned the wall facing the desk, telling the story of happier times when there were no wars, no political battles to be won or lost. Just two young boys playing on their bicycles, one a little older than the other and racing in front. Other pictures of the two attired in fancy dress, arms round each other's shoulders and with posed smiles beneath their false moustaches.

Then there were the pictures of the boys enjoying their chosen sports - football and rugby - as they got older, and moving on to their respective passing out parades: Jack with in mortar board and gown, and Hud on the parade ground in military dress.

The framed history of the two brothers' lives continued around the room and ended with a portrait of the older brother's successful ascension to the rank of cabinet minister, taking the viewer through marriages, christenings and funerals on the way.

Hud sat for a few minutes in silence, staring almost blankly across the expanse of their lives together and contemplating life now without his brother's guidance. There was an emptiness that he felt deep within him that he had never known before. A feeling of remorse and devastation which was only combated by the heat of anger that welled when he remembered who it was that had confessed to the murder of his brother. The egocentric turmoil created by his sadness and the simultaneous fury raged, and it took all his inner strength to remain aloof from his feelings.

But Hud realised that he needed to remain calm, to fight back his emotions. He understood the importance of focussing his energies and channelling his aggression toward a final goal, to see the whole picture and treat a stressful situation without emotion. He needed to stay cool in the heat of adversity, to stand back and observe and plan his attack. Just as he would on the battlefield. Just as he had done on so many occasions before.

He had stopped running from an unseen enemy.

The smell of coffee woke him from his trance: that and the soft touch of Judy's hand on his shoulder. She looked at him as he took the waiting mug from her, and then she looked around the room at the pictures which Hud had been studying just seconds earlier.

'I always loved this room, Hud' she said, mirroring Hud's feelings.

She stood close, close enough so that Hud could feel the heat of her body under her chemise, while they both took one last look at a previous life.

Hud stood and leaned close to kiss Judy on the cheek, before they walked through to the kitchen where Judy had prepared breakfast from the contents of the freezer.

They ate in silence, the cooked ham and croissants filling the spaces where conversation should have been. Hud could feel what Judy was too scared to say and so finally said it for her.

'I know it's a risk, what I'm doing. But it's the only way that I can possibly get out of this thing alive… that we can get out alive. And no, before you ask again, you can't come with me.'

'I know, Hud. But promise me you'll take care. Promise me you'll return. Say it like you used to' she pleaded.

Hud took a final swig of his coffee, draining the mug dry, and rose to his feet. He lifted the revolver that he had stolen from their guard the night before from the table and played with it in his right hand, releasing the magazine, checking the cartridges, and then replacing in the handle of the Heckler.

He walked across the kitchen to the rear door of the building before turning and speaking.

'I'll be back before you know it. I haven't done with looking into your eyes yet' he said, before winking, blowing her a kiss and then turning away to go to the garaged Citroen.

Judy was pleased that he still remembered how he had said goodbye every time they had parted. And how each time he had gone, he had returned safely. But she couldn't help thinking this time was different. This time he was on his own out there, he didn't have an army backing him up. This time it really was all or nothing. She looked at her watch before taking the dirty plates to the sink to wash.

It was nearly midday.

It was time for Judy to phone Amy and let her know that both she and Hud were safe, and to explain that they were using her house to hide away for a while. Hud had suggested that she call when he had left, knowing that the conversation with her best friend would take her mind temporarily away from what Hud was about to do.

As she lifted the phone and dialled Amy's mobile number, Judy watched Hud disappear down the drive in Jack's Citroen and at the end of the cul-de-sac turn left toward central Paris. Then he was gone, and Judy found herself speaking to Amy.

Amy sounded confused, and certainly surprised to hear that Judy was in Paris and had broken into Jack and Amy's French house. Amy spoke in a staccato voice as she arranged to come to the big house.

'Look, Judy, I'm in Paris... I couldn't take the intrusion anymore. The press... it's awful... what they are saying about Hud.

'I needed to get away. And so I came here. I stayed at a hotel last night, and was coming to the house for a few days. I'll be there a little later.

'I'll see you soon' she finished.

Judy was pleased that she would not be alone, and began busying herself in the kitchen trying to keep her mind from wandering to thoughts of Hud. Soon Amy would be with her and they would console each other.

Judy poured herself another black coffee, and walked through to the lounge flicking the television on as she passed. She sat and tuned into France 24.

The flight of the murderous fugitive from England was now the biggest news in France, and was overshadowing even the signing of the new European Treaty.

As she waited for Amy to come, Judy watched the screen in front of her. She knew that any news of Hud would appear on the French news channel first, before being aired around the world.

While Judy was on the phone to Amy, Hud continued his drive to Paris, taking care to observe the speed restrictions and watching for any sign of being followed although he thought it would be unlikely. Anyone searching for him would be concentrating efforts on locating a couple in a white box van, and would not be suspecting a single man in a dark blue Citroen.

At Jack's Hud had been able to sleep, eat and shower, and now felt more refreshed than he had for days. He wore Jack's clothes, and thanked good genetics for the similarity in build between the two brothers. The white collar of a well pressed shirt overhung the neckline of a navy blue sweater which complimented his dark trousers. His pistol was tucked in the rear of the waistband, and he could feel the cold metal pressing through the tail of the shirt as he sat upright with both hands on the steering wheel, taking directions from the car's integrated satellite navigation system.

It did not take long through the thin Sunday traffic to reach his destination, and he was soon parked on the Rue des Nations Unies looking at the multi storey block ahead of him. The building was granite grey to the front, and sand coloured blocks at the side, with various slogans in French, English, and Arabic in bold white lettering upon the huge expanse of sheet glass that hid the workers behind.

One slogan caught Hudson's eye immediately: "Au-dela de L'informatio" translated into English as "Beyond the News". Which is exactly where he wanted to find himself today.

The building seemed quiet, and beyond the entrance Hud could see there was a solitary security guard on the front desk, doubling as reception clerk. Giant television screens sat silently flickering their news in the adjacent windows, and above the broad entrance sat a glass tube that rose from the first floor to the top of the building, giving the edifice its uniqueness.

Hud readied himself to take the security guard, moving his pistol to the front of his waist as he slipped out of the car's seatbelt. He looked first one way and then the other along the street, ensuring that there were no pedestrians to spy his movements. When he had satisfied himself that he was alone in the street, he opened the car door and stepped across to the entrance, announcing himself to the guard as he entered through the large swing door.

"Ah Bonjour, Monsieur,' he said, striding briskly toward the front desk, 'Ou est Monsieur Gerrard?' he asked thinking of the first name that entered his head.

The guard looked up at Hudson approaching, before looking down at the screen in front of him, searching for a Monsieur Gerrard.

Before he could react, Hudson had vaulted the desk. As he did so he bought his left heel crashing into the temple of the guard, who reeled backwards as his chair toppled to the ground under his weight. Hudson rose to his haunches waiting for the response, but none came. The guard was out cold.

Hudson ripped the telephone cable from the back of the switchboard console and away from the floor box to which it fed using it to tie the guard's hands behind him, before then rolling the guard under the desk and out of site and replacing the chair in its upright position.

He looked around the lobby from his crouched position, and at the same time played with the mouse that controlled the camera views available to the guard on the four screens that sat in their own miniature plinths atop the desk. Hud could see that on Sunday the building operated with a skeleton staff, and was able to see that the main desks were located on the fourth floor. The lack of staff suited his purposes perfectly. He was about to give France 24 a world exclusive, and the fewer people to hamper his exit, the better.

Before making his way to the elevators across the atrium, Hudson removed the bunch of keys from the unconscious guard and placed them in his pocket. He pressed the lift call button, which immediately illuminated a fluorescent blue, and the journey of the elevator was confirmed by the changing pitch of the whirring motor echoing in the lift shaft as the elevator car sprang to life.

He travelled upwards until the opening of the doors signalled the elevator's arrival at its destination. Satisfying himself that no one was paying attention to the elevator's client, he used one of the keys that he had taken from the guard on the ground floor to disable the lift. With the butt end of his revolver he broke the key in the lock so that the lift could not be reactivated.

In front of him was a narrow corridor that led to the rear of the building, glass walls separating the passageway from the newsrooms beyond. He could see that most were empty, even though the monitors that would normally be manned by a plethora of researchers and analysts flickered their readiness for work underneath the tube lighting of their individual cubicles.

Hudson could see a cameraman behind a lens at the far end of the right hand office, where a lone newsreader sat reading from an autocue. Behind the newsreader sat a half dozen researchers trying to look busy. Hudson knew that much of the news broadcast on a Sunday lunchtime would be a rehash of the week's major items, rather than any new news. He walked the corridor to the office door, and swinging it open he pointed the barrel of his revolver toward the newscaster. The camera pivoted round to point at him, as he spoke.

'Arretez vous!' he commanded the reader to halt his work.

The newsreader stopped, mouth agape, before starting to rise. When he spotted the pistol pointing in his direction he fell silent, raised his hands and regained his seated position. The colour drained from him as Hud spoke.

'Do you speak English?' he asked.

The newsreader sat silently, with his arms still raised. Behind him the researchers had realised what was occurring, and had ducked behind their desks. Hud repeated his question again, this time with more urgency in his voice.

'Oui! Yes, I speak English!' the newsreader answered, perhaps forced by the threatening waving of the pistol in front of his face.

'Good!' exclaimed Hud. 'What's your name?'

'Maurice Le Verne' came the reply.

'Well, Morris,' said Hud, deliberately using the English pronunciation, 'I want you to tell all those people back there to come and stand behind the cameraman here' he pointed with his gun.

As the newsreader repeated Hud's instructions in French, the four male and one female researchers made their way slowly to the front of the studio and then beyond the camera which by now was capturing the whole scene, panning back and forth.

Hud knew that it would only be a matter of minutes before the studios were surrounded, and so hurried the proceedings along shouting 'faster' and 'move', which Maurice translated in a panic to his colleagues.

When everyone was in the position he wanted, he took a seat beside Maurice and told the newscaster to translate as he spoke. All the while, Hudson kept the revolver deliberately in sight of the camera and the watching audience, and continually pointed at his new best friend, Maurice the newsreader.

'Although I have dark hair, I am sure you all recognise the man on your television screens. For those of you who have been on another planet for the last week, my name is Peter Hudson.

'I am here today to tell you why I had no choice but to murder my brother, Jack – the UK Foreign Minister – and a man that was subsequently found in my apartment in London. I am also responsible for the death of a man on the streets of Paris in a car accident, and also have murdered the ex-detective Claude Duval, who, as I speak, lies in a pool of his own blood in his home here in Paris.

'I had no choice in these murders. All of these men, and others besides, were trying to stop the work I have been undertaking.

'And now it is time that I told you of the work of which I speak.'

Maurice struggled to keep pace with Hud's words, but Hudson did not slow. He was on a roll, and had rehearsed this speech over and over in his head. He had to make it plausible, and part of that believability was to force the translator to rush. So that the words Hud spoke did not sound fake, but as if he were shooting from the hip. He carried on, paying little heed to the struggling translator, all the time keeping his revolver pointed closely and in camera at Maurice.

'When I first toured Iraq with the British Army in the first Gulf War, I struck a friendship with a man named Omar Ali bin Akhbar. He showed me the futility of our ways in the West, how our decadence and capitalism is against the way of Allah. We hold material possessions above the morals of our children and ourselves, and it is now time that Jihad cleansed Europe of our Western corruption.

'Those that have died at my hands have given themselves for our cause, for they knew not what they were doing when they threatened to expose the Jihad they learned of.

'Now it is time to let the people of Europe know, the day of judgement is upon you all. Through the holy war we wage, we will cleanse the souls of your politicians.

The lawmakers that degrade the name of Allah will pay the price, and their sins will be absolved.

'My brothers of Islam and I have taken the measures to ensure that now, once and for all, the final day of reckoning has come upon the infidels.

'Your governments will be destroyed within their seats of power. Across the whole of Europe, bloodshed will wash away the sins of the people. And Allah will descend to show you the way.

'The unholy Union of Europe will be cleansed in one day of judgement. A day that Allah has given to my brothers and I to take away the sins of your people.

'And the whole of Islam will rejoice come Wednesday, for the day of judgement will have passed. And you will have seen the error of your ways, and we will have taken the war mongers away from this world, and sent them to the next in absolution.

'Your parliaments will be no longer, and Allah will come to you and prepare all the peace loving people of Europe for the path to righteousness.

'Praise be to Allah!'

As he roared the last sentence, Hud spent two rounds into the ceiling, plaster falling on the watching researchers who sheltered close to the floor.

He could see by the look on their faces, his words had struck a ring of truth with those that were cowering behind the camera. He hoped that the watching audience in their homes would feel the same fear.

He guessed that France 24 would spin the tapes out to other channels around the world. There would be analysis of the tapes, and experts would be called upon to give their witness to the authenticity of his words. There would be a clamour from the public demanding that bombs be found and disabled.

This is what Hud hoped would happen. Now all he could do would be to hide and wait.

He heard sirens approaching outside.

He needed to move fast.

Without hesitation he pulled Maurice up by the collar, still with the gun at his temple. He pushed his way past the timid crowd of researchers and made for the stairs next to the elevator, pushing the newscaster ahead of him as he went.

Maurice was calling not to be shot, and moved in terror, taking the stairs two steps at a time. They reached the bottom and Maurice fell to his knees, begging for mercy.

Hudson looked at him, and realised how weak civilians were. He leant in and spoke calmly.

'When they get here, tell them that the first to go up in smoke will be the home of your National Assembly. Do you understand?' he quizzed.

After his captive had answered feebly in the affirmative, Hud told him to crouch with his back to him. He ran out the building and gunned the C6 away as sirens approached from the opposite direction. Now he needed to get away as quickly as possible, and then lay low until nightfall.

And he knew exactly where to head, where he needed to be.

Behind him he heard the melee of police cars screeching to a halt and imagined the France 24 building being surrounded by armed gendarmes, each hoping that they would be France's new hero, the one who captured Peter Hudson.

What Hudson needed now was to find the evidence necessary to get himself out of the hole he had dug himself, and put Mark Chatfield firmly in it. The only place he could think he might find such evidence was where he now headed.

He needed to get back into the Paris headquarters of Schengen: only this time not as a prisoner. For the first time Hudson felt the momentum was running with him.

It felt good to be in control.

THIRTY THREE

Hudson parked the car tight and close between two large vans in the side street adjacent to the rear entrance where Chatfield had taken him and Judy. It took him several attempts and a lot of to-ing and fro-ing, but he was satisfied that from the main street his brother's car could not be seen.

Although it had not been long since his intrusion into the France 24 building, he could not be sure that the pictures of him holding a newscaster at gunpoint would not already be feeding to terrestrial television. And so, in some semblance of disguise, he pulled a Paris St Germain baseball cap as far down his forehead as he could.

He rifled the glove compartment and took out the service manual in its black leather binder, and made sure that his pistol was safely secreted in his waistband before leaving the car and heading round to the front of the Schengen headquarters.

When there he found the large dark oak door firmly closed, but fingered the buzzer. He kept his head bowed so as not to give himself away to the closed circuit camera that sat above and to the left of the doorway. He buzzed a second time before an impatient voice answered.

'Oui. Qu il y a?' the unseen voice asked who was there.

Hudson answered in French.

'Un pacquet pour un Monsieur Chatfiield' he held the leather binder up in the air as he spoke.

The line went quiet, before the concierge's voice replied telling him to wait a minute.

'Attendre une minute, s'il vous plait.'

Hud clenched his hand around the handle of his revolver as the heavy door was unbolted from within, and the door creaked open slowly. The guard had his back slightly toward Hud with the exertion of pushing the door open, and unseen was smashed over the back of the head with the butt end of the pistol. He fell to the floor in a crumpled heap, and Hud stepped over him to get off the street before pulling the guard back and closing the door behind him.

He waited, his back pressed against the door and breathing heavily for a few seconds, before moving further into the foyer. He trussed up the guard with telephone cable before walking up the stairs to search the building, pacing softly along the carpeted floors, and checking each office separately before closing its door and moving on.

When satisfied he was alone he returned to the ground floor where the guard was coming round. Hud held a finger vertically over his lips to tell the guard to make no noise, before gagging him with his own tie. He took the keys from his belt and tried them in the lock of Chatfield's office.

None worked. He would have to find another way in. He looked around the door feeling with his fingers as he did so, but the frame was solid steel, and the door flush to the edge. It would be incredibly difficult to crow bar, so he searched higher looking at the ceiling above.

He pulled a chair over and stood on it so that he could reach the tiled ceiling with the butt of his pistol. He tapped around, and where the ceiling took a step down with the contour of the underlying floor, the tapping turned from a dull thud to a baritone echo. He had found his way in.

He left his vantage point and moved behind the lobby desk and into the room beyond where the desk clerks would take their breaks. There he found a couple of metal legged chairs, a filing cabinet which had seen better days, and a half eaten ham baguette upon a rickety old table. A typical rest room for front desk security, the opulence of the lobby hiding the monkish décor reserved for a company's menial employees.

He opened the top drawer of the filing cabinet, and rummaged through its belongings but finding nothing of any use. He continued searching through each drawer, top to bottom, with each more difficult to wrench open than the one before. Finally he came to the lowest drawer which dragged across the stone floor as he pulled it open, making a scratching noise like fingernails against a chalkboard that sent sharp sensations from his teeth through his jaw.

He pulled the contents out of the rusty steel tray with a harshness that belied his increasing anxiety. Finally he found what he was looking for amongst the various small hand tools that he knew all security guards kept at hand. He picked the claw hammer from its hiding place and returned to the chair in front of Chatfield's office.

The security guard was still where he had left him, hidden from view behind his desk, bound and gagged.

He looked uncomfortable, and Hud remembered how he had felt when in a similar position in the building's cellar. Still, he could take no chances and this innocent bystander would have to remain tied.

He took the claw of the hammer and with a wild swing he dug it into the gypsum ceiling. Two swings later and he had made a hole big enough to get the entire claw through. He levered downwards, using his weight as counter, and the board began to crack. Pieces broke free as he repeated the exercise several times over before then using his hands to complete a rough circular hole big enough for him to fit head and shoulders in. He pushed his head into the void, and looked around.

There were wires and cables within the gap moving in all directions, some toward the office he needed to gain access to which disappeared under what looked like a solid wall. He squeezed his arm through with the hammer gripped tightly in his hand, and tapped against this wall. It gave a little as he did so, and so he hit harder. The hammer had pierced the board, but had hit something soft beyond.

He pulled himself from the hole in the ceiling, and began to rip away at the board above him with his hands, until finally there was a hole that extended three or four feet in circumference and Hud could see the false wall above Chatfield's office door.

He worked the hammer into the small hole he had previously made and began picking out a mustard yellow polystyrene foam that he recognised as soundproofing. It was hard work with his arms above his head, finger nails digging away along with the hammer's claw. A sweat began to build, the saltiness running into his eyes.

Several times he rested for a few seconds, willing the lactose that had built up in his elbows to dissipate, and taking water on board from the security guard's unfinished luncheon. By the time he had dug a hole large enough for him to fit through, the once immaculate lobby more resembled a building site. Pieces of plaster board lay strewn on the dust covered floor, and surrounded by small bricks of the yellow foam. Hud's hair had turned from dyed black to the salt and pepper of an ageing man, and he now stood with bare torso and breathing heavily from the effort of the previous hour, contemplating his next move.

Climbing on the chair once more, he stretched his arms upwards and hauled himself into the small space that he had created. Resting his chest on the concrete joist that sat above the office door, he swung his legs up and over. The space was tight, and he could not get a great deal of force into his kicks as he bought his feet down repeatedly onto the plaster that sat above Chatfield's office. Time and time again he tried until eventually his foot went through, the swinging motion dragging his body through the hole after it, as he crashed into the office below. As he fell he gripped the edge of the wall, so that he hung there suspended with his feet banging against the inside of the heavy door. Letting go he fell the few inches remaining, landing softly on the plush axminster carpet below.

He felt for the light switch in the darkness, and when he located it with his fingertips he allowed his eyes to adjust to the ensuing brightness, before turning to see the red leather furniture that he had previously only seen on the screen in the room below. The room was how he remembered, the sofa and chairs in the middle and around a coffee table, with a work desk toward the rear of the space.

Upon the desk a map of Europe sat open. Hudson walked over to examine the chart, and noticed each capital city had been marked. He sat where Mark Chatfield usually sat and looked around, wondering where to begin.

He looked around the office, admiring the deep oak panelling and white marbled walls. Every inch of the office screamed "success". But Hud knew that this success was false, built on lies, deceit, and corruption. Success that had been paid for by bribery and murder. The murder of his brother included. And Duval.

He palmed the remote control for the television screens and pressed the standby button. All six monitors flashed their obedience, coming to life as one. And on all six screens Hud saw himself, holding a gun to an innocent newscaster's head. Then on one screen the picture changed to the Palais Bourbon, surrounded by French Police, and cordoned off to the public.

He looked again at the trappings of Schengen's success. Now that success would start unravelling, and Peter Hudson wanted to ensure that Mark Chatfield paid the price for his crimes. Without evidence, there was nothing to associate Chatfield or Schengen to the widespread carnage that would be seen to be Al Queda led. It would be Hudson that would pay the price.

He started by breaking open the lock to the drawers in Chatfield's desk. He guessed that any important documents would be close at hand, and he wasn't disappointed. In the top drawer, Hudson found his brother's file. He flipped through the pages, to find it intact.

It was a start, but he needed more.

There was the map that lay still open on the desk

which, although it had various markings on depicting the capitals where bombs had been placed, would not be conclusive evidence.

He rifled through more drawers and cupboards, and when half way through came to the drinks cabinet. There in front of him sat a full bottle of southern comfort, next to a half finished bottle of Cardhu whiskey. He picked the bottle up, and held it in his hand. He had not had a drink for days, since he and Judy had been alone in her room at the George V. He suddenly felt the craving for the buzz that a shot of alcohol would give him.

Just the one.

He spun the top of the bottle, and placed the lip of the neck to his lips. It smelt good.

Then he thought of Judy.

Of how she hated his drinking, and what it had done to them.

He replaced the cap on the bottle, screwing it as tight as he could, and placed it back in the cabinet. He looked long and hard before closing the door and confining the bottles to the darkness of their hiding place.

Strangely, he felt good about himself. Stronger. He felt more complete, more able to face a world that had been turned upside down.

He continued cracking open locked drawers and cabinets before arriving at one which had been padlocked. He levered the lock off with the claw hammer.

Inside were hanging files, all in manila and each one an inch or more thick. They were labelled by country, and placed in alphabetical order.

He lifted the one labelled France, and spread it on the desk.

Inside were lists of names: police, politicians, celebrities, military generals...the list went on, each with a paragraph or more detailing responsibilities in the new order. He ran his finger down the list until he came to the one name that he knew was connected to Schengen: Rousset. He read the paragraphs that followed with some interest.

"Rousset, Jacques. Prefect of Police, Paris.

"Aided by planted evidence, and information leading to the whereabouts of several art dealers with artefacts lost during the Second World War. Arrest and conviction rate led to rapid promotion, finally promoted to Prefect when his predecessor died in a fatal car accident (Schengen, MC).

"Good, loyal servant to become Head of Homeland Security in France."

This was exactly the evidence that Hudson was searching for. Evidence that would prove Chatfield's association with murder. Evidence that would prove beyond doubt the existence of Schengen, and the power that it possessed in Europe.

He took the files from the cabinet and arranged them in neat piles on the coffee table in the middle of the room. He placed the open map on top, and stuffed his brother's file in the back of his waistband before pulling a chair across so that he could lever himself back through the hole in the ceiling that had been his point of entry.

Once he had put his shirt and sweater back on, he went over to the guard that had clearly been struggling to break free from his binds. His wrists were chaffed red raw, and his shirt was damp with sweat. Hud leaned forward to him, and removed his gag. He made no sound, but lay with a look of terror on his face as Hudson pointed his revolver at him.

'Poor guy. Mixed up in this, all so you can earn an honest living. What a shame your employers don't do the same thing.'

Hudson looked at his watch. It was almost eight in the evening, and the light would be fading outside. He walked to the main entrance and opened the door carefully.

The street outside was deserted. He strode back toward the guard who cowered away, hugging the wall behind. Hudson lent over him and placed a hand against the wall, toying with his pistol in the other. Fear erupted across the guard's face as Hud bought the arm that held the gun swiftly down.

Bells started ringing as soon as the glass casing of the emergency button smashed.

It was the second time that Hud had caused a fire alarm to sound during his stay in Paris. The first had been to mask his escape from the George V. This time it was to bring the emergency services to rescue a timid guard, and a certain amount of evidence from a locked office.

Hud smiled to himself as he pulled away from the kerbside. Soon he would be back at Amy's house, and the hell that he and Judy had lived through the past few days would be over.

THIRTY FOUR

The journey to his hideaway at Jack's house had been largely uneventful, and Hud had amused himself by flicking from one channel to another on the stereo radio of the Citroen as he drove. The airwaves were awash with the latest news from Paris, and Maurice the newscaster was basking in his fifteen minutes of fame.

A great swath of central Paris had been cordoned off from the public as the authorities searched for the fugitive, and Hud had found it necessary to take a detour wide and south before cutting back across the Seine at the Pont d'Austerlitz.

Once he had negotiated the higgledy-piggledy side streets of the West Bank, Hud had found the remainder of his journey to be plain sailing. He arrived in the North East Parisian suburbs where Judy would be waiting for him a little more than half an hour after he had left the ringing fire alarm at Schengen's Headquarters.

News of Hudson's exploits was just beginning to filter through the now regular bulletins, and it was now being reported that Peter Hudson had left a security guard tied and hurt in an office building in the Rue Paul Valery. Police had now cordoned this area in their frantic search for the murderer who had also become a terrorist suspect.

His appearance in the News 24 studios had stirred up something of a hornet's nest, and Interpol was now managing a hive of security activity across Paris. As he pulled into the Elm lined street where his brother's French residence stood, Hudson's head swum with the power that his actions had wielded. It seemed as if every police officer across the city was involved in the hunt and capture operation, whilst anti-terrorist teams had been rushed to the National Assembly with their sniffer dogs and bomb disposal equipment.

His plan, which he had concocted in his own mind whilst he had been driving the box van some hours earlier, had begun to work. Hud knew that in this day and age of uncertainty, no one was willing to take a risk with national – and international – security.

He needed now to return to hiding, to hope that the evidence he had uncovered after stealing into Chatfield's office would be found by uncorrupted officers, and that he would be found to be innocent of the crimes to which he had falsely confessed on international television. He now realised what it was that Judy was so scared of. What if the evidence was buried? What if no one believed the real truth?

He sat with the Citroen's engine ticking over almost silently, once more watching the large house at the end of the street in the darkness, knowing that he needed to get off the street and to the sanctuary where Judy would be waiting for him. He felt the strong urge to take himself immediately to where he could talk to her before handing himself in, and putting his trust in justice.

But something held him back. His instinct told him it wasn't safe.

He looked down at the file he had placed on the passenger seat. The file that had ultimately cost his brother his life, and that had dragged him and Judy into the chaos of the last few days. He cursed it, and yet at the same time he knew it could be the difference between survival and demise. It was the paperwork on which his innocence would be based.

He wiped the mist from his windscreen with the back of his hand, an arc of clear glass appearing through which he now peered. Something seemed wrong to him.

Hud killed the engine and sat alone in the darkness. Outside the wind blew, and the tall Elms creaked their resistance. The sky was dark with thick clouds that threatened rain speeding across the night, and the house that Hud watched sat still and dark.

Then a light as the front door opened and two figures first appeared - one slightly in front of the other - and then disappeared with the closing of the door behind them.

Hud sat motionless for what seemed like a lifetime, but in fact was just moments before the darkness was pierced once more, this time by the headlamps of a car speeding away from the house, down the drive and into the road. He ducked out of sight as it hurtled past, a blur of chrome and black picked out only by its own lights.

Hud watched in his rear view mirror as the crimson rear lights faded in the distance.

Judy!

He turned his attention back to the house in front of him. He needed to get in, and fast.

If anything had happened to her! She had been right, he should have allowed her to travel to Paris with him. How could he have been so stupid?

His heart beat fast, his breath shallow as he fired the car to action and floored the accelerator. The wheels screeched against the tarmac as rubber burnt from the tyres. He skidded down the gravel drive, coming to a sharp halt in front of the house and sprinting from the C6 to the front door.

He pounded his fists violently on the solid wood, not caring for his own safety but only concerned about Judy. Why had he left her alone in this house?

He stopped and listened. Nothing. The silence was agonising. He bent low and peered through the letterbox.

Beyond the light of the hall, he could see a body lying motionless. He called through and looked again. Once more, nothing. No sound back, no movement. He cursed himself, his brother, but most of all he cursed Mark Chatfield, as his feet pounded against the gravel and then the lawn on his way to the rear of the house.

He tried the door. Locked.

He hit the glass hard with his elbow, shards falling to the floor within, and he pushed his hand through the hole and turned the key that was in the lock on the inside.

He moved quickly through the house to where she lay, face down, tied and gagged. He turned her over and staggered back with the shock.

It wasn't Judy who looked back at him. It was Amy. He came quickly to his senses and worked fast on her gag.

'Amy! Judy? Where is she? What are you doing here? What happened?' he fired questions at her as his hands struggled with the knots that held her, and his mind struggled with her presence.

'He took her! Hud, I'm sorry…We…we didn't stand a chance. He was on us before we could do anything' tears collected in her eyes as she spoke.

Hud held Amy close, to comfort her before continuing. He asked the next question, knowing the answer before he spoke.

'Who took her, Amy? Who?'

'I thought he was your friend, Hud?' she asked straight back.

"Mark Chatfield!" thought Hud, anger rising inside him.

'Where, Amy? Where have they gone?' he asked in desperation.

'Hud, he said that you had ruined everything for him. That he would make you pay. What is he going to do Hud? What's this all about?' she screamed, hysteria taking hold.

Hudson shook his sister-in-law by the shoulders, begging her to be calm.

'Amy, think! Where? Did he give any clues?' he asked, hope sounding in his voice. He would never forgive himself if Chatfield harmed Judy.

Amy went still, looking in Hud's eyes, trying in vain to remember something, anything, that would lead them to Chatfield. Then finally she spoke.

'Schengen!' she screamed at Hudson.

'He said something about taking her to "Schengen", wherever that is. He said that the Director would know what to do! Hud, what does he mean?' she asked, confusion in her eyes.

He didn't answer, but grabbed her by the hand and led her to the Citroen waiting on the driveway outside.

'Get in' he told her. 'I'll explain on the way'

He started the car and roared away from the house, in the direction that minutes earlier his one time friend Mark Chatfield had driven with Judy. As he neared the end of the road he popped the glove compartment open.

'Take the map book out, Amy. Look for Schengen in the index. It's a small town near the borders of France and Germany. Where they both meet with Luxembourg. That's where we need to get to: that's where Chatfield is heading.'

She did as he told her, and having found it started navigating taking them first east toward Reims and then through the open countryside of Eastern France and on to Luxembourg.

Amy did not talk much, but concentrated on navigating whilst Hud had to work hard not to travel above the speed limit. The last thing he wanted was to be stopped by French motor cops. Even though he had to make good time, giving a lucky break to a cop behind a wheel was not on his agenda.

And so they drove much of the route in silence, although Hud did manage to find that Amy was in France to escape the media attention she was receiving back home. He didn't blame her for that, and promised to return with her for his brother's funeral.

They stopped once to refuel, and for Amy to freshen up a little. She bought two hot coffees back to the car, for which Hud was grateful. The exertions of the past days were starting to take their toll on him, and he drove the rest of the way with the window down, which played havoc with the map spread across Amy's legs - although she managed exceptionally well. She explained to Hud that her and Jack used to drive the route often, taking the opportunity to spend weekends in Luxembourg when spending the summer Parliamentary recess in Paris.

By the early hours of Monday morning they were at their destination. Their arrival at the small town of Schengen was heralded by the monument to the Schengen Treaty, three rectangular rusted steel obelisks each with an opaque gold star in its cavity, and sitting alongside a grey circular cobbled area with stone stars set within. The Moselle River ran fast and deep next to the monument, and as they drove over the nearby bridge a row of sand coloured houses with black slate roofs came into view. In the distance a church spire broke above the horizon lit by the lunar orb that now shone brightly in the clearing sky. They stopped halfway across the bridge, the sound of the engine running disturbing a town asleep.

'Where do we go now?' asked Hud of his companion.

She shrugged.

'Drive around?' she asked. 'There must be a clue somewhere. Its got to be a large estate, off the road perhaps' she offered, more hopefully than with certainty.

And so they drove, slowly in and out of the town examining any likely looking estate. Dawn was slowly breaking, the sun was starting to poke its head above the hills, when Hud stopped in front of a gated entrance that they had passed a half dozen times already.

There was something familiar about the great stone columns that held the gate in place that Hud had noticed before but not paid a great deal of attention to. He sat there with the engine buzzing, and his head doing the same as he racked his memory trying to recall the insignia. Then it came to him.

This was it. This was where Chatfield had taken Judy. He was certain.

'This is the place' he said to Amy, with assurance.

'How do you know?' asked his passenger.

'I just know' he said, staring at the crest carved into the red stone and picked out in black.

He had never seen the insignia before, but was familiar with it. He remembered the description of the St Andrews cross with the arrowheads that Judy had described to him: the tattoo that had been emblazoned on the neck of her attacker back at Hud's apartment in London.

The same tattoo that Judy had also seen on Mark Chatfield's neck.

He knew that inside the chateau beyond the iron gates he would find Chatfield and Donat. He knew that Judy would also be there.

He hoped that she would still be alive.

THIRTY FIVE

The pair took themselves out of the car and climbed over the locked gate. Hud knew that they would have to approach carefully, and took his pistol in his hand as they walked crouching low to the hedge, so keeping out of sight of the guard standing in the portico of the mansion at the end of the winding driveway.

The chateau stood square and erect, like a castle standing sentry to its surrounding land, its building blocks carved from granite centuries before.

On the ground floor were the trappings of refurbishment, large balustraded windows with leaded detail above ornate beds of sun-coloured daffodils and magenta gerbora.

Balconies adorned each of the shuttered windows on the first floor, whilst the four semi-circular turrets that marked each corner of the fortress remained with their small windows which once would have been used by archers within to repeal the feudal Lord's enemies.

There was a crispness in the early morning air which made their breath form small tornadoes of mist before spiralling upwards and evaporating in the half moonlit void, as they strode silently toward the house. The hoot of a tawny owl cut through the mist, her call resonating through the wooded land beyond their quest where the guard stood motionless and coming more sharply into focus as they approached with stealth.

Hud signalled for Amy to stay still and low behind him as he listened to agitated voices that drifted from inside the house. The guard paid no attention to the arguments from within, preferring to take the opportunity afforded by the preoccupation of his master to light a cigarette. He took a deep drag before looking skywards to expel the smoke. As he held the butt by his side in between his thumb and forefinger, Hud saw the sub-machine gun that hung from his shoulder.

He was close now, perhaps less than ten yards away, but not close enough to make his play. Amy was some way back, resting on her haunches. It would have been easy to shoot the guard, but that would have alerted the occupants to the presence of danger. No, he had to find another way. Before he had time to think, Amy was almost upon him striding purposefully toward the guard, heels crunching on the drive, and speaking in rapid monologue. Hud had forgotten how fluent her French was.

The sentry seemed taken aback, moving toward Amy as if commanded to do so. Within moments he was face to face with Amy, having stubbed his cigarette under the leather of his boot, and with his hand on the butt of his gun.

Hud moved instinctively, hurdling the hedgerow and lunging at the startled guard. In his hand he held a rock that he had gathered from the ground which had made his hiding place, and he now bought the heavy flint up and across the chin of his foe. Blood sprayed up as skin was torn, the guard immediately lifted off his feet by the force of the blow and falling back.

Hud was on him like a man possessed, and rained blows to his chiselled features until the man lay limp, his face swollen and bloodied.

Hudson ripped the gun from the guard's shoulder, and threw the strap over his head.

He looked at Amy, who stood in shock. He wanted to tell her how stupid she had been, but there was no time. They had to move quickly. He placed his hand on her arm, and asked her in a whisper if she was all right. She nodded, with fear in her eye but also a gritty resolve. Hud didn't have to think about giving her a weapon. Although she had executed a move that could have backfired terribly, she had shown she was a brave woman who was prepared to die to help save Judy. He took his pistol from the back of his waistband, and handed it to her.

'Let's go' he commanded.

She followed Hud, who hung low as he moved across and under the window. From inside he could still hear the argument continuing between the two men, unaware of the impending attack.

They crept round to the back of the chateau, where Hud tried the iron handle of the stable door that opened to a large area used for the dirty boots and outer garments that might be worn by country gentlemen as they walked their estate. The door opened smoothly, and Hud led Amy through the darkened rooms and corridors of the chateau toward the light and noise in the room at the front.

When they reached their quarry, they stood outside the large oak door that separated them from the room beyond. A shaft of light spread from the crack at its base, and shadows passing back and forth complimented the aggravated pacing of one of its inhabitants. From the sound of the pacer's voice, Hud could hear that it was Chatfield who was the more emotional of the two men.

'Director, this was the only way! You've seen for yourself the news of the break-in at our offices in Paris. You know that I too am now a hunted man, and that our plans are blown.

'Our only hope is to take Hudson and pin everything on him.

'In the meantime, much of the Schengen's wealth has already been transferred to safe numbered accounts in Switzerland as you instructed us to do before the planned attacks tomorrow.

'We can rebuild. The empire is not lost!' Chatfield was clearly on the back foot, and Hudson felt good at hearing that Mark had lost the arrogance and confidence that he had exuded just forty eight hours earlier in the basement in Paris.

He kept his ear to the door as an older voice answered in steadier more considered language.

'And so your big plan now is to bring your tormentor here, to my home. And to do so you use this woman as bait.

'You have desecrated my house by bringing her here.

'You have jeopardised my safety, my wellbeing. In one week you have put at risk decades of my work.

'You have failed the memory of your father, and the fatherland.

'How can I trust you to put right the mistakes that you have made?'

'He will come, Director. I am sure of it. The only thing that he has ever really cared about is Judy. He will want to be the hero, to save her.

'And when I have him, I will crush him in the palm of my hand. We will rise once more, with greater speed and sense of purpose than ever before. The Fuhrer's prophecy will come to bear. Europe, under our guidance will be all powerful.'

The footsteps came closer to the door, and Hud braced himself for attack. He heard Chatfield close, as the door handle moved downwards.

'Now, Director, with your permission, I must go and prepare for his arrival.' It was a statement rather than a request for leave, and as he spoke the light from the room flooded the hallway as the door opened.

Chatfield stood no more than a foot away, framed by the doorway, eyes wide at the sight of Hudson before him. He fell back landing with a thud against the stone floor, the blow from the butt of the sub machine gun falling heavy into his chest.

Hudson entered the room, standing with the sole of his right boot firmly on Chatfield's beating breastbone and the barrel of the gun threatening to explode in his face. He surveyed the room, eyes moving from one corner to the next before returning to study his captive.

Judy sat bound to a wooden captain's chair in the middle of the room, gagged so that she couldn't speak. But she was alive, and the look in her eyes told Hud that she was fine. He would release her soon, but first needed to deal with Chatfield and the Director.

The furniture was black leather and oak, the stone floor a deep crimson. In the middle of the far wall was a fireplace big enough to stand in. Logs gathered from the estate stood piled in a pyramid on one side of the hearth, and in the centre the firepit glowed with the embers of burnt wood.

Handcrafted casing carried books along the adjacent wall. Books that paid homage to the greatest emperors and warmongers the world has ever seen: books that told the life stories of the like of Genghis Khan, Napoleon, Alexander the Great, and Hitler. Tomes that played out the lifetimes of the British, French, German, and Roman empires accompanied the biographical entrances.

The walls were adorned with portraits of people that Hudson recognised from his brother's file: Doenitz, Jodl, and Keitel. In pride of place was a likeness of their beloved Fuhrer, Adolf Hitler himself.

Lit by the single bulb burning brightly under a reflective shade hanging from the ceiling, and in a wheelchair behind a great oak desk near the fireplace, sat a wizened old man: Pierre Donat. Less commonly known as Klaus Doenitz. Although much older than the only photograph of him he had seen, Hud recognised the harsh eyes and square jaw of the face that had been circled in red in attendance at Karl Doenitz's funeral.

The Director.

The man who had, with the help of his Father before his death and unbeknown to millions, steered Europe on the course it had taken since the end of the Second World War. A course that would soon have seen the creation of an Empire, the Fourth Reich.

The man who - days earlier - had stood on the edge of ultimate power, but now stared into the abyss of dishonourable failure and financial ruin – all thanks to the man that now held him and Chatfield at gunpoint. He now spoke to Hud, with an air of authority that the situation did not confer upon him.

'Ah, Mister Hudson, how nice of you to drop by. Mister Chatfield and I have been expecting you.

'Although we have never met, I believe that I do not need to introduce myself: I understand that your brother, the dear and recently departed Jack Hudson, made it somewhat of a mission of his to discover my identity. An unhealthy interest that ultimately cost him his life.'

Hud considered his answer for a few seconds before speaking. He was in the driving seat, and he was sure as hell going to let his host know that fact.

'Herr Doenitz, the pleasure of our meeting is all mine. As I am certain that Mr Chatfield has informed you, it is as a direct consequence of my brother's work and his subsequent misfortune – for which your colleague here will pay the price – that we meet in such unfortunate circumstances for you.'

As he drew to a finish Hud saw that the look of relief, which had been so evident in Judy's eyes after he had burst in, had rapidly disappeared. Now all he saw was fear and panic. She was looking behind him, toward Amy.

Before he could turn he felt the cold steel of the pistol's barrel against his neck, and as he froze Doenitz began to speak again with the same authority that his voice had held before. This time that authority was warranted.

'Mister Hudson, allow me to introduce a very close friend of mine – and an even closer friend of Mr Chatfield's. I believe you know her already.

'Now, would you kindly throw your gun toward me?' Doenitz asked Hud, in a "do it or else" kind of way.

Hud held steady a second, and Amy pushed the barrel hard into his neck. He complied with the request to disarm.

'One other thing before we talk a little more. Please take your foot off the chest of my young protégé. You know him as Mark Chatfield. I know him as the grandson of my father's dearest friend and comrade, Alfred Jodl. One of many that were wrongly accused and executed at Nuremburg.'

Again Hud complied, but not before pushing down with as much weight as he dare. Chatfield winced before getting to his feet, sneering at Hudson as he rose.

Chatfield grabbed Hud's collar, and pulled his right hand back clenching his fist as he did so.

'No! I will not allow it! We must be civilised, Mark' the command came quickly from the old man, and Chatfield held still. His eyes threatened, and then he released his grip and took a pace back.

Doenitz now held a revolver, pointing at Hud, that he had retrieved from the right hand drawer of his desk. As Chatfield relaxed, so too did the Director's voice as he now gave instructions to Amy.

'Amy, I can only assume that Fritz has been disabled in some way. Please, could you give your pistol to Mark before you go and take care of him? We have business to conclude that a lady should not bear witness to.'

Without taking her eyes, or the business end of the pistol, from Hud she waited until Mark had taken charge of the weapon before easing from her position of power. She lent into Mark, who leaned down to receive the kiss, before looking at Hud once more.

'He's ten times the man that your brother was, Hud. And how do you think he was able to get close enough to kill him?' she stated matter-of-factly, as if it should all make perfectly good sense to her brother-in-law.

All he could do was stare, before asking the only question he could think of asking.

'How long?'

'How long?' Amy mimicked. 'Your brother spent too much time on trying to make the world a better place, and not enough time on making his wife a woman. Mark and I first made love at your wedding, Hud. You could say that you, and that bitch over there, introduced us.

'Now there's irony for you' she finished with a wry smile before turning away and leaving Hud's fate behind her.

Hud knew now why Amy had proved such a good navigator. She had been to this place before, but not with Jack her husband. She had travelled here with her lover, Mark Chatfield. His blood boiled, he wanted revenge more than ever, but was powerless to do anything about it.

All he could do was stare at the man who he had once been proud to call a friend. He hated him, and would not take his eyes away from him. He wanted his chance to kill him with his bare hands.

Mark just stood, grinning widely, the two men unblinking as Doenitz began to talk again.

'We had plans, big plans: to make Europe whole again, an entire Nation, an Empire to rival any of those that have gone before.

'We worked so hard for so many years.

'My father devoted his life to the cause, hiding behind a life of retirement and writing. He engineered my "death" and ensured no one lived to tell the world that I never was a member of crew on that Fast Boat. Friends of mine died that day, and I accepted that it had to be so: for the greater cause, for the good of the Reich.

'The wealth that we rescued from Russia, The Amber Room. So many good men died that night to protect the secret, to protect the prophecy.

'My father knew that funds would be needed after the war to continue the work of the Fuhrer, so that Germany may reach its true destiny.

'A destiny that would see Schengen lead Europe as the super power of the World. The prophecy of the Fourth Reich would come true.

'But then you, in less than a week, wreck all those years of hard work. Our power base wiped out. All the politicians; all the captains of industry; high ranking officers across the armies of our peoples. The police, and security personnel. Everyone that we have cultivated over so many years, so much hard work, so much cost.

'Everyone, everything! Gone!

'And its all your fault. And for that you must pay. I must make an example of you, so that others that follow in your footsteps will know the consequence.'

Hud heard the first of two shots, and dived to the floor. The room around him fell into darkness, the echo of the gunshots subsiding. And then, seconds later the door opened and a swath of light broke through the gloom as Amy rushed in.

He looked up, Amy running past him to the limp body that lay nearby. She fell to her knees and cradled Chatfield's head in her hands, unable to catch her breath, blood seeping from her lover's neck and his eyes fixed at a point in space. Tears burst from the corners of her eyes, the sting of mascara reddening them immediately.

Hudson rose to his knees, glass from the shot bulb above his head cutting into his hands as he did so.

He looked round the room. There was no sign of Doenitz.

A hidden door behind the cumbersome oak desk swung ajar a few inches. He thought of following, but where could the old man go?

He rushed to Judy, picking the discarded sub machine gun from the floor as he went. Ripping her ties from her, he held her in his arms vowing never again to lead her to such danger, and promising that he would always keep her safe.

The roar of an engine from behind the house woke Hud from his momentary bliss.

Doenitz!

He had a car hidden out back! He can't get away, he mustn't get away! He looked at Judy, and she could see in his eyes the determination to finish the job that was once always there. She didn't have to tell him to go; he knew he had to stop him from escaping. His instincts took him away from her, out to the front of the house as the open top Mercedes came careering round. The thick black tyres underneath the heavy black metal monster cut a deep pathway through the gravel drive, the rear end turning outwards as the car negotiated the steep arc of the low wall that skirted the house.

Time stood still as Hud fixed on Doenitz's maniacal grey eyes through the windscreen. He must stop him! He mustn't let the twisted evil of an ageing Nazi break free to wreak its will on an unsuspecting world.

Hud raised the gun, preparing to shoot but as he squeezed the trigger his leg was pulled from under him. Bullets shattered the windscreen but missed their mark. The car spun as Hud hit the ground, twisting as he did so to spy the hand that caused his fall. The blood stained grin of Fritz the guard looked at him for a split second, before Hud stamped the boot of his free foot on Fritz's nose. Even above the noise of the Mercedes, Hud recognised the crack of shattering bone. Fritz let his grip falter, his hands reflexing to the pain, yelping in agony as blood sprung from his face and through his fingers.

In one continuous motion, Hud spun to his feet and leapt to the rear of the car as it made to speed past him. The toes of his boots made uneven channels in the stones below as he tried desperately to swing his legs up and into the car. He could see deranged eyes staring back at him in the rear view mirror as with one last effort he was in the car.

Hud tried in vain to stop his weapon from falling away, but as Doenitz first swerved one way and then the other the sub machine gun pulled free from his grasp and hit the drive that was now speeding past under the motor.

He saw Doenitz reach to the passenger seat.

His pistol! He still has his pistol!

Hud dived over the leather, his arms outstretched. His fingers wrapped themselves around the hand that held the gun, before it could be used.

Now Doenitz was driving with one hand on the wheel and his other trying to unload a couple of rounds from his weapon. But it was no good: the English pig was to strong! His grip was like iron!

Hud was upside down now, struggling to control Doenitz's frenzied movements. For such an old man he was powerful. Hud's legs waved uncontrollably above the headrest, as he tried to spiral his shoulders round to gain a better hold.

Then a shot rang out. The car swerved without direction, as on impulse Doenitz's driving hand released its grasp of the steering wheel and reached for the pain searing through his leg.

Hud was flung from the car, landing with a roll on the grass embankment beside the driveway. He looked up in time to see the Merc slam into the wall that ran the opposite length of the gravel road.

As if in slow motion the car turned over, somersaulting with gymnastic ability. And then it exploded into a fireball as it crumpled against a thick oak that sat beyond the wall.

Out from the flames crawled a smaller fireball, orange and red flames spitting from the half human shape until finally it collapsed beside the burning wreck.

A second and third explosion threw bits of the car in the air, like ash from a volcano.

Finally it was over. Hud turned to face the chateau where out front Judy stood, pistol in hand and waiting for Hud to return to her.

It was time to give himself over to the police. It would not take them long to arrive, and when they did would be the moment that Hud started to prove his innocence.

EPILOGUE

Hud opened his eyes. The half-light of the breaking dawn coloured the room in hues of gold and orange.

It had been three months since the day he had learnt of his brother's death from a news report on his television.

Amy had made a good witness for his defence, confessing all she knew about Chatfield, Doenitz and Schengen. Consumed by grief she had not felt the need to lie anymore.

During the weeks that followed the end of Doenitz and Chatfield, across Europe there had been mass arrests of people in power and positions of authority. Many prominent generals had resigned almost en masse, and a certain Prefect Rousset from Paris had been suspended from duty pending investigations into what was termed "irregularities".

Hud turned his head away from the clear morning sky and felt his face warmed by Judy's gentle breathing. Her long blonde hair fell in silken stands on his chest.

He looked at her, admiring her beauty as she slept.

There had been other times since their divorce that they had come together. But this felt different.

Their lovemaking had been slow, measured. They had taken time with each other's bodies, rather than the fast and furious sating of carnal needs as on the previous occasions.

It had felt more like they wanted each other, and not like they needed each other.

On the few times they had been together sexually since their divorce, Hud had always woken to an empty bed. This time she had stayed the whole night. And still she slept. He thought he saw a look of contentment on her face even while she slept that had been lost for a long time.

He gently stroked her cheek, and her eyes opened. She looked at him, looking into his soul as only she could.

'Hud, don't read too much into this. Let's just take things nice and slow.'

He knew she was right, that they couldn't rush or make any hard and fast plans for the future. But something had changed in him, and in her. He could see it. He could feel it.

'Routine and normality', he thought, saying out loud, 'Who needs them?'

'What?' Judy asked.

'Oh, I was just thinking out loud'

'What is it, Hud?' Judy questioned.

He looked at her, into her beautiful eyes.

'Life is for living, and that's what I want to do.

'One day at a time.

'No past, just now. Today.

'If I'm lucky they'll be a tomorrow. And if I'm not...well then I always had today.'

She wrapped her arms around him.

They kissed, and fell gently to sleep in each other's arms.

Their bodies, like their lives, entwined around one another.

AUTHOR'S NOTES – fact or fiction?

This book is written first and foremost as a work of fiction, and as such I hope that it has proved to be a book which you have enjoyed for the story it tells.

However, in its writing I wanted very much to be able to create a story not only that might be termed a "ripping good yarn", but also one that might make the reader think "what if?" In order to do this it was imperative to have the backbone of the tale built around factual information.

It was with this in mind that in its writing I spent as much time, if not more, in researching some of the finer details contained within as I did in constructing the story, the characters, the plots and sub-plots themselves. Of course, I have used a certain amount of literary licence to meld the facts together in order to produce the fiction.

One of my favourite authors, Michael Connelly, has put in print that when writing a novel an author should not only seek to entertain the reader, but also to impart some knowledge on his audience. Indeed, he goes so far as to say "the reader *wants* to learn".

With this in mind, I want to outline just a few of the more pertinent facts without which, of course, this novel would not have been possible. Before you read further, I would like to thank you for taking your precious time to read my work. I hope the reading gave as much enjoyment to you as its writing did to me.

Eisenhower insisted that only Generals of the highest military standing should be permitted to sign the surrender papers that ended the Second World War in Europe in 1945. Of these, only Doenitz survived the Nuremberg trials with his life, although he spent ten years in jail for war crimes.

Doenitz's sons, Klaus and Peter, were both killed during World War II, although his eldest son's body was never recovered after reportedly killed aboard a fast boat in the English Channel. Some reports say that all hands on deck perished whilst others say that there were half a dozen survivors. Klaus was most definitely not among those that survived, if indeed there were any survivors.

The Amber Room is a certainty. However, it is uncertain what became of it after the German occupation of Russia during the hostilities of the War. Some believe that it was bombarded and blown to smithereens, whilst other theories include that it was taken away by the Germans before it fell into Allied hands. Small parts of the room are reported to have turned up since its disappearance, although there has been no conclusive evidence that the room still exists in its entirety. To this day it remains one of the great unsolved mysteries of the Second World War.

The Treaty of Rome, which established the founding of the European Community (later to become the European Union) was signed a year after Doenitz was released, in 1958.

Karl Doenitz died in 1980, and was buried with the respect of a national hero. His funeral was attended by many that served with him, and for him, during the Second World War as well as high ranking German and European officials of the day.

With regard to the trading methods and monies of so called financial boutiques, trading houses, and hedge funds: whilst this book does not go into fine detail, the outline contained herein is accurate, although to the best of my knowledge there is not a financial trading company with the name Schengen.

Schengen is, however, a geographic area that has been designated by treaty as a free trade area within the continent of Europe. That is to say goods, services, and people are free to move between the designated Schengen countries without recourse to any form of border control. The treaty that created this was signed at a small town called Remerschen, which was renamed Schengen after the treaty was signed in 1985.

Of course, this is only a minutia of the detailed research upon which this novel stands, but is what I consider to be the most pertinent facts behind the fiction. I do not wish to inhibit your enjoyment by piecemeal regurgitation of my research, which would undoubtedly be able to fill the pages of a further book.

Finally, the only remaining pertinent fact that I have not summarised in this Author's Notes is the existence of a far right wing organisation in Europe that was born from the ashes of the Third Reich. And for that I will let you ask yourself one simple question: is the existence of such an organisation pure fiction, or could it indeed be fact?

Coming soon
Peter Hudson returns in

BLOWBACK

At the retirement party of his old Commanding Officer Peter Hudson is entrusted with the care of Drew Smith, an ex colleague who had been left mentally scarred by capture in Afghanistan. But Smith commits suicide, or so it seems.

Hudson returns home to find a hand delivered package of photographs from an unknown source. Photographs that hold the clue to an explosive mix of greed, power, and wealth.

Seeking the truth behind Smith's death, and the secret behind the photographs, Hudson is thrown into constant threat from the underworld and the politicians who want to control it.

Only by fighting back can he hope to survive.

To discover more about Peter Hudson, and find when Blowback will be available for purchase please visit:
www.peterhudsonthrillers.com

Printed in the United Kingdom
by Lightning Source UK Ltd.
135269UK00001B/46-111/P

9 781438 906454